THE TERRA GAMBIT

BOOK EIGHT OF THE EMPIRE OF BONES SAGA

YOWLING
CAT PRESS

BOOK EIGHT OF THE EMPIRE OF BONES SAGA

THE TERRA GAMBIT

Fortune favors the bold!

TERRY MIXON

BESTSELLING AUTHOR OF *BEHIND ENEMY LINES*

The Terra Gambit
Copyright © 2018 by Terry Mixon

Published by Yowling Cat Press ®
Print ISBN: 978-1947376083
Edition date: 05/14/2018

Cover art - image copyrights as follows:
DepositPhotos/Tristan 3D (Daniel Kurle)
DepositPhotos/innovari (Luca Oleastri)
DepositPhotos/100502500 (Natalia Romanova)
DepositPhotos/TsuneoMP (Junichi Shimazaki)
DepositPhotos/CoreyFord (Corey Ford)
Donna Mixon

Cover design and composition by Donna Mixon

Print edition interior design composition by Terry Mixon and Donna Mixon

Editing services by Red Adept Editing
Reach them at: http://www.redadeptediting.com

Audio edition performed and produced by Veronica Giguere
Reach her at: v@voicesbyveronica.com

TERRY'S BOOKS

You can always find the most up to date listing of Terry's titles on his Amazon Author Page.

The Empire of Bones Saga
Empire of Bones
Veil of Shadows
Command Decisions
Ghosts of Empire
Paying the Price
Reconnaissance in Force
Behind Enemy Lines
The Terra Gambit

The Empire of Bones Saga Volume 1

The Humanity Unlimited Saga
Liberty Station
Freedom Express
Tree of Liberty

The Fractured Republic Saga
Storm Divers

The Scorched Earth Saga
Scorched Earth

The Vigilante Duology with Glynn Stewart
Heart of Vengeance
Oath of Vengeance

Want Terry to email you when he publishes a new book in any format or when one goes on sale?
Go to TerryMixon.com/Mailing-List and sign up.
Those are the only times he'll contact you. No spam.

DEDICATION

This book would not be possible without the love, support, and encouragement of my beautiful wife. Donna, I love you more than life itself.

ACKNOWLEDGEMENTS

Once again, the people who read my books before you see them have saved me. Thanks to Alan Barnes, Michael Falkner, Cain Hopwood, Kristopher Neidecker, John Naiser, Bob Noble, Andrew Olivier, Jon Paul Olivier, John Piper, Bill Smith, Tom Stoecklein, Dale Thompson, and Jason Young for making me look good.

I also want to thank my readers for putting up with me. You guys are great.

1

"I left her there," Jared Mertz said. "This is my fault."

"Have you met my daughter?" Emperor Karl Bandar of the New Terran Empire asked his son. "Kelsey has a streak of what we'll generously call impulsiveness. If she thinks she has a better plan than you, she's likely to execute it and then beg forgiveness while you pick up the pieces."

Jared stared at his father for a few seconds and then laughed softly. "I suppose you're right. Still, I should've seen this coming. I let her talk me into leading the attack on the Dresden orbital to recover the data on manufacturing the Marine Raider implants. I figured they'd be in and gone before trouble came looking for them, but I was wrong. Again."

The two of them were sitting in the Emperor's private quarters at the Imperial Palace, sipping on aged whiskey. Jared had left his task force at the sealed Erorsi flip point a day ago and come home alone to report.

Based on the FTL probes they'd deployed as they'd fled the Rebel Empire, the enemy had only been about twelve hours behind them when they'd transitioned to Erorsi and put the flip-point jammer there back into service.

Even though he'd destroyed the FTL probes as his fleet had fled, he'd decided to leave the ones in the system just past Erorsi intact. He positioned them far enough out to avoid any chance of detection and could always send the self-destruct signal if anyone seemed to have detected them.

Jared had waited in the Erorsi system with his fleet in case the Rebel Empire made a concerted attempt to force their way through, but they hadn't. The FTL probes didn't have the best view of the enemy using passive scans at extremely long range, but he could tell that most of the Rebel Empire ships were setting up around the Erorsi flip point.

Based on the amount of debris that had come through, they'd sent several waves of probes to test his defenses. No ships had attempted to flip, so the complete lack of response had spooked them. That wouldn't last.

The flip-point jammer set up a gravitational resonance in the wormholes that allowed travel between star systems up to hundreds of light years apart. Nothing had survived the transit. Eventually, they'd figure out what he was doing, and then the real fun would start.

His people would have to take the flip-point jammer down for maintenance, but that day was over a month away. He'd worry about that when he had no other choice.

"We'll just have to hope she finds another way home," the emperor said. "I have every confidence in Kelsey's resourcefulness. Besides, she has Commodore Anderson and *Audacious* to help her get the technology home.

"The Raider implants might be the most useful militarily, but learning how to build AIs could help win this war. That would make all the trouble worthwhile."

The fact that the Dresden Orbital had held facilities to build sentient AIs had been a game-changing surprise, one they couldn't pass up. Kelsey had stolen the entire orbital with a ship used to transport large vessels that couldn't move themselves and fled in the only direction open to her.

The Fleet carrier and swarms of fighters in her belly would make for a very stout defense as well as an improbably strong arm of attack. Jared knew the Rebel Empire didn't use fighters. It would be a very unpleasant surprise for anyone that chanced across his sister.

"For the time being, Erorsi is secure," Jared said. "The downside is that they know exactly where to find us now. They're going to build up quite a Fleet element on the other side of the Erorsi flip point, and they'll keep probing it.

"Sooner or later, they're going to catch us while we're performing maintenance on the flip-point jammer. Then they're going to come through and try to swamp us."

His father nodded. "We'll keep your entire task force there. In fact, we'll transfer as many ships and fixed defenses as we can from Harrison's World to back them up. That's going to leave Commodore Meyer shorthanded, but such is life."

Sean Meyer had once been an executive officer for one of the worst Fleet commanders Jared had ever met. Meyer could be arrogant and condescending. To his pleasure, Jared had discovered the commodore was also an exceptionally capable man.

"He'll manage. I'll make certain that Erorsi stays secure."

"Actually, you won't. I have a different mission in mind for you."

Jared raised an eyebrow and sipped his drink. "What might that be, Majesty?"

"I thought I told you not to use titles when we're alone."

"When you start giving orders, this isn't a social call anymore."

Karl Bandar laughed. "You're an interesting mix of contradictions, Jared. While I certainly believe we need to keep Erorsi secure, we also have another very important mission that requires the most capable commander possible."

"You mean sending a destroyer from Harrison's World to give an annual status report to the AIs?"

Jared and his original makeshift force had managed to ambush and defeat the artificial intelligence controlling the Harrison's World system. He'd very much like to keep the other Rebel Empire AIs in the dark about the change in management.

The AI had been housed inside an old Fleet sector base called Boxer Station. After the civil war that had destroyed the Old Empire, the triumphant AIs had brought all the wrecked ships that had survived the fighting to orbit the station and created a gigantic graveyard.

He and his people had worked with the leadership on Harrison's World to bring the repair bays at the station back online. That allowed them to begin recovering and restoring the ships that were least damaged. Even the first of those had provided a very powerful fighting force for the New Terran Empire and their allies, the Pentagarans.

The crown princess of Pentagar—Elise Orison—was Jared's wife, and he wished he'd had the opportunity to spend more time with her after his return from the Rebel Empire, but he'd had to make do with just one night of her coming to visit him in Erorsi. She wouldn't be pleased to learn the emperor was sending him away again so soon.

"Understood," Jared said. "As far as I know, the automated destroyer the Harrison's World AI sent to report every year goes to a specific system and transmits a very basic report of all the events that occurred since the last report.

"We have records of everything sent since the AIs suppressed Harrison's World a decade ago. It should be a simple matter to send a captured ship to deliver a forged report."

Harrison—the newly formatted AI on Boxer Station—would be able to create a report that raised no electronic eyebrows. The friendly AI had none of the murderous core rules that its predecessor had. He was firmly allied with the New Terran Empire.

And allied was the appropriate word because the Imperial Senate had recognized AIs as individuals worthy of all the rights and responsibilities of citizenship. Boy, had that caused a ruckus. Jared just wished they had more of the sentient computers to help them.

"Exactly how often have plans proceeded precisely as we wished?" the emperor asked. "No, I think it might be best to send a team of our very best people to be sure this critical mission goes off without a hitch. And you, my boy, are the right man to lead it." The older man grinned. "I realize that command of a destroyer is a big step down for an admiral, but I think you'll remember what needs to be done."

Jared laughed. "Considering I was commanding a destroyer just a couple of years ago, I think it'll all come back pretty fast. When do you want me to depart? I need to get back and brief Charlie Graves about taking command of the defenses at Erorsi."

"Immediately," his father said. "The fast courier will take you straight to Boxer Station. Then she will deliver new orders for Commodore Graves to assume permanent command at Erorsi. The mission is scheduled to depart any day now, so you need to get familiarized with this new ship and assemble your crew at once.

"And with the Rebel Empire now aware of our presence, the chances that you will need to improvise are even greater than normal. I think we need to plan on things working out differently than we imagine." The older man leaned back in his chair. "I said immediately, but I suppose we can have dinner first. I wouldn't want to send you out on an empty stomach."

* * *

COMMODORE SEAN MEYER considered Coordinator Olivia West across her dining table for several moments. "I don't think so."

"Don't be ridiculous," Olivia said then took a sip of her wine. "Of course I'm going."

Sean and she were supposedly having a *working* dinner at her residence on Harrison's World. He suspected no one was fooled by their charade, but he had to keep up appearances. The two of them had discovered a spark while they worked hand-in-hand to restore Harrison's World to its former glory. He hadn't been involved in a serious relationship for many years.

She had lost her fiancé years ago. Fleet Captain Brian Drake had taken his own life on the flag bridge of the superdreadnought *Invincible* when the System Lord suppressed Harrison's World a decade ago, making it impossible for their rebellion to succeed.

The man had held on as long as his supplies had allowed inside the superdreadnought that they'd secretly restored. Then, once he and his people had no other option, they'd taken the painless way out.

The fact that Olivia and he were lovers now didn't change anything, he told himself. Her presence on board the ship wasn't necessary. He didn't need to risk their strongest ally in the region. Even he had to admit that sounded like a lame excuse.

He gave the ruler of Harrison's World a quelling stare. It bounced off her smug expression ineffectively.

Sean sighed. "Why in the world would I send you on a mission involving a Fleet ship? You wouldn't know the first thing about what to do in a crisis."

"Wrong. I know exactly what to do first in a crisis. Stay calm."

"Let me rephrase," he said repressively. "What would you contribute to the mission? We're sending a destroyer to send an automatic message and then come back. It's not going to interact with anyone."

She pointed her fork at him. "Are you certain of that? Just because it hasn't happened before doesn't mean it won't happen this time. What will you do if you're required to have inside knowledge of how the Rebel Empire operates? You need someone who knows."

"We already have someone like that. Commander Michaels, the computer specialist we captured at Erorsi. If they need specialized information, he'll have it."

"That assumes the emperor will allow him to accompany you," she said. "That's doubtful. In any case, meaning no offense to the good commander, he's only of the middle orders. If your ship has to deal with someone from the higher orders, it's a completely different—what's that term you use?—kettle of fish."

"Perhaps sometime you can explain why anyone would keep a kettle of fish around and exactly how they differ from one another. No, you need to have someone on hand who can explain what the rulers of the Rebel Empire are actually thinking. That means me."

He wished he could argue, but she was probably right. In any case, he knew by now that he was going to lose this fight.

"Admiral Mertz arrives tomorrow," he said. "The Emperor appointed him to command the expedition ship. I just got word of that a few hours ago. If you're going, then I'm going, too. It should be a short trip, so my absence here won't make any difference."

She raised an eyebrow. "And you think that Admiral Mertz is going to just allow the station commander to go along on this mission?"

He grinned. "You're not the only one who can be persuasive. We need to have the very best selection of people aboard. I feel confident that I can wiggle my way into the executive officer's position. I have quite a bit of experience in the role, you know."

"Weren't you fired the last time you were an executive officer?" she asked archly. "I seem to remember hearing a story about you being thrown into a cell. Well, two cells, if you count when I did it."

Sean grunted sourly. That had certainly been true. He'd rescued Princess Kelsey and Jared Mertz from his previous commander, Captain Wallace Breckenridge, and been thrown into the brig for mutiny.

Then the AI had captured *Spear* and many of the crew had been sent to Harrison's World. Olivia had locked them all up in a prison camp. One he'd escaped from, but he didn't think he needed to mention that little detail right now.

"I do hope you realize bringing that up is going to cost you," he said with a grin.

Olivia set her wineglass down and smiled back at him. "And what is the price that I shall have to pay? Does it, perhaps, involve some late-night entertainment?"

"Considering this might be the last evening we'll have to ourselves, you're damned right it does."

2

___

Crown Princess Elise Orison wasn't a happy woman. Her sources inside the Imperial Palace at Avalon in the New Terran Empire had told her that Jared's father was sending him off on another mission.

Not exactly the news a newly wedded woman wanted to hear when it involved her husband of only a few weeks, particularly when they'd only had stolen moments to celebrate alone. Well, they'd had one night after the wedding, but it was so rushed that it barely counted. It had been divine but far too brief.

The night she'd come to visit him at Erorsi was even worse. The threat of imminent attack had hung over them, distracting him when she wanted his undivided attention.

Jared was a serving Fleet officer, one critical to the defense of both the New Terran Empire and her own Kingdom of Pentagar. His focus had to be on the war with the Rebel Empire, but that didn't mean she couldn't arrange for a little more time at his side.

By all accounts, the journey to deliver the message would take six days, and then they'd spend the same amount of time coming back. Two weeks sharing their marital bed, even with his attention focused on the mission, would just about satisfy her. For now.

That was how she found herself waiting for him in the Nova system aboard His Majesty's fast courier *Lance*. The quarters were cramped, but such was the nature of a ship designed to get from one place to another at the fastest possible speed. The little vessel was mostly drives. That meant her closet back at the palace was bigger than her current accommodations.

Not that she cared. She was focused on work. A princess's duties were never done.

A rap at the hatch drew her attention from the report she was reading. She rose to her feet, crossed over, and opened it.

Lieutenant Commander Gerald Parker, the ship's commanding officer, stood outside. "My apologies, Highness, but we have a priority message for you."

"You could have just sent me a message through your implants," she reminded him.

He grimaced. "I'm still trying to get used to the idea, and it's only a few steps from the bridge to your door. Just contacting you seems rude when it took scarcely ten seconds to come in person."

She smiled and shook her head. "I suppose it makes no difference. What's the message? Admiral Sanders needs something? My father? Maybe even Jared?"

The young officer shook his head. "It's from Omega, actually. He indicated that he needs to speak with you in person as soon as practical. His words."

"Truly? And he asked for me?"

"He did, Highness."

"Then I suppose I'd best go see him straight away. I assume you have a suit I can use?"

He nodded. "All ships are now equipped with hard suits that can survive in the radiation here for just such a contingency. We have three. Shall I accompany you?"

Elise shook her head. "Not inside, no. You can fly me over, though."

An hour later, she stood on the hull of the alien space station, looking at the bright gas circling the black hole where the sun in this system once gave its worlds life. Never in her wildest dreams had she ever imagined seeing such a thing.

"Welcome to my station, Highness," a male voice said through her suit's com system. "The journey through my hull is disconcerting, but safe. Are you prepared?"

She waved at Commander Parker. He stood in his ship's sole cutter watching her.

"I'm ready, Omega. And it's a pleasure to finally meet you."

"As it is for me. Here we go."

The hull deformed under her, sinking in to deposit her into a corridor filled with liquid. Water, so she was told. Omega had come from an aquatic species before he'd volunteered to physically become part of the station.

"You're right," she said. "That *was* disturbing. What did you need to speak with me about?"

"That is something of a complex issue. There is a chamber around the ring where an environment suitable for humans is maintained. It would be much simpler if you were there. Turn right, and it is only a few minutes away."

Moving through the liquid in the heavy suit taxed her skills, but she managed to slowly make her way around the alien ring. That gave her plenty of time to think about where she was going.

The story of the chamber she was heading for was gruesome. Omega's station had been designed to capture the power of his race's star and create bridges to other realities. That was how his people had escaped the death of their world. They hadn't had flip drives.

Her people were slowly adopting the term "flip point" in place of "space-time bridges" simply because it was less formal. Before the arrival of the New Terran Empire destroyer *Athena*, the Pentagarans hadn't had interstellar drives and had been trapped in their own system, so not many people needed to use any term to describe them at all.

In any case, after the explosion of the sun in the Nova system, the station seemed to have been somehow linked to all others of its kind across the multiverse. In effect, they became a single station with Omega as the being in control.

Something about the bizarre situation made the skin of the station impenetrable and indestructible. It also meant that people from any universe where the station existed could make the trip inside it, if they solved the riddle of opening its skin.

In those days, Omega had been unable to communicate with humans. He had no basis for establishing a dialogue with the humans trapped inside his station, people that were variants of others Elise knew. People that had died building that chamber she was heading for while they waited for rescue that never came.

Carl Owlet—Sir Carl, she corrected herself—had managed to crack that secret, just like so many others the brilliant young man had solved. He'd also found the dead bodies of a number of people he knew in the chamber, including several versions of himself. That had to be eerie. And macabre.

Elise arrived at the hand-built airlock leading into the compartment and started cycling herself in.

"Once you get inside, I think it best you know that you aren't alone," Omega said as the water began draining from the lock.

"What?" Elise straightened in surprise. "Who else is here? Our ship was the only one in the system."

"True, but there is a visitor from another reality."

Elise started to ask again who was waiting on the other side of the hatch but stopped herself. It was already swinging open. She might as well find out the old-fashioned way.

She also made a mental note to explain the difference between pleasant and unpleasant surprises to the alien when she had the opportunity.

To Olivia's mind, her original tour of the destroyer had been a tad underwhelming. Of course, it had been converted to computer control and no longer had the fittings for human habitation at that point.

The Fleet personnel of Boxer Station were rapidly correcting that deficiency, and she wanted to see her new quarters. Lieutenant Logan Butters, one of the base's engineering officers, was escorting her.

They exited the cutter that had delivered her to the destroyer in its repair slip. The inside of the ship seemed much the same as she remembered, but men and women were bustling about and getting everything prepared for the human crew.

"How long until the ship is ready to depart?" she asked her guide.

"It could leave tomorrow, Coordinator, but the refurbishment will be complete the day after that. Call it forty-eight hours. They've reserved one of the senior officers' cabins for you."

"I do hope that no one was displaced to make room for me."

He shook his head. "No. They're running with a reduced crew, so they didn't need all of them. The automated systems will allow them to get by with roughly two-thirds of a normal crew."

They stepped into the lift, and he sent them up. Moments later, the lift doors slid open, and they continued down the corridor.

He went a little farther and then gestured at one of the hatches. "This is it. I've taken the liberty of linking the controls to your implants."

Olivia sent a signal to the hatch, and it slid open. She walked inside and schooled her expression. It was even smaller than she'd imagined. Well, she'd make do.

They'd moved standard Fleet furnishings in, so she had a bed, a desk, and all the other aspects of life she would need for the next two weeks. Everything had probably come from ships in the graveyard. Including the bed.

Sleeping on something belonging to a long-dead Fleet officer was a little ghoulish. That might take some getting used to.

"I took the additional liberty of providing all the consumables you'll need," the lieutenant continued. "They're stashed in compartments in the bathroom and in here. Let me show you."

Over the next half hour, he gave her a detailed tour of her

accommodations and demonstrated everything. Much of it was already familiar to her, but some was new and strange. It would take a little getting used to.

Once she was satisfied she had everything committed to memory, she turned to face him. "Could we see the bridge?"

The officer nodded. "Of course. This way."

It was on the same level and just down the corridor. She imagined that the designers had wanted to put the senior officers right at hand in case of an emergency.

The hatch leading in was open. Unlike other parts of the ship, the bridge work was finished. All the modifications for human control were in place.

Olivia marveled at how much smaller it was than the flag bridge on *Invincible*. Cramped didn't begin to describe the difference.

She took a great liberty and sat in the commander's seat. Everything was so intimate. She could almost read the screens on the other control consoles.

The main screen showed the interior of the semi-open repair slip on Boxer Station. A man on a small sled zipped by, probably delivering something to the massive ship just visible behind him in the next slip.

That was the superdreadnought *Implacable*. The battle damage that had killed her was still all-too visible down her flanks. The crew had committed suicide by dumping their air when the AI-controlled ships had brought her to heel.

The idea of so many people still floating unrecovered in the ships of the graveyard turned her stomach. She knew how their friends and family must have felt. Intimately.

Fleet Captain Brian Drake, her lover a decade ago. The memory of his suicide still tore at her heart, even though Sean Meyer had brought her feelings back to life.

She'd seen Brian and his comrades buried with every bit of pomp and circumstance. The same was true with the dead from *Implacable*. The ship was going to be the nucleus of the new fleet based here at Harrison's World. It seemed only right.

That left the millions of bodies still entombed on tens of thousands of derelicts. Recovering them and seeing them laid to rest would take decades. Well, they'd been waiting five hundred years already. What were a few more?

At one time, Fleet in the New Terran Empire had buried their dead at a monument called the Spire. There was no way that could continue, so she had overseen the dedication of an identical monument here on Harrison's World. Located in the area around one of the cities destroyed by the AI during the suppression of her world, it had space for all of the dead they might find.

"I'm surprised to find you here," a voice said from behind her.

She turned in her seat and found Sean standing beside the hatch. Lieutenant Butters was nowhere to be seen.

"I must've gotten lost in thought," she said as she rose to her feet. "This little ship isn't much to look at."

He smiled. "Yet she'll fight hard if she needs to. The mettle of a ship isn't in her hull; it's in her crew. Have you had lunch? We can drop in on the mess hall and see if the cook is any good."

"Can we replace him if he isn't?"

Sean laughed and held a hand out to her. "I'll see what I can do. Come on. We'll eat, and then I'll give you the grand tour."

3

J ared frowned as he examined the display over the captain's shoulder. The bridge of the fast courier *Javelin* was small, and he already missed his spacious flag bridge. Even *Athena's* control center had been bigger.

"What are they doing?" he asked, more to himself than anyone else.

"Looks like they're waiting for us," Lieutenant Calvin Fassbinder said.

"Well, I suppose I'd best find out what this is about," Jared said. "Might I borrow your seat?"

The young man rose and took one step away. That put him almost against the bulkhead. The bridge was that small.

Jared sat and switched the view to the communications controls. The Pentagaran ship sat near the flip point linking to Avalon, where there was zero chance they'd miss Jared's transit and they were close enough that the incredible radiation density wouldn't overwhelm his signal.

Even with the suddenness of his orders, they'd known he was coming. Jared knew that because they'd asked for him by name. They hadn't said so, but he suspected they either had orders to lure him to Pentagar, which he would have to reluctantly decline, or they'd brought his wife out to see him. That would make refusing her entreaties even harder.

Well, that was why they paid him his exorbitant salary. He opened a com channel. "*Lance*, this is *Javelin*. What can we do for you?"

The image of the ship vanished, replaced by Lieutenant Commander Parker's face. The man smiled. "Lord Admiral Mertz. A pleasure to see you as always, Highness. Your lady wife requires some of your time on a matter of urgency. And delicacy."

That caused the corners of Jared's mouth to twitch upward. "I see. Well, I do have *some* time to spare, though not nearly as much as I might like. I'll be over in a few minutes."

The other man's expression became more serious. "Bring your guards, Lord Admiral. All of them."

Parker killed the channel before Jared could ask why.

With a shake of his head, he relinquished the console. "I'll need your cutter, Lieutenant. Let me go collect my guards. My wife must be more annoyed than usual."

The other man gave him a look. "That's why I'm staying single, sir."

"You say that now, but you'll find the right person eventually. Never say never."

The trip back to his quarters was quick. On a ship this small, getting anywhere fast was never a problem.

As they were going directly from Avalon to Harrison's World, only needing to transit the Nova system, he didn't have to worry about actually spending the night in the cramped cabin. His father had sent him out first thing in the morning after their dinner, so he was good to go.

His staff was holed up in the small compartment. His guard complement consisted of a mixture of Imperial Guards and marines. There were situations where one or the other group might be more appropriate.

Lieutenant Colonel Adrian Branson was in overall command of the mixed unit. He sat on the bed beside Major Karalee Smith, the marine detachment leader.

The two of them were more co-leaders than superior and subordinate, so Jared had wisely decided to keep his mouth shut about their budding relationship.

Frankly, he was surprised he'd figured it out on his own. Elise was much better at that sort of thing than he was. He hadn't even noticed Kelsey and Talbot were a couple until someone pointed it out to him.

The third person sitting on the bed wasn't a guard. In fact, he wasn't even an Imperial citizen or in any branch of the military at all.

Alexander Alexander—Double Alex to his friends—was Jared's Pentagaran manservant. There'd been discussion about giving him both a Fleet steward and a Royal manservant, but he'd drawn the line at one person.

Hell, one was too many, but he'd seen himself losing that fight. A good officer knew when to perform a fighting retreat.

Alex could be a little obsequious when he chose, but in private, he'd shown himself able to unwind a little. There was a spine in there somewhere. Out of all the choices presented to him, Jared thought their personalities might mesh the best.

This trip on the destroyer was sort of a test. If Alex didn't drive Jared insane in two weeks, they'd probably be able to do this. If not, he'd send the man packing and find someone else that his wife approved of.

"I'm headed over to the Pentagaran fast courier *Lance*," Jared said as he opened his closet. "I was told I needed to bring my guard."

Branson heroically managed to avoid rolling his eyes. "Of course you need to bring your guard, Admiral."

The two of them had had a long discussion on the use of titles. The Imperial Guard officer preferred "Highness" since Jared was technically a prince of the blood and the Prince Consort of Pentagar, but he'd accepted Jared's decree to only use that during unambiguously social affairs.

So, the man had acquiesced to using his rank in all other circumstances. That defaulted to almost every situation, which pleased Jared to no end.

"I see what you did there, but I mean he made a *point* of telling me to bring you. That's weird."

The Imperial guard's eyes narrowed. "Then we'll go over in force. I'll summon the ready squad." His eyes flicked to Major Smith. "You get everyone else ready to come over if we need them."

The slender woman shook her head. "Won't work. We only have a single cutter. You need to have it there at all times in case you have to retreat in a hurry. We don't have suits to make the jump in this hellish environment, either."

The man in Imperial whites scowled but nodded. "Then we pack everyone into the cutter. Everyone. Get them there."

The marine rose without a word and strode out of the compartment.

While they'd been speaking, Jared had pulled out his gun belt. He didn't go armed as a matter of course—unlike Kelsey—so he'd left it in his closet. He certainly didn't think he'd need a weapon now, but it was prudent to bring it.

A few minutes later, the entire security detail was crowded into the cutter. It was an exceptionally tight fit.

All told, he had over four dozen people in his security detail, so they could handle multiple shifts and situations. A cutter was designed to comfortably seat three dozen people in the passenger compartment. It turned out one could hold everyone on his security staff. Barely.

Double Alex took one look at the sardine can and headed for the cockpit, declaring he would ride at the flight engineer's station. A wise man.

Jared evicted the co-pilot and took over control of the flight. "Remind me to make sure we have a pinnace as our small craft going forward," he told the Pentagaran. "It has a lot more internal space. It has to, to deliver seventy marines in powered armor."

The man nodded. "I've already done so, Highness. One suitably modified for dual use, as I doubt you'll be needing marines every trip."

Jared exchanged words with *Javelin*'s bridge and detached the cutter. The trip to *Lance* would only take a few minutes. That still gave him plenty of time to worry.

What the hell was going on over there?

* * *

WORK WAS CONTINUING on preparing the destroyer for human habitation and control, but Sean was satisfied that she was far enough along for a test flip to be certain everything was functioning correctly.

He'd consulted with Fleet command about renaming the ship. *R-4587* just didn't have snap to it. With their concurrence, he'd secretly rechristened the ship.

Sean suspected Admiral Mertz would approve of her new name: *Athena*. The original would finally be sent to the breakers at Harrison's World and remade.

"We're at the weak flip point, Commodore," Commander Janice Hall, their helm officer, said.

The position was a big step down for a woman who'd recently commanded a light cruiser, but she didn't seem to mind. And since the ship's captain would be an admiral, well, it wasn't too big a downgrade in comparison.

"Take us over as soon as we get the green light from our escort."

Sean had chosen to have one of the fully operational ships flip with them, in case there was a serious failure. Not that he expected any trouble, but the Nova system was not the place to have a breakdown.

The light cruiser *Brazil* had recently finished her trials and was heading for Avalon. He figured the two ships could travel together to the artificial flip point that Omega had created. By then, he'd be sure of *Athena*'s stability.

"My compliments to Commander Meissner, Wanda. Tell her we flip in sixty seconds."

"Aye, sir," Commander Wanda Dieter, their com officer, said. "She reports that they'll be ready."

"Battle screens up, Commodore," Commander Evan Brodie said. Their tactical officer was grinning.

"Excellent," Sean replied with an indulgent smile. Something about the man excused his occasionally excessive exuberance.

Sean tapped his console and opened a link to engineering. "Are we there yet?"

"Obviously not, sir," Commander Katheryn Pence said. The chief engineer's tone was mildly acerbic, but neither of them were overly bothered by their antics. She's served aboard *Spear* with him for years. "We are, however, ready to flip at your command."

"We flip in… fifty seconds."

"Copy that. Engineering out."

The hatch to the bridge slid open, and Olivia West walked in, accompanied by the ship's doctor, Commander Emmett Dishmon.

"Am I in time?" she asked.

"Barely," he said with a nod. "Have a seat. Forty seconds to flip."

The new arrivals secured themselves at the observation consoles just in time.

"Flipping the ship," Hall said.

The familiar twisting tore at his guts. It lasted only an instant but still made him grimace.

The view from the main screen had changed. Instead of a star field, everything was a haze. The radiation and stellar matter thrown off in the titanic explosion that collapsed this system's sun into a black hole had flooded the outer system with this crap. It only cleared up once one reached the inner system.

"*Brazil* reports a good flip," Dieter said. "They're ready to proceed."

"Set course for the inner system and take us in," he ordered.

He turned to face Olivia. "How was your first flip?"

She stuck out her tongue sourly. "I'm glad I took Doctor Dishmon up on the shot. I can't believe you do that all the time."

"Fleet implants make it more tolerable. The civilian modules you have might not be up to the task. Before we had any implants at all, this was a real pain in the ass. First timers usually lost their lunches."

Her face took on a look of revulsion. "Heaven protect me from that. How humiliating."

"It was like a rite of passage," he mused. "We'll have to come up with new ones now."

"You know that's hazing, right? Can you do that?"

"Within certain limits, a little. You should hear what the fighter pilots do to their new recruits." He shuddered theatrically. "Trust me. This is nothing."

Doctor Dishmon was rubbing his chin. "I think I have everything on hand to update most of her implant components to Fleet standards. Maybe all of them. If not, I can get the missing equipment before we depart Harrison's World. Would you like an upgrade, Coordinator?"

"I'd never considered it before," Olivia said. "Should I?"

"The nanite package is worth it all on its own," Sean said. "I say you should do it. After all, you're normally so busy that you couldn't block out the time. Why waste the opportunity?"

She considered that and then nodded. "Then I will. What does the procedure entail?"

"I'd go in and swap out the implant processors, but the cranial wiring is the same for both Fleet and civilian," Dishmon said. "You'd get some upgrades in processing capability and only half a day of light duty to make sure everything is calibrated.

"During that time, the new nanites will propagate. Once I insert the new population, they'll override the civilian units and take over. That means I need to swap out the nanite fabricator, but that's hardly worth mentioning.

"It would be different if you were getting Raider implants. Not that we could do them, mind you. Those would keep you down for a while and take multiple sessions over six weeks."

He saw Olivia shudder. Knowing what he did of how the heir had gotten her implants, he understood.

"No," she said. "I think Fleet-level implants are quite enough, thank you. Perhaps we can get them done now? Then I'll be fully back to normal by the time we get home. I'll have a last flurry of things to take care of before we head into the Empire. Excuse me, the Rebel Empire."

Dishmon glanced at Sean, so he nodded his approval.

"Absolutely," the doctor said as he stood. "We can start right now, Commodore."

She stepped over and kissed Sean. "Don't worry. I'll be fine."

It amused him how the bridge crew were studiously working on their consoles after Olivia left. The woman really knew how to push his boundaries. He wasn't the kind of man that appreciated public displays of affection, so she'd made absolutely certain everyone now knew they were an item.

Well, that would be obvious as soon as they started visiting each other at night. A destroyer was a small community, far too small for secrets like that.

Knowing her, she also wanted to get the word out back on Harrison's World. Olivia West did nothing by accident. Everything was always planned and considered.

Sean smiled. He'd have to take the chance to turn the tables on her with some surprising behavior. Fair was fair.

"Yes," he said dryly. "Coordinator West and I are seeing each other. Carry on."

"We're not the ones carrying on, sir," Evan said in a sotto voice.

Everyone laughed, including Sean. "Touché. Now, how about we get this ship on the move? I'd like to get things wrapped up before the admiral gets to Harrison's World. Make it happen, people."

4

Olivia thought the procedure to update her implant hardware to Fleet standards took very little time and seemed to be a simple process.

At first glance, everything felt the same. She supposed that the differences in performance speed and capability were subtler than she'd imagined. As long as they made the flips more tolerable, she could live with that.

Doctor Dishmon ran a set of diagnostics on her after the procedure. "Everything looks good. Remember to take it easy for the next twelve hours. Your new nanites are settling in, but I'd like to get them established before you need them."

"I'm not seeing much difference between them and the ones I had before," she said as she sat up. "Am I missing something?"

"The Fleet version has significantly more redundancy and will perform better when you have a lot going on. In general use, both are fast. I'd wager you see the difference after you really get to put them through their paces."

She nodded. "That sounds good. I suppose I should let you get back to business."

He laughed and gestured at the mostly empty medical center. "I don't have a lot of customers right now, but that's how I like it. I'm sure I can find some paperwork to handle. Fleet loves paperwork."

Olivia started to make a joke about the nonexistent paperless society, but an incoming call preempted her attention. It was Sean.

"We have a situation developing," he said tersely when she accepted the call. "Can you meet me at the docking level?"

"I'm on my way," she said, waving to the doctor as she strode into the corridor. "What's wrong?"

"I'm not sure. Admiral Mertz is already here and is meeting Crown Princess Elise on her ship at Omega."

That sounded innocuous. "They're married. I think he's safe enough."

"Then why did they make sure he brought all his guards with him? All of them."

"You're right. That does sound odd. Why don't you ask him?"

"I did. He's heading over via cutter and has no idea. I tried to get the details out of the Pentagaran commander, but he said it was best not to say. I think we need to head over and see for ourselves."

Olivia stepped into a lift, and it whisked her down to the docking level. "Did you tell Admiral Mertz you were coming? Is he concerned? Might there be something wrong with the princess? What if we need a medical team?"

"Commander Parker told me no one was injured but to have a medical team on standby. Nothing urgent, but it sounds damned odd."

The lift opened, and she stepped out to find Sean waiting for her. Together, they headed for the nearest cutter.

"They're being very mysterious," she said as they entered the cutter.

An ensign was waiting to see them strapped in. He gave Sean a nod and stepped into the cockpit. Moments later, the cutter detached from *Athena*.

"We should arrive a few minutes after the admiral, but I asked him to wait for us," Sean said. "This makes me nervous."

They spent the next few minutes pondering what could be going on but arrived at the Pentagaran ship as clueless as when they started.

"Admiral Mertz's cutter is undocking to make room for us," he said. "We'll find out pretty quick, I suppose."

The docking seemed to take forever, but they were actually standing in just a few minutes. When the lock opened, she found Admiral Mertz on the other side. He had his guards with him. Dozens of them.

"Don't you think this is overkill?" she asked as she stepped out.

"Coordinator," he said with a nod. "I suppose so, but Commander Parker said Elise had instructed him to tell me to bring them all. I'm not sure what's wrong."

The lift doors opened, and Commander Parker stepped out. "My timing is good. Welcome aboard, Highness, Coordinator. I'm sorry to have been so mysterious, but Her Highness was very specific that I not say what the situation is."

"Are we in danger?" Jared asked.

The man shrugged. "I'm not precisely sure I'd call this situation immediately dangerous, though it might have elements that I haven't grasped yet. If you'll accompany me to the main deck, I'll give you a rundown of the basic elements I know."

"Why isn't Elise here?" Olivia asked. "Is she okay?"

"I saw her not ten minutes ago, Coordinator. She is fine."

Jared turned to his guards. "Follow me up."

"I think not," a man in New Terran Empire Imperial Whites said. "We send a team up first, and I go with you."

"Is all this really necessary?" Sean asked Parker.

"I believe so, Commodore," the other man said gravely. "Basically, we arrived here a few hours ago, and Omega summoned Princess Elise. She didn't come back alone. It seems we have a visitor."

Olivia frowned. "A visitor? From Omega?"

Jared's face showed he'd grasped the situation. "From another universe. Oh, crap."

The lift returned from taking the first set of guards up. Parker, Jared, the guard commander, and she went into the lift with a few more guards. The trip up took only a few seconds. They rejoined the other guards.

"I see you've grasped the basic situation," Parker said. "Her Highness is waiting in our wardroom with our guest. She is concerned that this meeting might go… badly."

"Who is it?" Jared demanded.

The hatch slid aside, and Olivia looked inside the room. What she saw sent a cold chill through her. Crown Princess Elise of Pentagar waited there, with a very familiar figure beside her.

The short woman in black armor had her helmet off, and Olivia recognized Princess Kelsey Bandar. Only, this woman was not *their* Kelsey. This woman had a deep scar on the left side of her face and some kind of artificial eye under a metal plate.

What Olivia could see of the woman's natural face didn't hold the cheerful expression she would've expected. No, this woman glared at them all with a look of mixed anger and revulsion.

"Just my luck," the new Kelsey said in a low growl. "The Bastard."

* * *

JARED STOOD THERE in shock for a moment before he roused himself. "Kelsey. I suspected we'd get visitors from other realities, but I hadn't considered you might be the first."

She tensed. "Don't be familiar, Mertz. You don't get to use my first name. Only my friends do. I am your crown princess."

The sense that he was caught in some strange nightmare washed over him. He opened his mouth to tell her that wasn't how it was but stopped himself. This might have been how they'd turned out if things had gone differently.

Obviously, it was exactly how they'd turned out in her universe. He'd best keep in mind that this was *not* his sister. This was Crown Princess Kelsey Bandar, a woman who obviously loathed him.

"Forgive me, Highness," he said with a small bow. "I will, of course, respect your wishes. Might we come in?"

The woman glared at him before stepping back.

Elise stood there, a stricken look in her eyes, one she masked almost as soon as he'd seen it.

He wanted to take his wife into a hug, but he needed to keep his eyes on the unpredictable threat in the room. This Kelsey obviously hated him and, based on her armor, had Marine Raider implants. She could kill him anytime she chose.

Interestingly, she showed no sign of recognizing Olivia West. Yet, unless things were very different in the other universe, she'd come through Harrison's World to get to the Nova system.

He started to step into the compartment, but his guards moved in first. By some unspoken cue, the Imperial Guards moved to the side of the compartment that Kelsey stood on, and the marines backed him up. Their hands were close to their weapons, and the tension in the air went up.

"Stand down," Kelsey told the guards in white. "Call off your dogs, Mertz."

Jared made a gesture, and they all relaxed just a hair. Interestingly, she only seemed to associate the marines with him. He decided not to correct her misapprehension and communicated his intent over his implants to the guards.

Keep things low key. She's not associating the Imperial Guard with me, so let's keep it that way for now.

Colonel Branson looked unconvinced but nodded almost imperceptibly. His implant response was very direct, however. *We'll play it your way, Highness, but she's not our princess. If she makes a move on you, we'll come down on her.*

Let's hope it doesn't come to that. He stepped cautiously into the wardroom and gestured to his companions. "You've already met Elise. This is Commodore Sean Meyer and Coordinator Olivia West."

Kelsey's natural eye narrowed again. "Mind your manners, Bastard. That's Crown Princess Elise to the likes of you."

The absurdity was almost too much, but this wasn't the time or place to educate her.

"Of course. Forgive me, Highness," he said to Elise.

Anger flashed in her eyes but also horror and sadness. His wife swallowed and nodded. "Of course, Admiral. Shall we all sit? This might take a while."

Kelsey ignored her and walked over to Sean. For him, she had a smile. "This is a well-deserved promotion, Commodore. It's good to see you again, Sean. Even if you aren't precisely the same man I know."

If her reaction shocked him, he hid it well. "It's good to see you, too, Highness."

She shook her head. "We're long past that, my friend. It's been Kelsey for years now. In my universe, we're the very closest of allies. I certainly hope that's true here, too."

"It is," he said with a smile. "I'm just trying to make sure I don't make a mistake because of what I know about you here."

"For you, I'll forgive any lapse," Kelsey said, momentarily taking his hands into hers in an obviously intimate gesture.

Olivia narrowed her eyes, but Kelsey was turned so she couldn't see it. The expression had vanished by the time the princess turned to face her.

"Coordinator West, I'm sorry to say that I don't know you. Is that a title in the empire here?"

"In a manner of speaking," Olivia said evenly. "I rule Harrison's World as part of the New Terran Empire."

Kelsey opened her mouth to say something but stopped herself. When she finally spoke, it was with great sadness. "I see now why I don't know you. In my universe, the AIs sterilized your world. By the time my people and I arrived, there was no one left to meet. I'm very sorry to have to tell you that."

Olivia wilted. "I see. I wonder if we managed to ambush the AI there and that caused it to go even farther than in this universe."

"We couldn't tell," Kelsey said with a shrug. "If it's any consolation, we destroyed it along with the old Fleet station it was using as a base."

Princess Kelsey sighed, turned to the table, and sat at its head. "So many things didn't work out as we'd hoped."

Jared considered sitting at the other end of the table, but he suspected that would cause more instinctive hostility from his sister. Instead, he chose to sit in the middle of the table. "You came to visit us for a reason, Highness. What can we do for you?"

She pinned him with a cold stare. "You can help me save the empire. I realize that might not be your first instinct, but I urge you to try it as a change of pace."

This had gone far enough. If he didn't draw a line in the sand, she'd walk all over him.

"First, with all due respect, you don't know me. The Jared Mertz in your universe is not who I am. If he's anything like me, he loves the empire and would give his life for it. You demand respect from me, so remember that it is *you* who are the guest here, not me." How he managed to say that without an edge to his tone, he had no idea.

It still didn't stop her from sneering. "Please. You're still the same toad here, I'll wager. A man who wants to steal the empire from the rightful emperor, the man you tried to kill. Did you succeed here? I can't imagine how else you'd style yourself an admiral."

Rather than react with the anger he felt, he simply shook his head. "I can't speak for your universe, but I never tried to kill anyone here. I simply protected myself when your brother tried to have me murdered. I serve the emperor with all my loyalty."

Kelsey laughed. "How can you say something so absurd? In my universe, you're a damned regicide and traitor."

"You're no longer *in* your universe, Highness. As hard as it is to believe, we're close friends and allies here."

She leaned forward with a palpable rage. "Never. How could that be when you killed my... her father?"

Sean cleared his throat. "That's probably easier here since your father is still alive and on the throne."

Kelsey's head whipped around and she stared at him. "What did you say?"

"Your father still rules here," Sean said in an even tone. "What Admiral Mertz says is true. In our universe, you and he are close friends and family. Together, you fight against the AIs."

"Is that true, Elise?" Kelsey asked slowly.

"Very true. Are we friends in your universe?"

Kelsey nodded. "Friends and allies, yes." Her expression darkened. "I only hope you're still okay there."

"Then listen closely when I tell you that Jared Mertz is not your enemy here."

"How could you know? He made a career of fooling everyone around him before he betrayed everything he supposedly held dear."

Elise smiled. "I know him better than anyone. He's my husband."

The silence was profound.

"I've obviously fallen through the looking glass," Kelsey said. "The world is turned upside down."

"I'm sorry that our history in your universe is so bad, Highness," Jared said slowly. "But we're the people you have to work with. Why did you come?"

Kelsey jutted her chin out defiantly. "As much as it galls me, I need your help to save the empire. I have to go to Terra, and *you* have to help me get there."

5

_____

Elise's eyes were on Jared as Kelsey asked for their help. This had to be surreal for him. This was his sister that hated him. She longed to intervene, to tell Kelsey that all the things she'd said about him were wrong, but this was not the time or place.

Hell, she might even be wrong. The Jared in Kelsey's universe might be the bad apple she said. Or this Kelsey could be as paranoid as her brother had been here.

If her father was dead there, that probably meant Ethan Bandar ruled the New Terran Empire. She certainly hoped he wasn't the same kind of man he'd been here. That would've been an unmitigated disaster.

Which, on reflection, certainly sounded like Kelsey's situation, based on the few hints she'd picked up. Really, they needed to get to know one another before these preconceptions ruined any chance they had of working together.

Elise cleared her throat. "We really should get to know one another better before we continue. Everyone seems to think they know everyone else, but it's obvious that nothing is what it seems.

"Before we make any errors that cannot be easily forgotten or forgiven, I think we should take a step back and give Kelsey time to accept this is not her universe."

Kelsey opened her mouth to argue—Elise could see it in her eyes—but looked at her more closely before she spoke. "Perhaps that would be for the best. I wish I could speak to the emperor, but that would take far too long."

There was a longing in her eyes. The man was dead in her universe. How could she not want to see him again?

"Would you like to speak with him?" Elise asked. "We can make that happen in a few hours."

The comment left Kelsey thunderstruck. "What?"

"We have our ways," Jared said, rising to his feet. "I think it best we do exactly that. If you'd care to speak with my wife, I'll make arrangements to get you face-to-face with your father on Avalon."

Elise stood. "Jared, make that happen. Kelsey and I will talk. Everyone else, out."

Everyone except Kelsey and Elise filed out of the room. While they did so, Elise gave orders to Commander Parker over her implants to coordinate their travel with Jared. The flip point to Avalon was only a few hours away. That might be enough time to figure out the strange woman who looked so much like her friend.

Or maybe not.

Once the hatch closed, Kelsey leaned forward and focused her attention on Elise. "Is it true? You married the Bastard?"

Elise have her a stern look as she resumed her seat. "It's true, and I would take it as a great personal favor if you stopped calling him that."

The other woman's expression was a wild mixture of disbelief, revulsion, and anger. "They can't be that different. That just isn't possible."

"You told us who Jared Mertz is in your universe, or at least who you *think* he is. Let me tell you who he is here. He's the man who saved Pentagar. You did, too, but that's beside the point.

"He also performed miracles in keeping the New Terran Empire safe and whole. He's not a traitor here. Exactly the opposite. He's a national hero. Did you see the Imperial Guards? Why do you think they were here?"

The woman's good eye narrowed. "I thought they were here because the… Admiral Mertz assumed some kind of Imperial power."

Elise shook her head. "Assumed, no. Was granted, yes. By your father. And before you say it, he wasn't under any compulsion. Your father pushed these awards on my husband over his strong resistance."

"I *can't* believe that," Kelsey said slowly. "The man is as power hungry as they get. What precisely did my father supposedly push on him?"

After a long, steady stare, Elise spoke. "A number of things. A knighthood, a duchy, and he inducted him into the Imperial Family as a prince of the blood. The guards are his by right. I should make him take some of mine, honestly. He's the Prince Consort of Pentagar, too."

Kelsey rubbed her face. "This can't be *real*. My scientists told me that Omega could bring me to a universe not so different from my own, but that was obviously a mistake. This is a land where everything is backward.

"How could I be friendly with the likes of him? He murdered my father and tried to kill my brother. He abandoned the New Terran Empire in its moment of need. *Abandoned?* Hell, he stuck a knife in its back."

"I can prove how close you two are here with one video," Elise said quietly. "Would you like to see my wedding? It was yours, too. We had a double wedding just a few weeks ago."

The news seemed to stun the other woman. "Married? Who would I marry?"

"Talbot."

Kelsey blinked and frowned. "I don't even know anyone by that name. How could I marry someone I don't know?"

"Of course you know him. He was your strong right hand when you were learning to deal with the implants the Pale Ones forced on you. He was a senior sergeant on *Athena* back then."

The other woman shook her head almost violently. "No. That was Lieutenant Angela Ellis on *Ginnie Dare*. She's my rock."

"She still is, even here," Elise said with a nod. "In our universe, you're away on an important mission together. She's your executive officer on *Persephone*."

"*Persephone?*"

"The Marine Raider strike ship we recovered."

Kelsey sat bolt upright, her eyes wide. "You found a Marine Raider ship? Was the computer intact?"

"It is," Elise said with a wry smile. "It makes you crazy since it won't accept anyone other than you as its captain. And since you haven't found it in your universe, it did have complete specifications of your implants in its memory."

She considered mentioning the other memories waiting inside Ned Quincy's implants but rejected the idea. This wasn't the time to explain that taking in a dead man's memories would create a sentient AI in her friend's head.

"Things *are* different here," Kelsey said. "I think I'd best see this wedding."

Elise had the official video in her personal implant storage, as well as her personal recordings. She sent them all to Kelsey.

The other woman sat back and turned her focus inward. The look of incredulity that spread across her features would've been comical under other circumstances.

A minute later, Kelsey came out from under the spell and stared at Elise with a truly horrified expression. "I honestly don't know what to say right now."

"Perhaps its best if you say nothing," Elise said. "Instead, let me tell you what's happened here without asking questions or telling me how I can't be right. That can come later. For now, you need to hear it all."

"I suppose I have to," Kelsey said as she leaned back in her seat. "White is black, and right is wrong. This is bizarro world."

* * *

SEAN ESCORTED Admiral Mertz over to *Athena*. It would return to Avalon with the fast courier the admiral had come on, the Pentagaran fast courier *Lance*, and the light cruiser *Brazil*. He had no doubt everyone wanted to see how this would play out.

Once they were safely aboard, Olivia took charge. "To the captain's office. I think we need to talk this over while we have a stiff drink. Perhaps a *very* stiff drink."

Mertz snorted. "There isn't enough alcohol in the universe—any of them—to make this less crazy."

"You're telling me?" Olivia asked with a shake of her head. "She just told me that the plan I put so many years into working on *Invincible* got everyone on my world murdered. My view of the universe is a little shaky right now, too."

"I'd imagine," Mertz said as he headed for the bridge. "Who is in command, Sean?"

"Me, until you assume command. I'm hoping to wrangle the executive officer's slot before I'm done, though, so alcohol is to my advantage."

Mertz laughed softly. "I've always had a completely different idea of how being plied with drink worked. And you don't need to convince me. I suspect our mission might expand before this is all over. With your seemingly excellent relationship with... ah, the other Kelsey, you'd be an invaluable asset to have in my back pocket."

"Admit it," Sean encouraged. "You almost said 'Evil Kelsey,' didn't you?"

"I did," Mertz admitted with a shake of his head. "I can't ever do that. It's not accurate, no matter what all the movies of things like this portray. Worse, it makes it far too easy to make a serious mistake in judging her."

The lift they'd climbed into deposited them outside the bridge. Admiral Mertz was about to pass through it and go toward the office, but Sean stopped him and gestured at the plaque beside the hatch.

Mertz looked at it and did a double take. Then he smiled. "You're a sneaky man," the admiral said. "You got Fleet Command to rename her *Athena*. I appreciate both the sentiment and the fact that you recovered the original plaque. I'd know it anywhere."

"It seemed appropriate. I suspect there will always be a ship of this name on active duty and that it will be a plum posting. The people following in your footsteps will have a lot to live up to."

Sean gave the bridge crew a high sign and led Admiral Mertz into the office, where he closed the hatch behind them. Once they were alone, he opened the small bar.

"If you're like me, I suspect Kelsey's taste—our Kelsey, that is—in entertainment is coloring your perceptions. This isn't the Mirror, Mirror universe. At least I hope not."

"What happened to her face?" Olivia asked. "Why didn't she get her eye regenerated?"

"Maybe she couldn't," Mertz said as he accepted the drink Sean offered him. "We really don't know the first thing about her universe. Perhaps they didn't get access to all the Old Empire technology. Or something went wrong.

"Of more concern to me is what she wants us to do. There's only one reason to go to Terra. She knows about the key and the override."

Sean frowned. "What key and override?"

Admiral Mertz smiled. "It's a secret that I could get into a lot of trouble for revealing, but you both need to understand the importance of what we're talking about. Emperor Marcus sent the Imperial Scepter to Avalon with Lucien.

"It's not just a symbol of the emperor's power. It's an actual key to the Imperial Vaults under the original Imperial Palace on Terra. Inside that, there exists a physical override that can force the primary AI at Twilight River to submit to our commands."

Sean considered that as he sipped his whiskey. "That's incredible. If we get our hands on that, we could end this war once and for all."

"That's a big 'if,'" Olivia said, crossing her ankles as she leaned back. "Terra is a long way from Harrison's World, and Twilight River is almost on the other side of the Old Terran Empire. The current occupants might be loath to allow us free transit.

"Plus, Terra is locked down much more thoroughly than Harrison's World was. The AIs don't even allow humans into the system. Even supposing we found a way in, we'd still have to sneak onto the planet past numerous computer-controlled stations and into the ruined palace. What if they flooded the planet with something like the war machines?"

"We can't live our lives as if everything is impossible," Mertz said. "If we give up before we start, we'll all die for sure. Frankly, everything we've managed to accomplish so far was impossible when we started. Yet, here we are."

Sean had been considering the new situation while they spoke, and she turned the conversation back to Olivia. "How will this help the new Kelsey?

Even if we get the override, what's to say it will work in her universe? If the device is even slightly different, it probably won't function the way she hopes."

Admiral Mertz shrugged. "I have no idea. If I know my father as well as I think I do, he'll order us to help her, if it doesn't put us in a bad place. Obviously, our universe has to come first. We can't let her take the key until we use it ourselves.

"That presents a whole new level of challenge. She's a Marine Raider. If she resorts to force, we're not going to be in any position to stop her without killing her."

"Her and a lot of other people," Olivia muttered. "This is a mess. Are you sure the emperor will side with her on this?"

"Pretty sure," Mertz said with a nod. "Come to it, I support her, too. Those are our people, and she's my sister. Even if she hates me. Even if I'm a cad or worse in her universe."

"Do you think the two of you can work together?" Sean asked delicately. "She *really* hates you. I'm talking Crown Prince Ethan levels of animosity."

"Somewhere under there is my sister," Mertz said with a shrug. "I have to believe that I can eventually convince her I'm not the man she thinks I am. That isn't to say that it will be easy."

"No, it'll be just as hard as convincing Ethan I had no designs on his throne. And we all know how well that worked out."

The three of them considered one another and downed their drinks.

6

_____

Kelsey still couldn't get her mind around what these people were telling her. Of course, she'd known that *some* aspects of alternate realities would be different. Just not *this* different.

After speaking with Elise for more than an hour, she asked for a place she could think. Alone. They'd speedily provided her with a cabin and some quiet, if not peace.

She wanted to reject everything her friend had told her out of hand, but that would've been stupid. But she couldn't just accept it at face value either.

The biggest sticking point for her was, of course, the Bastard. He *couldn't* be the hero here. He'd killed her father and tried to kill her brother. Hell, he'd tried to kill her before he'd deserted with his followers. Even now he was off somewhere, plotting to seize the throne from Ethan.

So that begged the question, how could he have fooled everyone here so thoroughly? Elise was no idiot. For that matter, neither was Sean.

She'd always trusted the man's judgement, and he'd never ever been one of the toadies that coddled up to the Bastard. How could he be in the man's camp now?

Yet this was the reality she had to deal with, one where the Bastard had them all under his spell. One where she had to get the assistance that her people needed to survive over his inevitable sabotage and backstabbing.

On the plus side, her father was still alive here. She could warn him what a viper he'd taken to his breast before it was too late.

The thought of seeing him again made her cry, a weakness she couldn't afford to let anyone see. Not here. Not ever.

Her father's assassination had started the civil war no one had seen coming in the New Terran Empire. One it could ill afford. Sadly, it had also thrust her brother onto the throne before he'd been prepared to shoulder the burden.

Mistakes had been made. That was inevitable when fighting two powerful enemies at the same time. But that boat had sailed. There was no going back to do things over. Not in *her* home.

A rap at the hatch made her jump. "Give me a moment."

She rushed into the bathroom and washed her face. Once she was satisfied she looked as normal as possible, she opened the hatch. Sean Meyer stood outside.

He smiled at her. "We're in orbit around Avalon. The admiral has asked that I escort you to the Imperial Palace. He felt this wasn't the time for the two of you to work out your differences."

"As if the two of us will ever 'work out our differences,' except on a battlefield where I leave his smoldering corpse behind."

The vehemence she felt didn't surprise her, but it was more than she'd wanted to show. She had to at least *pretend* to get along with the Bastard until she got what she needed.

"I can see how that might seem to be a difficult task," Sean said with admirable aplomb. "I'm grateful we don't seem to have such baggage."

Kelsey sighed. "You've always been a good friend and wise advisor to me. I have to confess that I don't understand how things here are so *wrong*. My father is truly alive?"

He nodded. "And in excellent health. God willing, the Empire will have him at the helm for many long centuries."

She frowned. "Centuries?"

He raised an eyebrow. "We still have a lot to learn about each other. I can't see how you don't know why that is, but I can discuss it with you on the way down. I'm afraid I must insist that you leave your armor behind."

Kelsey had expected that. "I want your word that it will be returned to me once I have finished meeting with my father. It's irreplaceable."

"Done," he said at once. "And the same is true of your weapons. I realize that you're technically a weapon, too, but I have to trust that you don't intend your father any harm."

"Absolutely not," she said with a firm shake of her head. "I would die to protect him. I couldn't the first time, but I won't allow him to be hurt again. Ever."

He nodded. "I've taken the liberty of getting a uniform for you." He gestured for a crewman to bring it to him and then handed the folded garment to her. "You can leave your armor in marine country. It'll be safe there."

Kelsey seriously doubted the uniform would fit. She was far smaller than most women. Still, it would do until she could get something in her size.

She allowed him escort her to marine country. It was set up exactly like the one on *Ginnie Dare*. How she wished Angela were here with her now.

The strange sense of déjà vu lasted until she stepped into the changing room, and what she saw stopped her dead in her tracks. The bulkheads held rack after rack of powered armor. Dozens of suits.

"Is something wrong?" Sean asked, a slight frown on his face.

"Where did you get these?" she asked reverently. "Do they work?"

"They wouldn't be of much use if they didn't," he said dryly. "You act as if you'd never seen anything like them."

She ran a hand along the arm of one of the massive suits. "Only in video images."

Thank God there had been none aboard *Courageous* when the Bastard had stolen her. That would've been the end of the New Terran Empire.

After staring at the armor for a few seconds, she turned to face Sean. "Where did you find them?"

"The graveyard around Boxer Station. Didn't you say you'd been there?"

She felt herself frowning. "Graveyard? I don't understand."

He gave her an odd look. "The mass of wrecks left over from the Fall. The AIs brought everything that survived there and put them in wide orbits around Boxer Station. We think there are around fifty thousand derelicts."

"Fifty thousand—" She snapped her mouth closed as her eyes widened. "There were no ships there. Hell, there was barely a station even before we blew it up. Are you joking?"

He shook his head. "It's where this destroyer came from. The same for most of the new ships in Fleet. All this armor was recovered there and refurbished."

Her throat squeezed shut as if someone were choking her. She felt faint. "Nothing like that exists in my universe," she said softly. "This is an Old Empire ship? Like *Courageous*?"

"It is," he said with a nod. "We have the newly repaired light cruiser *Brazil* with us, and that isn't the only ship in orbit around Avalon, though most of Fleet is at Erorsi."

The absurdity of the situation made her laugh bitterly. "I doubt you'd be interested in my old, beat-up armor then. Look at these things. Oh, what we could do with something like this."

She was grateful the Bastard hadn't found a place to rearm the stolen Old Empire battlecruiser. With enough missiles, he'd have conquered the New Terran Empire by now.

"I suppose I'd best get changed," she said with the shake of her head. "I can't wait to see what other revelations you have for me."

"I can see we need to make a pass by *Gibraltar* before we head down. I'll let you change in peace."

He stepped out of the chamber and left her with several marines. Not all of them female.

She cleared her throat. "If you gentlemen would excuse us, I need to get out of this."

They shared what looked like confused glances, and the men departed. The two women who remained would be barely enough to help her get the armor off, but she'd manage.

"Do you want to use the rack over here, Highness?" one of them asked.

"I've never had a rack. How does it work?"

They got her into the contraption, and it made getting out of her armor a damned breeze. She'd have to get her people busy making something like this.

The women's eyes widened when they saw her body, and both stepped back. Kelsey was sadly used to that kind of reaction, which was one of the reasons no one *ever* saw her naked.

Puckered scars crisscrossed her entire body, a never-ending reminder of when the Pale Ones had stolen her innocence.

She was eternally grateful the doctors on *Spear* had managed to get her face, skull, and hands regenerated. She missed her left eye, but the artificial one worked well enough, even if it was hideous.

The other blessing was that the scientists had restrained her wild rage until they'd scrubbed the corrupt code from her implants. The mere thought of being a slave to the AI's programming again made her quail.

She'd kill herself if that ever seemed likely. The damned things were still a threat but one that she hoped they beat before too much longer.

Ignoring the stares, Kelsey stripped off her underwear and dressed. She was astonished to discover that the bare uniform fit as if it had been made for her. As short as she was, that *never* happened.

Once she was dressed, she had the marines bring Sean back in. "I'm ready to see my father."

* * *

To say Jared's father was surprised to see him again was an understatement. They met in the same private room they'd dined in last night

The older man raised an eyebrow. "Did you forget something?"

"You might want to pour a drink and sit down before I tell you."

That sent the other eyebrow up to join its companion. "This doesn't sound promising."

The emperor sat—minus drink—and gestured for Jared to join him. "What's wrong?"

"Not so much wrong," Jared said as he sat, "more like sideways. Something that isn't inherently good or bad but wasn't planned for. We have a visitor from another reality via Omega. It's Kelsey."

Karl Bandar considered Jared for a bit without saying a word. When he did speak, his voice was soft. "I knew that was a possibility, but that hardly prepares one. Is she like our own Kelsey?"

Jared gave him a long stare and then shook his head. "I don't have time to get into the specifics because she can't be more than an hour behind me, but events didn't progress in her universe the same way they did here. Let's just say that her opinion of me tilts more toward how Ethan felt."

His father grimaced. "Oh, Jared. I'm so sorry. I know how close you've become and that has to hurt."

"More than you can imagine, but that's hardly the only difference. Things have not gone nearly as well in her universe as here. I can't speak to the specifics, but Elise was able to figure out a number of differences.

"We'll have to work out a timeline at some point, but I'm guessing they haven't actually met the Rebel Empire in direct combat just yet. They didn't get the ships at Boxer Station. The AI there sterilized Harrison's World, and there were no derelicts. No AI, either. Just rudimentary defenses.

"Honestly, I don't think *Courageous* was in as good a condition, either. Kelsey was hurt at some point and has an artificial eye. Their regeneration tech must be deficient, and her nanites need looking at.

"In any case, they don't have the battlecruiser now. Evil me stole it. Sometime around when I killed you and tried to kill Ethan, if the story is to be believed. Ethan is the current emperor there, by the way. I'm the one trying to steal the throne."

"Amazing," his father said sadly. "That's what Ethan said here, too, yet we both know he was unbalanced."

"I have no idea," Jared said with a shrug. "This Kelsey might not even know. In the end, it hardly matters. She believes what she believes, and she's come to ask us to do something. She knows about the key and the override."

"That *is* awkward," the emperor admitted. "We need them for ourselves. Yet, if I could help her, I would. In some sense, her people are my people, too. The very least I can do is hear her out. She's my daughter. If I can find a path that saves our people and helps hers too, I'll take it."

Jared nodded, but inside, he worried that they just didn't know enough about the enigmatic Kelsey to make a decision like that. Was she telling them the truth, or did she have ulterior motives of her own?

There was only one way to discover the truth. They had to let things play out. Meanwhile, he'd take what precautions he could.

"Before you meet with her, we need to think about security," Jared said. "She's got Kelsey's implants, and all our computers will recognize her as the heir to the Imperial Throne. We have to come up with a way to restrict her authority."

The emperor nodded. "An excellent point. Luckily, we have a solution to that. I'll speak with the Imperial physician and have him declare her medically unfit. I'll have to tell the senate and get their backing, but Breckenridge will understand. This isn't about my daughter here—and she isn't even in the same region of space—so I think the two of us can work something out."

"Send Elise to talk with him," Jared urged him. "She and Breckenridge have managed to develop a good working relationship. And she was waiting for me in the Nova system when the new Kelsey showed up on Omega. She's up in orbit now."

The emperor nodded decisively. "Talk to her while I deal with your sister. Your *sort of* sister? You and she have my full backing in bringing the senator around.

"And start planning for a more ambitious mission into the Rebel Empire. I think you might be taking a much longer trip than we'd first intended."

7

Olivia was waiting for Sean and Kelsey when they arrived at the docking level. She silently approved of seeing the smaller woman in something other than her armor. She wondered briefly why her armor was black rather than gray but decided that really didn't matter.

She stepped forward as they approached. "I've decided to join you, unless anyone objects. I've never seen Avalon in person and would like to."

"Of course," her lover wisely agreed. "If the two of you will board the cutter, we'll get started."

Sean sat on the other side of Kelsey from Olivia. "Once we undock, I've instructed the pilot to make a pass by Orbital One on the way down. I think you'll want to tap into the cutter's scanner feed."

The cutter bumped a little as it came loose from the destroyer and began moving under its own power. Olivia had tapped into scanners before, but it was still a new and interesting process for her.

Even though she'd been born to a social class that implanted their children at a fairly young age and she'd been so equipped for her entire adult life, she'd never had the opportunity to use a ship's scanners before the New Terran Empire came to visit.

The higher orders had the odd habit of working around their implants rather than with them. She'd begun wondering if that was an intentional change in the social structure made by the AIs. They needed the implants to control the leadership of the Rebel Empire but didn't want them actually becoming a threat.

She turned her attention to Kelsey. "You said that my world was dead in your universe. The AIs destroyed it. Could you tell how long ago?"

The smaller woman shrugged. "Recently. Decades, probably. There wasn't a whole lot left to put together. I'm sorry."

Olivia was still in shock about the events on her world in the other universe, but they felt like someone else's story.

"It's not your fault. If anything, it's mine. I was part of the resistance. We planned to rebel against the System Lord. Ah... the AI ruling the system from Boxer Station. I suspect it didn't work out nearly as well as we'd hoped."

"That sounds like something of an understatement," Kelsey agreed. "We found the weak flip point in Erorsi almost by accident and had to retreat through it later. A few flips more, and we came across your world, though we didn't know its name.

"The planet had three stations in orbit with orbital bombardment weapons. Someone had used them to exterminate the population. No area was left untouched, and we found no survivors. It was horrible."

Olivia nodded, feeling a bit faint. "We'd intended to restore a mostly intact ship from the graveyard in secret and depose the system Lord. In this universe, we never got a chance to try. Something or someone tipped off the AI, and it locked us down. I wonder if we managed to try in your universe, and that was our reward."

Kelsey shrugged. "The old Fleet base was mostly intact but had a lot of battle damage. The damage looked recent, too. It fought us, but we managed to sneak up on it, and a lucky shot set off one of its fusion reactors.

"There were no signs of other ships in the system. We blew up the orbital stations to be sure they couldn't hurt us. We found the weak flip point leading to that horrible system with the nova and figured out how to use the battle screens to get a ship over.

"Thankfully, that was one of the technologies we managed to keep when —" Kelsey clamped her lips shut. "Well, let's just say that it's hell when you have something like that snatched from your grasp."

It made Olivia sad to see how much pain this Kelsey had gone through. She'd thought what her friend had endured was bad. This only proved how lucky they'd all been.

"So," Olivia ventured, "how are you handling the Rebel Empire there?"

"I assume that's what you mean by what's left of the Old Empire," Kelsey said. "We worked with the Pentagarans to ambush the freighter bringing supplies to Erorsi. The destroyer was tough, but Captain Breckenridge used *Courageous* to turn the tide."

Kelsey raised her eyes and stared at Olivia. "To answer your question, not well. I was there in Erorsi when an overwhelming number of Old

Empire ships—probably under control of something like the Pale Ones—came into the system and attacked everything in sight.

"My ships were out near the weak flip point, so we fled that way. The Pale Ones and those computers don't know about the weak flip points. Thank God."

Olivia had a decent idea of the timeline there. Something just didn't make sense. Well, a lot of things didn't make sense, but one thing in particular stuck out to her. "You and the expedition were trapped in Pentagar space. If Jared Mertz wasn't with you, how did he steal *Courageous*? I thought he staged an attempted coup on Avalon. He can't be in two places at once. Did you find another way home?"

Kelsey shook her head. "No. We're still looking for a way."

Olivia shared a glance with Sean. This Kelsey only thought she knew how bad things were. If the Rebel Empire had succeeded in taking Pentagar in her universe, they might find out about the weak flip points.

"I'm very much afraid the situation in your universe is significantly more dire than you imagine," she said. "The Pale Ones are an aberration. Something left over from the Fall almost by accident.

"The AIs that control what's left of the Old Empire are sentient. They subjugated the humans that survived and have brainwashed most of them into being blind servants. The forces that came to subjugate Pentagar were manned by Fleet personnel from the Rebel Empire, not Pale Ones."

She allowed a moment for that to sink in. "They will have eliminated all resistance on Pentagar, but they won't mindlessly obliterate everything. They'll almost certainly hear about your arrival and how you saved Pentagar from the Pale Ones."

Kelsey swallowed noisily. "I have to pray that Elise and her people manage to keep that secret to themselves. Otherwise, the cost is everything I love."

They sat in silence for a bit before Kelsey continued. "To answer your earlier question, Mertz rebelled while we were gone. He and a number of renegade Fleet officers tried to seize power. My father was assassinated. Mertz tried to kill Ethan, too, but my brother is smart.

"Mertz escaped with perhaps a third of Fleet and made his way to Pentagar. We didn't know he was there. He used another officer to claim to be a rescue force. We were damned glad to see them and never questioned things."

Sean nodded. "We sent reinforcements here, too. With different results, obviously."

"We never suspected a thing," Kelsey said bitterly. "They slipped more than enough people onto *Courageous* and took her. Captain Breckenridge died in the fighting. Mertz seized control and left through the Erorsi weak flip point with all his ships. We had nothing that could hope to stand against an Old Empire battlecruiser, even one in the condition we found her.

"Eventually, the attack on Erorsi drove us after him. I've got Captain Breckenridge's original task force. That's it. We had a single set of battle screens. That was enough to protect one of the destroyers. That's how I was able to explore the nova and find the alien space station."

The other woman shook her head. "Only my armor was strong enough to resist the radiation so I could visit the station. The alien there told me about you, as hard as it was to believe, so here I am, trying to find any solution I can to save my people."

Olivia's heart went out to Kelsey. Her universe had really, *really* drawn the short straw.

Sean cleared his throat. "I hope we can help. We're passing by Orbital One."

That reminded Olivia that she should've been watching the scanner feed. The massive space station was right there. In close orbit around it was the newly reformed Home Fleet commanded by Admiral Yeats. And his flagship.

"Holy God," Kelsey said softly. "What is that?"

"That is the superdreadnought *Gibraltar*," Sean said. "Admiral Yeats's flagship. We recovered her and the rest of the new ships at Harrison's World. We're still getting the force together, and this is only part of it. Most of our ships are at Erorsi holding off the Rebel Empire. Admiral Mertz was in command of that force until he came back to perform a special mission."

Kelsey turned to face Sean. "No wonder you were able to resist him. Look at the size of that thing. Is she fully operational?"

"She is," Sean said with a nod. "But, Kelsey, Admiral Mertz recovered that ship. It wasn't even repaired when he led a force of over a hundred Old Empire ships back here to Avalon."

Her lover focused his attention on the princess from another universe. "I can't speak to events in your universe, but in this one, Jared Mertz sat on the flag bridge of a ship just like that one—the superdreadnought *Invincible*—when he entered Avalon orbit.

"Let me lay this out so I'm being as clear as possible. He had more than a hundred Old Empire ships under his command, and Fleet had nothing that could stand against even *Invincible*."

Sean relentlessly continued. "His fleet consisted of a superdreadnought, a Fleet carrier, six battlecruisers, eight heavy cruisers, twelve light cruisers, two dozen destroyers, thirteen Fleet transports, ten colliers with extra missiles and supplies, six Marine troop transports, sixteen fast couriers, twelve scouts, a dedicated science vessel, two hospital ships, four factory ships, a liner to carry civilians, and a Marine Raider strike ship. All Old Empire tech and manned to fight."

The silence that statement produced was profound.

"Kelsey," he said softly, "if Admiral Mertz wanted to take over the New Terran Empire, he could have reached out his hand and done so. No one could have possibly resisted. He turned all those ships over to Admiral Yeats and submitted to the emperor's authority willingly. Jared Mertz—at least our version of him—has no designs on the Imperial Throne."

Kelsey stared off into space until the cutter began descending into Avalon's atmosphere. Only then did she sit back and slump. "*Courageous* was more than enough to take the New Terran Empire," she said softly. "I can't believe this is true."

"There must be plenty of records," Olivia offered. "And you're going to see the emperor. He'll tell you."

Kelsey rubbed her face. "My father never saw Mertz for what he is. He died still wanting a relationship with the Bastard. As much as I loved him, my father was a trusting fool."

Olivia shook her head slightly when Sean opened his mouth to respond. "In the end, you'll have to decide what to believe. Perhaps in your universe, that's the way things are.

"In this one, Kelsey Bandar has stood back to back with Jared Mertz. Together, they fought the enemies of the New Terran Empire. All we ask is that you entertain the possibility that things here are different, that people and events might have progressed in a different manner than you remember."

"I suppose I don't really have a choice," the short blonde said. "I won't promise that it'll change how I feel, but there seems to be enough evidence that things in this universe are not the same as in mine. People here *might* be different."

Olivia heard the slight emphasis on the word "might." It was probably the best anyone could hope for at this point.

8

———————

Elise took a different cutter down to Avalon than Princess Kelsey, Sean Meyer, and Olivia West. They'd already left *Athena* by the time Jared had contacted her with this mission, and frankly, it was best the others didn't know what she was doing anyway.

Getting an appointment with Senator Nathaniel Breckenridge was as simple as calling ahead and asking if he had time to speak with her.

The same young woman who had met her on her first visit was standing beside the landing pad and smiling at her. "Crown Princess Elise, welcome back to Avalon. The senator is waiting for you."

Elise was thankful that her implant memory made remembering names and faces easy. She extended her hand to Jean Trouville, the aide to the Imperial Affairs Committee. "Miss Trouville, it's a pleasure to see you again."

The woman's smile brightened even more. "For me, too. I saw your wedding. It was *so* romantic. And your husband." She made a motion fanning herself with her hand.

That made Elise chuckle. "Jared is all that and more."

The aide led Elise into the Imperial Senate building. It was still a bit too modern for her taste, but her initial edge of dislike for the design had faded. Perhaps it had more to do with how she'd felt about Nathaniel Breckenridge at the time.

He was the powerful uncle of Captain Wallace Breckenridge, the man who'd betrayed them all at Erorsi, and she'd known him to be their enemy, someone so dedicated to power and wealth that he would work against them every step of the way.

And she'd been completely, *utterly* wrong.

Nathaniel Breckenridge had ending up working hard to help them meet their goals and been shot rescuing Emperor Karl Bandar. It wasn't often that Elise misjudged someone, but this had been one of those times. As Kelsey would have said, an epic fail.

The man was also Kelsey's biological father, something he hadn't known before the attempted coup. That was still something neither her friend nor the senator quite knew how to approach, but he would listen very closely to what Elise had to say.

Senator Breckenridge had also been the father to Crown Prince Ethan Bandar. He'd known that by the time he'd chosen to keep the mad prince off the Imperial Throne. While he hadn't directly had a hand in the man's death, she imagined it still kept him up at night.

This time, no one had any issues with her guards. The protocol had been established, and the Senatorial Guard knew the people in the Royal Guard. A number of guards from the elite Pentagaran unit lived on Avalon now, providing security for their embassy.

Miss Trouville led Elise to the same office she'd visited before and handed her off to the senator's assistant. He speedily passed her inside to the senator himself.

Breckenridge was already in front of his desk with his hand extended. "Crown Princess Elise, it's a pleasure and a surprise seeing you again so soon. Your wedding was magnificent. I hope you and Prince Jared find every happiness."

It felt as if everyone had seen the state wedding when she'd married Jared and Kelsey had married Talbot. The viewership numbers confirmed that. It was literally the most watched broadcast in both the Kingdom of Pentagar and the New Terran Empire. Only people living in caves had missed it.

She gave the senator a wide smile. "Thank you, and we both hope so, too. Also, thank you for agreeing to see me on such short notice."

"You said the matter was urgent. I've cleared my schedule, and I'm at your complete disposal."

Elise looked around his office. "I need to make certain the room is secure."

"It was swept for listening devices a few days ago, but I'll have my people come in and give it another look."

Once he'd tasked his assistant, she raised an eyebrow. "I'm curious. Do you find many listening devices? My people are absolutely paranoid about the things, but I've never asked what they found."

"Surprisingly, yes. In the last year, my people have found three. One was crude, and the perpetrator was quickly identified. The other two were of exceptionally high quality, and we still haven't proven who put them here, though I have my suspicions.

"The new technology makes finding them easier for now, but as it gets out to everyone, the bugs will become much more sophisticated. The senate has a room that's secure from eavesdropping. Eventually, we'll need more of them."

His eyes narrowed. "Do you think it best we use the room now?"

She nodded promptly. "Don't let me stop you from securing your office, but this matter couldn't be more important, and I don't want anyone to catch wind of it."

"How intriguing. Come this way then."

He led her down the hall to a room with a massive hatch. It looked like something she'd have expected to see on a ship protecting a sensitive compartment from destruction. Two members of the Senatorial Guard stood outside.

Breckenridge spoke softly with one of the guards. The woman signaled and stepped into the room once the hatch opened. A few minutes later, several men and women—Imperial Senators, she assumed—came out.

One of them jokingly accused Breckenridge of shooing them out to disrupt their plans to get some piece of legislation passed. He laughed and said he was actually inclined to support it, if they could come to agreement on a few details. They made an agreement to meet in a few days to discuss the matter.

"I'm sorry you had to disrupt their meeting," she told the senator as he led her into the room.

"Think nothing of it," he said dismissively as the Senatorial Guard searched the room for listening devices. "They'd already exceeded their reservation time. In case this is a surprise to you, politicians love the sound of their own voices."

Elise laughed. "I've noticed that. How long did you reserve it for us?"

"An hour. Is that sufficient?"

"You'd best make it two, just to be safe."

"Done."

Once the guards declared the room clear and departed, Breckenridge sealed the hatch and activated the antilistening equipment.

He gestured to the table. "I can get us refreshment from the small kitchen over there. If you need to take a break, there's a restroom beside it. We made sure that once a meeting started, no one would need to leave the room."

"I'm fine," she said as she sat at the table. She waited for him to sit next to her and then launched into events of the last day.

He listened closely and didn't interrupt, even though she could tell the news of a Kelsey from another universe shocked him.

"She's probably at the Imperial Palace now," Elise concluded. "She's going to want help, but that's not why I'm here. The problem is that every computer in the Empire recognizes her as the heir, and we *really* don't know her."

Breckenridge leaned back, his expression still reflecting his shock. "I can see where that would be a concern. There are no allowances made for people from other realities. At least people can be warned. Well, the ones who need to know."

He immediately shook his head. "No, that won't work either. The news would get out. Well, this is a complex problem. What can I do to assist?"

"The emperor has decided the simplest solution is to declare Kelsey medically unfit. That would allow him to restrict her authority. As the heir, that means such a decision requires the senate to approve the recommendation."

Breckenridge nodded slowly. "That might work, but it creates a different set of complications. As you said, politicians love to talk. That includes telling secrets to people that aren't cleared to hear them. Still, for something this important and delicate, it's possible we can keep word of the situation to a small group."

His eyes took on a haunted look. "On a personal level, I'm troubled by how badly this Kelsey has been hurt. It tears at my heart."

Elise nodded. "Mine, too. I don't think she knows about your role in her parentage, so you'll have to be very cautious when you interact with her."

That comment made his eyebrows rise. "You think I should meet her?"

"I do. The senate has to hear from one of their own. I think you should come with me to the Imperial Palace as soon as we finish here."

He chuckled ruefully. "I can't imagine she'll be pleased to see me, even if she doesn't know what I did with her mother."

"You might be surprised. From what I've been told of her story, she and Wallace were close allies."

"That's... troubling on a completely different level. My nephew was never the smartest Fleet officer. It brings her judgment into question."

With a shrug, he rose to his feet. "I suppose I'll find out. This can't wait. I should meet her and the emperor as soon as possible and get the ball rolling."

* * *

KELSEY WAS AMAZED at how intact the capital was. The images she'd seen from after the attempted coup had shown her a city partly in ruins. This place looked pretty much as she remembered it.

Oddly, there were some differences in the skyline. She was able to find half a dozen buildings that were changed in some way from what she remembered even without consulting her implants. That brought it home to her that this was not her universe in a way just being told couldn't manage.

She wondered again what the version of her from this reality was like, aside from having the worst judgment of people she'd ever heard of.

Yet, perhaps not in all things. The woman had fallen in love with a marine, someone who had filled the same role as Angela Ellis in her world.

That, she could understand. Angela was her strong right arm and firmest ally. If it were the same here with this Talbot, she could imagine how the relationship had developed.

She said nothing as the grav car left the city and headed for the Imperial Palace. The coup had left her home a smoking ruin. She longed to see it whole again. And to see her dead father once more. Even if he wasn't truly her father.

The thoughts threatened to make her good eye start tearing up, so she set that aside and looked at Sean. "What happened to my brother here?"

His expression became grim. "You did. Rather, our version of you. She allowed him to run to the system with the alien spaceship in it. Without battle screens."

That revelation made her suck in a deep breath. Her scientists had told her the radiation there was intense enough to kill everyone inside a ship in minutes. Hell, even the ship's systems would fail in an exceptionally short period of time.

She'd killed her own brother? That was unthinkable.

"Your universe might be different," Sean continued relentlessly, "but Crown Prince Ethan was paranoid here. Not in small measure, either. He believed *everyone* was out to get him and he poisoned your father. He then framed you for the crime."

"Perhaps that's what some people want you to believe," she responded, unconvinced. "I've known my brother my entire life. He is not a villain. He loves the Empire."

The Fleet officer shrugged. "Again, I can't speak to that. I wasn't on Avalon, but I saw the testimony before the Imperial Senate where they laid it all out. A number of people opposed your father naming you as the heir, and Ethan's actions had to be spelled out with hard evidence.

"There was a diary in his own image and voice, one he'd kept for years, documenting the various people he felt had wronged him. Of what he'd done to get even. Here, he killed people. Had them killed, anyway. Tell me, do you know Carlo Vega?"

She nodded. "He came with me on the expedition. He taught me everything I know about being a diplomat. I like to think he's a close friend."

"In our universe, your brother sent a gift from the palace to Jared Mertz in your father's name. Something, it happened, the admiral didn't care for, so he gave it to Mister Vega. One piece was poisoned. Carlo Vega died before you even found Pentagar.

"I watched the recording your brother made after the expedition left. I saw the hatred and glee at the likelihood Jared Mertz would die. In our universe at least, he was not the brother you know."

"I want to see it. All of it." She would see through the lies and deceptions. Of that, she had no doubt.

"I'll see to it," he said with a nod. "Along with the exhaustive verifications that prove none of it was doctored."

Since there was nothing left to say on that subject, they traveled in silence until the Imperial Palace came into view. It was miraculously intact, a sight she'd never expected to see again.

The grav car came down onto the main pad, and everyone exited. The Imperial Guard was out in force, armed for trouble. It both saddened and amused her that she was the threat today.

Her Marine Raider implants made her a force to be reckoned with, but she wasn't a danger to her father. Not only did she love and miss him, but she desperately needed his assistance, particularly if Coordinator West's tales about the Rebel Empire were true.

She'd left her precious armor and weapons back on their ship. If they wanted to take her, they could. A number of guards had neural disruptors that could kill or stun her before she could take them all out.

Lisa Devonshire, her father's majordomo, stepped out and bowed as if meeting a new Kelsey was an everyday occurrence. "Highness, welcome to Avalon. The emperor is eager to meet you. If you and your escort will follow me."

Seeing the familiar corridors intact as she passed through them was surreal. She allowed the sights to distract her from the heavy contingent of guards surrounding them as they proceeded toward the official audience chamber.

That wasn't like the father she knew. He hated the place. Every meeting that could happen under more intimate circumstances was done that way.

Maybe it hadn't been his choice, she decided. If they wanted to keep her under the gun, they'd need a lot of room to assure the emperor's safety.

"Do you have restraints?" she asked. "Arm and leg shackles that I can't easily break?"

Sean frowned and opened his mouth to respond, but Devonshire interrupted him.

"We do," the majordomo said as she came to a halt, stopping everyone around her.

"Use them before you take me before my... the emperor. His safety is paramount. It's not going to offend me. If you wanted to take me prisoner, you could do so right now."

"That isn't necessary," Sean objected.

The majordomo seemed to disagree as she gestured for one of the Imperial Guardsmen to bring over a set of handy restraints.

Kelsey smiled wryly at Sean. "Don't take it personally. I'm not. Hell, I'm a dangerously unknown and unknowable threat. I'd lock me up, too."

"This is only until we get to know you well enough to dispense with them," Devonshire said.

She allowed the guards to pull her hands behind her and lock her wrists down. A belt around her waist provided an extra point of attachment for the arm and leg restraints that followed.

The chains looked flimsy, but she took the opportunity to throw her fully enhanced strength against them. Might as well. The restraints kept her arms securely locked behind her. She wasn't going anywhere or hurting anyone without them being able to take her out.

Walking was more difficult once they resumed moving forward. The chains between her ankles only allowed for short steps. It was kind of funny, seeing the large group around her creeping down the long corridor at her pace.

After what felt like forever, they arrived at the main doors to the audience chamber. At their approach, the doors swung back, and half the guards entered, no doubt to join others already waiting.

Kelsey held her head high and strained to catch sight of her father. When she did, a giant fist clamped down on her heart, and she found she could no longer see out of her natural eye because of the tears welling up.

He was alive. Oh, God, he was alive.

And he was angry.

Her father hadn't been on the throne but pacing in front of it. At the sight of her, his face contorted with rage, an expression she rarely remembered seeing on the gentle man.

He strode toward her with his lips tightly compressed. "What is the meaning of this? Get those things off her this very instant!"

Kelsey only barely suppressed the laughter that threatened to burst out of her. How very like him.

"I asked them to do it," she said, her voice rough. "I may look like your daughter, but to them, I'm a potential threat. This way, you can be certain of your safety."

He brushed her words aside just as quickly as he did the guards who tried to step between them. "Take those damned things off my daughter right now. Right. This. Second."

The majordomo looked at her liege for a few seconds before she gestured to the guards. They quickly removed the restraints.

Kelsey opened her mouth to say the words she'd settled on as the best greeting from another universe, but only managed to squeak when he yanked her into a tight hug.

"Oh, my poor darling. What happened to you? You're safe here. Always and forever."

Her planned speech died as emotion overwhelmed her, and she sobbed on her father's shoulder. A shoulder she'd never expected to see again this side of death's veil.

9

S ean stood with Olivia as the tearful meeting between the emperor and his daughter from another universe took place under the watchful eyes of every Imperial Guardsmen in existence. Or so it seemed. Not that any of them could do a damned thing if something went wrong.

Thankfully, it seemed as if this Kelsey had no evil intentions toward the emperor. She merely clutched him and cried. From what Sean could tell, she'd been through more than enough to need the comfort.

"It's nerve-racking," Olivia said quietly, "not knowing how she differs from our friend."

He nodded. "I'm glad I don't have to make the hard decisions this time."

She poked him a little. "You're a Fleet commodore. They pay you to make the difficult decisions."

"Not this difficult," he disagreed. "The people in her universe are so far behind that I'm not sure we can change their outcome. And that's even if we had help to give her this very second. "By the time we're in a position to help her, the New Terran Empire might be under the Rebel Empire's heel there."

Olivia scowled at him. "You're a ray of sunshine on a dark day."

"I'm a realist," he countered. "Plan for the worst while hoping for the best."

"Have you considered who you are over there?" she asked.

He had but wasn't sure he could adequately put his feelings into words. He liked that he was someone Princess Kelsey considered a friend, but he'd seen how wrong about Captain Breckenridge he'd been here. His judgment was questionable.

Of course, she hated the one man who had saved the Empire here, so that Princess Kelsey was doing even worse.

"I hope I'm not much different. It sounds as if Captain Breckenridge died there, too. The circumstances were different, but I suspect I'm the senior Fleet officer in the ships with Kelsey. For her sake, I hope I do better this time around."

Someone behind them cleared their throat.

He turned and saw a man in a white lab coat. "Pardon the interruption. I'm Rueben Beecher, his majesty's personal physician. Might I have a few moments of your time?"

"Of course, Doctor," Sean said. "What can we do for you?"

"His majesty directed me to look into Princess Kelsey's medical condition. Ah... *this* Princess Kelsey. I see that she has some kind of prosthetic eye. Are you aware of any other health issues she might be suffering from?"

"I am," Sean said with a sigh. "I haven't personally seen them, but I'm told the regeneration of her original implantation procedure left most of the scars on her body. I'm guessing, based on that and some other things she said, but I don't believe her medical nanites are operational."

Olivia sucked in a deep breath, obviously horrified. "God," she whispered. "I've seen the video. Those are still there?"

He nodded grimly. "All over her body, with the exception of her head, hands, and arms. Several female marines saw them. Kelsey also had no idea what I meant when I told her that her father might rule for centuries."

His lover seemed to be thinking furiously. "That explains so many things," she said. "I'll wager without Jared there to come for her, the Pale Ones turned her into one of them. The good guys must've recaptured her and overwrote the corrupt code. We should've checked it before we came down."

"I suspect that is fine," the doctor said. "She has interacted with her own people and you without overt violence. Still, for the sake of everyone else's blood pressure, we'll verify that first."

Beecher narrowed his eyes and pursed his lips to one side as he considered Princess Kelsey. She was walking with her father toward a table he must've ordered brought in.

"I suspect they'll be talking for quite some time, so I'll have plenty of opportunity to prepare for an exam. If she'll allow it, I might be able to do something with her remaining injuries, though the amount of time that has passed will work against us.

"At the very least, I should be able to improve upon the ocular replacement. There's no reason it has to look so slapdash." The last word was said with a moue of distaste.

Sean wasn't sure how amenable the woman would be to allowing someone she didn't know to mess with her like that. If anything, this Kelsey might be even more averse to the idea than he was.

The Pale Ones had made her one of them and forced her to do things against her will. He only prayed they hadn't made her fight and kill her friends.

"Realistically, what do you imagine you can do, Doctor?" Olivia asked softly.

The man shrugged. "I can certainly get her nanites working. We have some of Princess Kelsey's on hand for study, and the fabricator is probably still inside this young woman. If we seed it correctly, the population should take hold.

"That said, it may be too late for them to repair all the damage done to her, even in conjunction with regeneration. Marine Raider nanites are incredibly capable, but even they have limits."

His eyes narrowed as he considered his potential patient. "I'd imagine the visible scarring can be dealt with, given time and repeated regeneration sessions. Those might not erase the damage at a cellular level, but we should be able to restore her physical appearance."

The man sighed. "And we can't forget the elephant in the room. She lost an eye. Even with Old Empire technology, that's probably more than we can undo. That said, I can create a lifelike replacement and regenerate the skin and muscle she lost around the injury. No one has to look like that."

Sean pondered the man's words and nodded slowly. "I can't speak for her, obviously, but I suspect she'll at least consent to an examination. I'll stretch that and wager she'll agree to have her nanites restored once she learns what they can do for her. She'll probably jump at the chance to get rid of her scars, too.

"As for the eye, I just can't say. I don't know how deeply she'll trust us. Not until she knows us far better than she does right now."

The man nodded, obviously already thinking ahead. "I can prepare for every aspect of care. If she rejects treatment, then I can try to sweet talk her. Or ask her father to do so."

He refocused his attention on them. "Thank you very much for your input. It has been quite helpful."

"Do you think she'll agree to all of that?" Olivia asked after the doctor had hurried off.

Sean shrugged. "Probably not, but all she can do is say no. Anything we can do to give her comfort is worth the effort."

The emperor and Kelsey were deep in conversation at the table. He had her hand in his and was saying something with an earnest look on his face.

Her expression was just what Sean imagined a daughter would look like if a beloved parent had come back to life and she wanted to remember everything.

He understood that, too. Even if everything worked out here, she'd one day return home and likely never see him again. He'd be dead once more. Lost to her forever.

Sean vowed to do everything within his power to help her.

* * *

JARED ROSE to his feet when his father came into the room. "How did it go?"

Emperor Karl rubbed his face tiredly and poured himself a very stiff drink at the small bar. He didn't speak until he'd downed half the glass. Only then did he turn to his son and sag a little.

"As well as could be expected, I suppose," the older man said. "God, she's so like my girl, yet hurt in ways Kelsey managed to avoid with your help. She's a wounded bird, and it breaks my heart."

His father sat in one of the chairs and slumped back. "After meeting her, I'm convinced she isn't a threat to the Empire or to me personally. You, on the other hand, had best keep your distance. I think she hates you more than Ethan ever did."

Jared took the liberty of pouring a drink for himself and joined his father. "I'd gathered that. Without unbiased data, she might have every right to those feelings. Other me might be a traitor and backstabber. I can see how my life might have gone in that direction if I'd developed different attitudes."

"I can't see that, but I'm glad things worked out the way they have. Your mother wanted to see Kelsey, but I convinced her that it might be counterproductive."

Jared snorted. "Considering how Kelsey feels about me, I can only imagine how she sees the woman you had an affair with. No, I think we should avoid unnecessary provocations. We have enough landmines already."

He resisted the urge to ask his father what help they intended to give. That the man would help was a given, but the specifics would come out in time and without his prompting.

"I'm told that Senator Breckenridge is on his way," the emperor said. "He's going to assess Kelsey and then take my recommendation to the Senate Imperial Affairs Committee. They'll fill in the rest of the Senate and hope that no one leaks the details."

"They won't," Jared said. "It's tied into Omega and the existence of alternate realities. They've kept that information under wraps. It's an Imperial secret, and they know we'll use one of the AIs to find the leaker. None of them is going to risk their careers over this."

"I love how certain you are," his father said dryly. "I'm usually the optimist. I hope you're right."

"If I'm not and the secret gets out, what does that really change? It won't hurt our defensive posture. Hell, most people won't believe it anyway. It sounds like science fiction."

His father considered that and nodded. "I suppose so. In any case, it's not as if we have a lot of choices about how we respond to her arrival."

Jared felt his lips twitch. Here came the compassionate response.

"The needs of the Empire—our Empire—come first, of course," the emperor said, "but we'll try to help her and this other Empire. We can best do so by getting our own house in order, stopping the AIs we have to deal with, and then turning our attention to her situation.

"I'm expanding your mission. We need to get to Terra and retrieve the override. Depending on the circumstances, we can then decide the best way of getting to Twilight River. Perhaps sneaking will work. Or it might require brute force. One way or another, we need the tools to defeat the AIs."

He nodded. "Did she tell you what they know about the key and the override?"

"We spoke briefly about them. She's aware the Imperial Scepter is the key to get into the Imperial Vaults on Terra. She also knows that it requires DNA from the Imperial Family. DNA she was shocked to discover she didn't have when Ethan tried to access their Scepter.

"Just like in our universe, neither of them are direct descendants of the Imperial House. Unlike in ours, there are no surviving cadet branches of the family. The only man who fits the bill there is at war with them, so they need other options."

"Based on her reaction to me, she didn't come looking for my help," Jared said. "She was hoping other members of the Imperial Family were still alive here. She's grasping at straws."

"No," his father disagreed. "She'd clutch at anything that will keep her head above water. Drowning people do that. Hope is fading there.

"Once we end the reign of the AIs, we won't need the override. We can certainly hope it works for them. I'll cheerfully give it to her then."

"What if it doesn't?" he asked. "What if the override is somehow different? They might fight their way to Twilight River and then it fails to work."

His father nodded glumly. "I'm hoping that during the process of acquiring the override here, she'll get all the data they need to do so in their own universe. The key isn't required to open the vaults. We have the complete plans. It would be difficult but not impossible."

"You're not suggesting that I—"

His father shook his head. "Absolutely not. Based on her reactions, you wouldn't be a welcome sight to anyone there. Under no circumstances do I believe you should go there. In fact, as much as I hate to say this, you need to take precautions.

"Desperate people do desperate things. I can foresee circumstances where she might be very tempted to kidnap you and force you to help her. Do not allow that temptation to bloom. She's an honest woman. I'd prefer we help her stay that way."

Jared had been thinking along the same lines. It wouldn't have been easy for this Kelsey to get him away from his ships and into Omega. Then she'd need to convince the alien to open a way back to her own universe.

Daunting obstacles, but as his father said, desperate people would take terrible risks. He should know.

"I think the safest way to scotch that plan is to lay it out for her," Jared said after he took a sip of his whiskey. "If she knows we're on the lookout for her to try something, then she won't. We need to give her hope, though. Despair is a terrible thing."

"That's why I'm sending her into the Rebel Empire with you," his father said as he set his drink down on the table between them. "She must be part of the success. I want you to take her back to Omega with you and assist her in gathering some of her people to join you. A trusted cadre but not a group that's a threat to you or your people.

"Limit the number of people on your mission that are duplicated. They won't have implants, so identifying them should be simple enough, as long as your crews are diligent and the computers keep track.

"If you send anyone to her side, be certain you have passwords and code phrases. And make sure Kelsey understands that. Once again, we'll keep the honest people honest."

Jared nodded his understanding. If she had her own people along, they'd learn what obstacles they had to overcome when they went for a repeat back in their own universe.

"Then you will complete phase one of your mission," his father continued. "Send the report the Rebel Empire expects from Harrison's World. That buys us critical time. After that, you'll probe toward Terra. That means you'll need the Imperial Scepter.

"I'll also send the small transport ring with you. Sadly, a situation may arise where you are forced to send the override back to your ships in a hurry."

Jared understood his father's meaning at once. It might become necessary to send the override back because they were trapped by the AI's forces. A suicide mission, in other words.

"Finally, I've changed my mind about how much force to send with you," the emperor said. "You're going to need *Invincible* and a strong escort in case the way is blocked or you have to provide a rear guard while someone sprints for home with the override."

That would be the worst-case scenario, if they got the override and had to make a stand while others got it safely away. It would be worth it, though.

His father leaned forward. "The best result is for you to slip onto Terra like you did Dresden. Then you could do the same while moving toward Twilight River. Use weak flip points to get into unexpected locations, if it seems safe. Use stealth to bypass enemy strong points when it doesn't. In any case, your orders are to retrieve the override and take the fight to the master AI."

"I'll do my best," Jared said, inclining his head. "Let me urge you one more time to allow Commander Michaels to accompany us. His assistance could be critical."

The emperor shook his head. "No. You may trust him, but I'm not quite there yet. Coordinator West will be a better source than the good commander in any case, and she's already on the mission."

Jared sighed. He really wished he could change his father's mind, but he'd just have to make do.

This mission was his most daunting one yet. So many things could go wrong. The way might be blocked. The Imperial Palace might be destroyed. The AI might be too heavily protected.

No matter how he went about this, the mission would be a long, difficult one. One fraught with risk. One he had to make happen.

10

K elsey stared at her father's personal physician—her other father, that was—with some confusion. "What are medical nanites?"

"Extremely small machines programmed to perform repairs on a continuous basis," he explained in what she assumed he meant to be a reassuring tone. "They come from a reservoir inside your body that continually refreshes them. Or that would if they were operational."

The thought of little machines running through her made her skin crawl, particularly ones installed by the damned Pale Ones.

"And everyone has that kind of thing here?" Judging from his expression, she hadn't entirely kept the horror she felt out of her voice.

"Yes and no," he said patiently. "Everyone with implants has them. That was true in the Old Empire, too, by the way. These are not harmful in any way. Far from it.

"That said, the Marine Raider implants come with nanites of greater capability. We're still studying them, but once again, there is *no* danger. Your doppelganger in this universe provided the samples I have on hand and has been living with them for years now without any ill effect whatsoever. Quite the opposite, really."

"How can you trust anything done by the Pale Ones?" she asked. "If I could undo everything they did to me, I'd jump at the chance. The idea of these things sends a shiver up my spine."

"Princess Kelsey didn't complete the procedure you went through," he said slowly. "I'm very sorry for bringing these traumatic memories back to you, but you need to hear this and consider it with as clear a mind as you can."

He took a deep breath and continued. "Princess Kelsey was scanned by the Pale Ones for implants and had them forcibly implanted. Admiral Mertz and his people rescued her before they altered the programming in her implants.

"I'm told that's the reason your nanites are dead, by the way. The computer controlling the Pale Ones didn't allow its slaves to have any healing capability other than what their bodies normally provided. We surmise the nanites might have had some negative effect in allowing it to maintain control."

He held up a hand when she tried to speak. "Let me finish before you reject the idea out of hand. The code I pulled from your implants is very similar to what our people worked out, but not identical. We'd need to overwrite what you have now to allow the nanites to function, which would also prevent them from overwriting it themselves, so we're not talking about anything that could even be done immediately.

"Yet you need to know the differences between your history and your doppelganger's. I have implant recordings and marine helmet cam video. It will be extremely upsetting to watch, but I can't think of any other way to bring this home for you."

He sent her a set of files through her implants. She was shocked. She'd had no idea that was even possible between people. She'd only used them to work her armor and weapons. Nothing else her people had would interface with the dammed things.

With more trepidation than she cared to admit, she opened the first file. To her horror, it was the same implant recordings she'd made automatically when the Pale Ones butchered her. She paused it almost at once and examined the still image.

The marines trapped with her were different. One of them was even familiar, that Talbot guy she'd married. No, that her doppelganger had married. It was best to get into the habit of thinking that way.

In her world, none of the marines captured with her had made it. Some had died in the fighting when Commander Roche came for her, sadly fighting for the Pale Ones against their comrades. Other had died during the implantation process. Those were memories she wished she could get rid of.

She'd had to fight her own people, too. They'd used neural disruptors to stun her. She was deeply grateful she hadn't killed or seriously injured anyone.

Struggling to keep from hyperventilating, she restarted the playback. The events deviated from what had happened to her almost immediately. The marines managed to distract one of the Pale Ones, and this Talbot fought one by himself to give her time to do something.

In the end, this Kelsey managed to kill the Pale One, and the marines ended the other one. She never went into the final machine. This other her was so blessed.

The next major deviation was when the rescuers arrived. They came much more quickly than in her world. There, she'd spent several days as a Pale One being brutalized in every way imaginable by the savages and the AI.

In this universe, only minutes passed. To her shock, the Bastard was there. How could he have come for her? That made no sense.

More amazingly, he seemed relieved to find her safe. He'd actually risked his life for her, something she would've considered impossible.

Unlike in her universe, she was awake to hear what happened as they fled the orbital and arrived on the destroyer. It couldn't have been *Ginnie Dare*. It was another ship.

The video ended there, so she opened the second one. It was a marine helmet cam. It showed the damage to her body just as she remembered it. The scarring had been there too long for the regenerators to deal with in her case.

She opened the final video and immediately knew why the marines with Mertz had recoiled. This Kelsey didn't have the scars anymore.

Kelsey refocused her attention on the doctor. "I see. Your Kelsey was very lucky. I think I hate her for that."

The man nodded sadly. "I suspected as much. Still, in conjunction with multiple targeted regeneration sessions, the nanites could probably eliminate the visible scarring that remains. There would likely be some internal damage left at a cellular level, but the amount of pain you suffer from it would be greatly reduced."

She allowed one corner of her mouth to rise. "I'm not in pain, Doctor. The drugs inside my implants keep it under control."

"That probably isn't healthy over the long term," he cautioned, mirroring what Doctor Guzman on *Spear* had said. "You really should take what I'm saying as sound medical advice."

"I will, Doctor. Forgive me, but I have to think about this for a while before I make a final decision."

The doctor stood right away. "That's all I can ask. Let me leave you to consider it and thank you for coming down."

She sat there after he'd gone, considering what she'd seen. The Bastard had actually come for her. Not to kill her, but to rescue her from the worst days of her life.

The mere idea boggled her mind. It was, quite literally, inconceivable.

Worse, it meant she needed to make a real effort to determine what the truth here was. This Mertz was obviously not the same man as in her universe. And that might be the hardest thing of all to accept.

* * *

ELISE INSISTED on accompanying Breckenridge to see Kelsey once she'd finished her consultation with the emperor's personal physician. If there was going to be trouble, she wanted to be right there to stop it. She'd arranged to use an intimate little seating room for the get-together.

She needn't have worried. Kelsey smiled widely when she saw Breckenridge and came over to hug the flummoxed man.

"Nathaniel, it is *so* good to see you," she told the senator warmly. "I can't tell you how long I've waited for this moment."

Elise had trouble imagining the senator at a loss for words, but all he could do was stare over Kelsey's shoulder at her in shock, his mouth moving but no words coming out.

"I take it you know one another," Elise said wryly.

Kelsey turned to her and seemed mildly scandalized. "Of course we do. His nephew saved my life. He sent me many messages and helped the Empire organize its response after the expedition. I still haven't made it home in my universe, but I feel as if we're family."

"Me too, Highness," he said in a strangled voice. "I'm just not used to you being so friendly to me. We work well together here, but there's... tension."

She stepped back from the senator and frowned. "Why? Is my doppelganger an idiot?"

He chuckled and shook his head. "Far from it. Might we sit? We've got a lot of ground to cover."

Kelsey sat and seemed relaxed. Perhaps that was because both Elise and Breckenridge were her close allies in the other universe and she felt at ease. Whatever the cause, Elise was happy there was no tension.

Breckenridge took control of the meeting. "I regret that we're meeting in a situation where I have to discuss business, but events are marching on, and we need to get in front of them. There is some concern that you represent a threat to the Empire. Our Empire."

The other princess considered that and nodded. "I'm an unknown outsider with a familiar face. You have no idea what I'm capable of. I get it. I can't do anything, though. You know who I am. It's not as if I've secretly replaced your Kelsey."

"That's where the problem comes in," he said. "With implants becoming more commonplace, so are the computers that interface with them. Computers that know you as the heir to the Imperial Throne."

Kelsey frowned. "I'm not following."

"Consider *Gibraltar*, the superdreadnought you saw in orbit," Elise said softly. "Its computer would recognize you as the heir. There's quite a bit of havoc you could cause. Computers aren't like people. They wouldn't know you're not *our* Kelsey."

That made Kelsey sit back and frown. "What the hell would they let me do?"

"I haven't the slightest idea, and no one else really does either."

"I'll grant you that is a problem," the other woman admitted. "What do you have in mind?"

"His Majesty has come up with a solution that shouldn't inconvenience you too much," Breckenridge said, crossing his legs. "He'd going to have the senate declare Kelsey Bandar medically unfit to serve as heir for the time being. Since our Kelsey isn't here, that won't cause anyone any problems."

"Okay," she said. "It makes perfect sense, though I don't understand why you're consulting me about it."

"I needed to meet you so I can answer any questions my colleagues have. And I wanted to see you for myself."

Kelsey nodded. "I felt you tense up, so my friendliness wasn't what you expected. Are we enemies here in bizarro world?"

"Our relationship is… complicated. Our Kelsey didn't have the best rapport with my nephew. He tried to imprison her and supported the coup attempt. Sadly, he was responsible for a lot of needless damage and loss of Fleet lives."

The other woman laughed a little bitterly. "Of course he was. Why is nothing the same between my universe and yours? So if we have a complicated relationship, does that mean we get along on some level?"

The senator gave her a lopsided smile. "We do, though not in the way you imagine. I'm probably about to cause other me some serious problems, but it sounds as if his life is going more smoothly than mine has. He probably deserves this.

"Elise tells me that you know the emperor isn't your father by blood. Due to some youthful indiscretions, I'm actually your biological sire."

Kelsey's eyes bugged out. "You're my *what*?"

No, she hadn't known. Elise reached out and took the other woman's hand in hers.

"It ended before you were born," Breckenridge said. "Neither of us knew this until the attempted coup, so we're still trying to figure out how we feel about it. Needless to say, our version of you is still angry with me."

"Then she *is* an idiot," Kelsey declared, rising to her feet and pulling the man up and into an embrace. "That's the first thing I've learned that actually makes my life better. I already respect you. While I miss my father every day, I couldn't be happier to have you be even closer to me."

It was hard for Elise to keep a straight face at Breckenridge's expression. Flummoxed no longer seemed adequate. Flabbergasted was better. Then Elise stopped trying and just laughed.

Kelsey gave her an odd look and then saw the expression on Breckenridge's face. That made her laugh, too.

"I've stunned you, haven't I? I'm sorry." The grin on the woman's face told a different tale.

"I may never understand you," he said in a bemused tone. "But no matter what universe you come from, I am and shall remain your friend and steadfast advisor, if you'll have me."

After one more hug, Kelsey resumed her seat. "I trust what you two say more than so many other people here. Let me ask you about medical nanites."

With growing horror, Elise listened as Kelsey told them of her current condition and what the emperor's personal physician wanted to do to address it. Elise pulled her into an embrace when she finished.

"Oh God, Kelsey. I've lived my life fearing exactly that fate. I'm so sorry."

"It's done," the other woman said sadly. "I'm going to have to live with it for the rest of my life. I'm ruined. A travesty of a human being."

"Don't believe it," Elise said. "Don't fall into the trap that this ends your life. It doesn't."

"Have you seen the horror they left behind on my body?" Kelsey asked with a shake of her head. "I've often wondered whether I'd be better off dead."

Elise stared into the other woman's eyes and held her hands tightly. "Listen to me very carefully, Kelsey. Let them put the nanites inside you. They'll heal your body. Maybe even more than the doctors expect. It's the right thing to do."

"Allow me to second Princess Elise," Breckenridge said as he too leaned forward with an expression of sympathy. "Our Kelsey has recovered mentally and physically. I know it seems impossible to imagine, but you are far stronger than you give yourself credit for. You can triumph over this adversity. Let us help you."

Kelsey looked at them both in turn and slowly nodded. "If you say to trust this doctor, I will. Would it be possible to have a someone I trust do this, if he's available? Doctor Guzman might not know me here, but I know him. I trust him."

Elise nodded. "He knows you and has examined our version of you. He's at Erorsi, but I can get him, I'm sure of it. Take one more piece of advice from me and allow Doctor Lily Stone to do the work. She was with you every step of the way here. She knows your implants almost as well as you do. If anyone can fix your body, she can."

The other princess seemed to shrink into herself. "Will you stay with me?"

"Every step of the way," Elise promised fiercely.

Kelsey wiped her natural eye. "Then I'll do it."

11

Olivia stepped off the cutter and into the landing bay on the hospital ship *Caduceus*, currently in Erorsi orbit. It was set up to have small craft come directly inside the hull to expedite patient care. It had a veritable fleet of specialized ambulance cutters to make that happen during emergencies.

Her trauma bays were clustered close to the landing bay to receive the most critical cases immediately. Thankfully, there was no current need for those services.

She'd been the obvious person to brief Commodore Lily Stone, the ship's commanding officer. Well, not precisely her commanding officer. She had a flag captain that actually commanded the ship, but Stone called the shots.

Doctor Stone stepped forward with a smile. "It's good to see you again, Coordinator. Welcome aboard *Caduceus*. I believe you know Justin."

"Doctor Stone, Doctor Guzman, it's a pleasure to see you both again. Can we go somewhere private? Time is short."

Stone gestured for her to accompany them as they retired to a briefing room.

Olivia made certain the hatch was locked behind them. The room probably wasn't as carefully screened as her offices, but no one should expect critical secrets to be under discussion on a hospital ship. Secrets like the ones she was about to spill.

Once everyone was seated, she started. "Sean is delivering orders from the emperor to Commodore Graves as we speak. They've decided to pull most of Jared's fleet back to Avalon and send them to Terra. You're coming along."

Stone seemed surprised but nodded. "Terra? We can certainly make that happen, but why brief us personally? We're doctors, not combatants."

"Because you're going to be working on a patient that has what I'll kindly call serious issues while the mission proceeds. One who it's critical we keep quiet about until the mission is under way. Perhaps even then. I'm not completely sure of how they'll want to play it."

The two physicians glanced at one another in obvious confusion.

Guzman took the lead in following up. "Why us? Are the doctors on Avalon not up to the task? The word I'm getting is that they're catching up with the new technology pretty fast."

"I suppose," Olivia said with a shrug. "The key here is your experience. Particularly Doctor Stone's. We have a woman who was forcibly implanted with Marine Raider implants several years ago and is now suffering from the complications it brought on as well as subsequent injuries."

Stone leaned forward. "I thought we'd taken care of the Pale Ones. The teams on Erorsi forced them to come to them and overwrote their implant code with the clean version. They treated the injuries they could and didn't find any recent converts, only the savages. Did they miss one?"

Olivia shook her head. "No. The patient is Princess Kelsey Bandar. Not ours, but one from an alternate universe. She came through Omega looking for help."

The news made both doctors sit up straight in shock. Stone recovered first. "That's astounding. Of course we'll help. Did you bring her records? I assume she's been examined by someone."

"The emperor's personal physician looked her over and recommended treatment," Olivia said with a nod. "Her history is somewhat different there than what we experienced. To the point, she wasn't rescued until several days after the Pale Ones implanted her.

"She was savaged by the monsters. Her nanites are inactive, she lost an eye and has some kind of crude replacement, and the surgical scarring was not regenerated except for her head, hands, and arms."

Stone's jaw hardened, and her eyes narrowed. "Leaving aside the emotional damage she has to have suffered, that will create a very challenging path to physical recovery. Why didn't she get a full regeneration treatment on *Courageous*?"

"Let's just say the expedition there was not the same one we went on. A lot of her personal history is different. Jared wasn't in command of the mission. Commander Roche and *Ginnie Dare* went with *Best Deal*. Things played out much differently."

"Obviously," Guzman said. "I can't wait to hear more about it, but I get why we're keeping this quiet. Someone from an alternate reality has come to see us. Amazing."

"We need to review her medical files and start developing a treatment plan," Stone said. "Activating her nanites has to be step one. We'll make sure her implant code is up to spec, insert some of our Kelsey's stored nanites, and get the new Kelsey's body to repairing what damage it can. Let me have the files."

It only took a moment for Olivia to send them. Stone threw them onto the wall screen.

"It looks so much like her, except for that eye," Stone said with a frown. "We can't regenerate something like that, but I can put in a replacement that will be lifelike. Oh, my heart is breaking. The horrors she must've gone through.

"*Caduceus*, secure all discussion in this room under the file KB2 and lock it to only myself and Doctor Guzman. Then connect me with Captain Kemp."

"File secured, Commodore," the computer said through the overhead speakers. "Connection open."

"Yes, Commodore?" a woman's voice asked.

"Prep the ship for movement, Deloris," Stone said. "We'll be getting movement orders shortly, and I don't want to wait a minute longer than we have to. In fact, contact Commodore Graves and inform him that we're deploying. Gather the chicks and get us all moving for Avalon at best speed."

"Aye, ma'am. Bridge out."

"Chicks?" Olivia asked.

"Hospital ships aren't supposed to fight, but we do have escorts to keep trouble off our backs. Two heavy cruisers, four light cruisers, and eight destroyers. They're supposed to shield us while we run like good little noncombatants.

"What else can you tell me about this Kelsey? You've met her. What challenges are we going to face?"

Olivia grimaced. "Her universe has it tougher than ours. She's not Jared Mertz's friend there. There was an attempted coup there, too, and her father was killed. Ethan Bandar is on the Throne.

"I have no idea if that's because the man actually pulled off a coup or if that Jared Mertz is a cad. Honestly, I don't think Kelsey knows either. She hasn't made it to her version of Avalon yet.

"In any case, Jared stole *Courageous* and fled. Harrison's World is a sterilized husk, there's no graveyard, and they're in an awful bind. The bottom line is that they have very little access to recovered Old Empire technology."

Stone shook her head. "This is going to be complicated. I assume she doesn't know me."

"No, but she knows and trusts Doctor Guzman. Elise has convinced her to let you lead the treatment, but she needs to have a face she trusts standing beside you. That's why she needs you both."

"This might not have a perfect outcome," Guzman said with a sigh. "Her recovery is probably going to be difficult and incomplete."

"That's why we're bringing in the best the Empire has," Olivia said. "With the technology on this ship and your combined experience, you'll make as much magic happen as you can. The emperor considers this Kelsey his daughter, too. He's counting on you. She's also counting on you, even if she doesn't know it yet."

Stone's expression firmed with resolve. "We'll figure something out. We always do. If you'll excuse us, we have a lot of preparatory work to get started."

* * *

SEAN WATCHED Charlie Graves as he paced around the office just off *Courageous*'s bridge. He understood some of the feelings the other man must be feeling. The new orders put him into something of a bind.

"We're not exactly full strength here," Graves muttered. "I don't know how many Rebel Empire ships we're going to accumulate on the other side of the flip-point jammer as things progress."

"I hear you," Sean said. "The Pentagarans have moved their ships here to back you up, so the overall strength won't drop that much, other than the fact they made a great reserve force that you no longer have."

Graves grimaced and stopped pacing. "Exactly what I was thinking. What's the schedule on refurbished units at Harrison's World?"

"We've built up a fairly sizable force," Sean admitted. "We're short on trained personnel, though. I discussed the issue with Admiral Yeats before he finalized everything. Most of that reserve will be on its way to Avalon to pick up crew within the next week.

"It can be here before the jammer needs maintenance. It won't completely replace what Admiral Mertz is taking, but it'll give you a credible force.

"It'll have a new command for you, too. Much to his annoyance, Admiral Yeats has decided he has to pass *Gibraltar* on to you, so you have the most powerful fleet command unit possible. I wouldn't be surprised if you got a bump to admiral along with it. Congratulations."

"That's not as shocking as it would've been a few months ago," Graves said, rubbing his face. "I'm basically doing the job now. It'll be nice having the extra firepower. I'll miss this ship, though.

"With as many admirals as we're going to have running around, I'll need a chart to know who outranks who."

"I wouldn't worry about that. I gather His Majesty intends to create a new position for overall command. In the next few days, you'll get notice that Grand Admiral Yeats is in charge."

"That makes sense and far better him than me." The other man walked to the screen mounted on his wall. It displayed a tactical representation of the Erorsi system.

"I'm not sure why the emperor wants to make a push to Terra, but that's his call to make. I think based on the requirements you've given me, the best plan is to send *Invincible* and her escort back with you.

"They're used to working as a team now. I'd rather Kelsey had them with her, but she doesn't. A superdreadnought, two battlecruisers, four heavy cruisers, six light cruisers, and a dozen destroyers should provide him a good screen.

"Combine that with four marine transports, six colliers to rearm everyone, eight fast couriers, six Fleet transports, and all twelve scouts, and he should have a pretty potent force at his command."

Sean nodded. "He'll also inherit a light carrier that just came out of the docks. So will you. We have all the files that Commodore Anderson put together on fighter doctrine. These ships are based on battlecruiser hulls, so they only have one squadron of fighters to deploy, unfortunately."

"A force of Thirty-six fighters is nothing to sneer at," Graves said. "I'll take them. Will the ships come with escorts?"

"Sure will. Two heavy cruisers, four light cruisers, and eight destroyers. They should have more, but we're light on repaired hulls and even lighter on crew.

"These ships will come close to tapping the last of Fleet's trained people. The plan is to implement heavy training on boosting skills in our current crews while new people are recruited.

"As repaired ships come online, the experienced crews will split to form the nucleuses of two ships and start over. We're going to keep going as long as we can, but that's going to require a lot of hard work on everyone's part."

"That's going to be rough on morale, but I get it," Graves said. "I'll manage with the people we have left, I suppose. If we can catch a break when we take the jammer down for maintenance, we'll have even longer to get new ships into play."

The flip-point jammer was the weak link here at Erorsi, Sean knew. While it was up, the wormhole was impassable. When it was down, the enemy could send probing ships through and attack in force.

"How long is the maintenance cycle?" he asked.

"Based on the few times we've done it, anywhere from four to eight hours. That's assuming there isn't a major problem."

"Mind some advice?"

The other man shook his head and came back to sit beside Sean. "Not a bit. Lay it on me."

"You're playing defense. Switch your mindset around into an attack strategy."

Graves frowned. "I'm playing defense because I have to keep them out of this system. What am I missing?"

"My suggestion for when it comes time to perform maintenance is to mass every ship you have here at the flip point. Not to defend it, but to attack while the flip point is open. If they send a probe through at an inopportune moment, go after them with everything you have.

"The Rebel Empire ships will back off and play defense. You set them on their heels long enough to perform the maintenance and then race back to Erorsi. Played right, they won't even be in a position to rush you."

Graves smiled. "Because we'll have rushed them first. That's brilliant. Thank you."

"My pleasure. I wish I could take credit for the idea, but one of my tactical officers on *Spear* came up with it in a simulation. She really deserves the credit."

"Send me the simulation details along with her name, and I'll do exactly that," Graves promised. "I just got word *Caduceus* and her escorts are pulling out. We need to get you to *Invincible* before she gets too big a lead on you. Speaking of that, why do you need a hospital ship?"

"Can't say," Sean said as he rose to his feet. "Not specifically for the mission to Terra, though. Emperor's orders."

"Can't say or won't?" Graves asked shrewdly. "I suspect there's something else afoot."

Sean smiled blandly and shook the other man's hand. "Give them hell, Commodore."

"I will," the other man assured him. "And good luck on your secret mission. Keep the admiral safe."

"He'll get everything I have. You have my word on that."

12

J ared stood outside the room where Princess Kelsey was meeting with her doctors via FTL com. He would rather not interrupt them, but he needed the other woman's attention. She didn't know it yet, but they'd be leaving to meet the hospital ship and all the other vessels at Harrison's World shortly.

The Empire had gotten lucky with the relay between Avalon and Pentagar. Though the distance was considerable—even individually over the two artificially created flip points—the repeater was able to connect to both worlds.

Maybe that was because both flip points were new, because the termini in the Nova system were adjacent to one another, or perhaps it was just a fluke. Only about half the repeaters worked in connecting systems more than one flip away from one another.

That meant half didn't. For example, the repeater to Harrison's World hadn't. Luckily, they both had single flip connections to the Nova system, and Omega didn't mind repeating the transmissions. He'd have done the same with Pentagar, but this was better.

Why the alien could do it and the automatic repeaters couldn't was a mystery.

Carl Owlet had suspected he'd misunderstood part of the new theory on FTL and believed he'd eventually solve the problem. Only he wasn't here. Ironically, he was far beyond FTL range inside the Rebel Empire with Jared's Kelsey.

Jared rapped his knuckles lightly on the hatch and waited for it to open.

He wasn't nearly as tense as his guards. By now, he suspected that this version of Kelsey was reevaluating him. He felt relatively safe that she wouldn't attack him.

The hatch slid aside, and Kelsey gave him a hard look. "I'm rather busy," she said brusquely.

Elise stepped up and put a calming hand on the other woman's shoulder. "I'm sure he knows that. Perhaps you should hear what he has to say before dismissing him."

Kelsey grunted a little and stepped back. She smiled when her gaze shifted to where Jared's guards were eyeing her worriedly.

"I'm not going to hurt him. You have my word of honor."

The half dozen guards at his back seemed unconvinced, but Jared motioned them back. "Her word is good enough for me. Wait out here."

He stepped through the hatch and closed it in Colonel Bronson's face as he tried to slip inside. Jared turned to fully face Princess Kelsey. The wall screen was on, he saw.

Lily Stone smiled at him. "Jared, it's good to see you again. I wish I were there in person."

"Me, too, but I'm going to have to end this consultation a bit early. The emperor is sending us to meet you and wants to see Princess Kelsey before she leaves. We'll meet you at Omega. Sorry."

The other woman shrugged. "We've accomplished about all I could honestly expect without being in the same place. This is as good a time to wrap up the consultation as any. Just give me a few more minutes."

Lily turned her gaze to Kelsey. "I understand that you have no reason to trust me, but I know your implant hardware inside and out. Hell, I know your body inside and out, right down to the cellular level.

"I also know this sounds daunting. That's because it is. I'm not going to sugarcoat this. We won't get you back to the same level of recovery that our Kelsey managed. There's been too much injury, and it's had time to set in.

"What I can promise you is that we'll do everything within our power to repair as much as we can. That's going to be huge. No matter what universe you come from, I will always do everything I can to keep you in the best health possible. I only ask that you trust me as much as you can."

The corner of Kelsey's mouth quirked up. "Believe it or not, I actually do trust you. Maybe it's the doctor vibe, but I honestly believe you're in my corner and will do everything you can. I'm deeply appreciative, Doctor Stone. Lily.

"You and Justin have my complete confidence. Whatever you recommend, I'll do. I only wish that I could take you home with me when this is all over."

Lily smiled warmly. "I don't want to steal His Majesty's thunder, but we *have* spoken about that. You're probably going to bring some of your people over to join you on this mission. I hope you can bring a full medical team or two to take a crash course with me and my staff.

"We've got plenty of spare equipment to send back with them. I wish we could send ships, but that isn't realistic. What we can do is transship cargo containers full of medical gear and the know-how to use it. Once you have the data and knowledge to manufacture your own equipment, the sky is the limit."

The expression on Kelsey's face was profoundly grateful. "Thank you. It will mean uncounted lives saved, and you will have my eternal gratitude. All of you."

"It's my deepest pleasure. I realize that you and Admiral Mertz don't precisely get along, but you need to know that he urged me to make this proposal to the emperor. He's been a strong advocate on your behalf and that of your people."

Kelsey's eyes slid over to him. "Has he now? I'm starting to worry that my feelings toward this version of him might be misplaced. Maybe."

She returned her gaze to Lily. "I make no promises about how I feel toward him, but recent events have given me food for thought. Your loyalty to him tells me something about his character, too.

"I'm nervous but ready to get this process started. I will never forget the kindness you do me and my people. Neither will the emperor. My emperor. Until we meet, farewell."

The call ended, and Kelsey turned to face him. "I can't make the same promise for you, but I do appreciate the assistance."

He bowed slightly. "Believe it or not, it's my pleasure. If you and Elise would accompany me, His Majesty would like to see you one more time before we leave for Harrison's World."

"I'm going to cry," Kelsey said sadly. "Seeing my father again was an unlooked-for blessing. Returning to a world where he's dead is going to open those wounds all over again." She strode to the hatch without giving him a chance to say anything.

Jared fell in behind her with his wife at his side. Together, they all headed to the final audience with Karl Bandar before they left for Terra.

* * *

KELSEY ENTERED the Imperial apartments with a heavy heart. As much as she wanted to see her father again, she knew he was dead. This version of him wasn't the man who had raised her, no matter how alike they seemed. Her father was dead and buried.

Not that her traitorous emotions cared. They knew he was her father in every way that mattered.

Karl Bandar rose to his feet as they entered. He smiled at her and gestured to the three chairs he had set up. "Kelsey, please join me. Jared, you too. Everyone else, wait outside."

She didn't like the idea of sitting down for a casual chat with the Bastard, but this wasn't her show. If she were going to get the tools her people needed to survive, she'd have to hold her nose and do it. At least he wasn't insisting they have dinner.

Once they'd all sat, her father considered her. "How did your consultation with Doctor Stone go?"

Kelsey shrugged. "As well as it could. The damage to my body has set in, and the prospects of a complete recovery seem unrealistic. Still, any improvement will be a welcome change."

"That grieves me deeply. When I first heard what had happened to you in this universe, I was heartbroken at the pain and suffering you'd endured. I now realize that my version of you got off lucky.

"Another thing the two of you share is that you're both stronger than you think. You stand up to adversity and force it to your will. You will overcome this."

"I appreciate that you think so, but you really don't know what my home is like."

She flicked her gaze toward the Bastard. "And I'm not convinced you know the people around you as well as you think, even if it's becoming apparent that this Jared Mertz isn't the same as mine. At least not openly."

Her father digested that before he shook his head. "I refuse to believe that. While I can certainly misjudge people, I saw how Ethan became at the end. I pray he isn't mad in your universe, but he drove the coup here. Even my Kelsey agreed."

"I really don't know how much weight to give things here," she said with a sigh. "The differences at Harrison's World illustrate that things are not identical between our universes, but so many things seem similar."

Mertz cleared his throat. "I can't speak to the other me. Honestly, I know with all the prejudice I dealt with in Fleet because of my parentage, I could've become bitter. I might be the bad guy there.

"What I can say for certain is that I'm not one here. I love the Empire and have zero desire to run it. Kelsey has become my sister in reality, and I love her. My father is a bit more intimidating, but I'm trying."

He turned to face her squarely. "What I can promise unequivocally is that I will do everything within my power to help you and your people, with the understanding that my Empire comes first."

"Perhaps it would be helpful to know precisely what you want us to do," her father said. "You came here with a plan in mind. Based on your earlier comments, I believe you're looking for the key and the override. Is that right?"

Kelsey nodded. "I was able to send information through the weak flip point and back to the Empire, just like you. We also found the information that allowed us to deduce that the Imperial Scepter was the key to the Imperial Vault on Terra and what that vault probably contained. Unfortunately, that's when the coup took place."

She gave Mertz a hard look. "You staged a coup. My father died in my universe. So did everyone with any hint of Imperial blood, except for you. The damage to Fleet and Avalon was significant.

"You took the Imperial Scepter and fled when you couldn't kill Ethan. Your ships guarded the weak flip point while you came through. You managed to convince Captain Breckenridge to let you onto *Courageous*, and then you and your traitorous cohorts killed him, stole the ship, and fled through the flip point leading to what I now know is the Rebel Empire."

She sighed. "I hope to eventually kill that version of you, but the key is lost. Even if I had it, I can't use it. When I found Omega and learned of your universe, I knew I had to beg your help. I need your key and someone with the right genes to unlock the Vault."

Her father leaned forward and took her hand. "I feel terrible for the pain you've suffered, both physically and mentally. It rends my heart. Yet I must look out for my people first.

"I cannot send the key with you until we have the override. Even so, it might be that our key is different. It might not work."

"Worse, you don't have the ships to get to the Master AI at Twilight River," Mertz said. "It will be heavily guarded, as will Terra. Without the graveyard, you'll need to use stealth, and that might not be enough to bypass the defenses."

"It's all I have," she said. "I refuse to just give up."

Her father nodded. "I've authorized the transfer of knowledge and hardware from our universe to yours. You can bring people over to receive training in using the equipment. That will make a difference.

"Once we get that started, you and some of your people may accompany Jared to Terra. The knowledge of what you have to face there may make the difference between success and failure back in your universe.

"Finally, once we have the override, you're welcome to our Imperial Scepter with my blessing."

"The key is useless without someone to use it," she said. "Doctor Stone told me that my DNA is identical to her Kelsey. That gives me hope that the Imperial DNA in my universe is the same, too."

"I'll wager we can figure out a way to short-circuit that lock," Mertz said. "My friends are very talented."

Kelsey very much doubted that, but saying so wouldn't help her cause any. She'd take what help she could get. "Thank you."

Her father rose to his feet. "Time is short, but I'd appreciate it if you dined with me. Just the two of us. Sorry, Jared."

"I understand," Mertz said as he stood. "I'll go to Orbital One and get *Athena* ready to move out." He inclined his head toward her. "I know this is hard, but I'm not your enemy, Kelsey. I'll do everything I can to help you."

She only wished she could believe the lying bastard.

13

Elise was waiting for Kelsey when she finished the meal with her father. The other woman's expression was closed, but she knew her Kelsey well enough to see the turmoil roiling under the doppelganger's calm expression.

It wasn't too hard to imagine any number of things getting to the woman, but odds were good that her father was high on the woman's list of deep thoughts.

Rather than intrude, Elise simply walked Kelsey out to the landing pad where a sleek grav car was waiting for them. In moments, they were flying toward the city and the spaceport.

Kelsey didn't say anything for the first few minutes but finally turned toward her. "You married Mertz. Why? Political survival? Because your people needed the Empire?"

Rather than being offended, Elise was glad for the opportunity to talk about Jared directly. Kelsey needed to understand who he was, or they'd never accomplish anything long lasting.

"No. Our version of you made a treaty that gave us a fighting chance. I married Jared because I really do love him."

Under other circumstances, the look of incomprehension would've been amusing. Okay, it still was.

"I just can't force myself to understand that," Kelsey said, disbelief clear in her tone. "I hear everyone talk about what a great guy he is, but my Mertz is a total dick."

Elise smiled. "That leads to a discussion of nature verses nurture. Is someone's personality determined in the womb? Or do the circumstances of our lives make us who we are? I'm inclined to believe the latter. Life is what we make it, and it in turn shapes us."

She turned in her seat to face Kelsey directly. "I've learned a lot about Jared since we met at Pentagar two years ago. That includes the circumstances of his birth and some of the ways it worked against him. Not only with the hatred you and Ethan gave him, but the slights his fellow Fleet officers perpetrated against him.

"Admiral Yeats admitted to me that, at the time of the exploratory mission, Jared would've been a senior captain rather than a commander if he'd been fathered by anyone else. Frankly, I'm amazed Jared isn't bitter."

"How do you know he isn't?" the other woman asked intently. "Perhaps he's a simmering pot of resentment inside with great acting skills."

Elise shook her head. "I have implants. I might not be able to read his thoughts, but I can certainly sense his moods. I was good at that even before I got implants, but linking with him allows me to be absolutely sure.

"In your universe, you're the only person who has implants. You have no idea what it means to interact with someone else who also has them. Particularly someone close to you. Allow me to demonstrate."

She initiated a call to Kelsey's implants. Previously, Kelsey had only received files. This should be a real education for the other woman.

Once Kelsey accepted the call, Elise spoke only with her mind.

This is what it feels like to communicate through the implants. It's almost like just talking. Do you feel anything about me?

Kelsey shook her head. "No. It's like you're whispering in my ear."

Elise nodded. "That's right. Even with implants, this is how most people communicate, but there is another layer for those who are *really* close. Frankly, it's asking a lot to even make this offer, but you need to understand precisely how sure I am.

"Implants allow extra depth for those in a relationship. Intimate mode. It's designed to sense emotions and even the physical body of one's lover.

"Not even close friends use this with one another because it's intensely personal, invasive even, when the two aren't actually intimate. Yet I need you to understand the true depth of my certainty. Are you willing to do this for a minute?"

Kelsey stared at her before nodding wordlessly. "We're close friends in my universe. I trust you."

"I apologize in advance. You can terminate the contact at any time you choose. You're always in control."

Elise offered her friend a connection in intimate mode. Moments later, Kelsey accepted.

The mental link expanded to include brushing up against Kelsey's emotions. She felt the other woman's uncertainty and doubt on a level that was beyond question.

She also had an uncomfortable awareness of her friend's body. In intimate mode, she was deeply connected in a way meant to enhance a lover's touch and to feel their reactions as if they were her own.

With Jared, that meant she could truly feel his physical reaction to her touch. Making love was like sharing his body. The intensity of the connection in those moments was an almost spiritual experience.

Kelsey reached out hesitantly and ran her finger down Elise's arm. The gesture was nonsexual, but the resonance between them in intimate mode caused Elise's body to tremble a bit and sent a jolt down her spine.

The other woman snatched her hand back as if the contact had burned her.

"I felt that," Kelsey said, her voice shocked. "I felt myself touch you and your reaction to it. How it made you uncomfortable. How it made you—" She clamped her mouth shut.

Elise ended the connection, relieved to once more be alone inside her own skin. "That's how I know how Jared feels. He's my husband, and I've been in intimate mode when he's spoken about any number of things. He's not your enemy or the Empire's in this universe. I'll stake my soul on it."

The other woman rubbed her face. "This is impossible. How can people live with that kind of intimacy? You… ah, make love with that turned on?"

Even the thought of that made Elise react physically, and she was deeply glad to have ended the contact with Kelsey. She didn't want to have the other woman experience the rush of arousal the very idea sent through her.

"Oh yes. I'd never imagined how it would be to not only feel one's own pleasure, but to feel someone else's at the same time… it's indescribable. I instantly know how he feels, even how my body feels to him. When we make love, it's almost as if we're one being, body and soul."

She shook the thought away. "But that's too personal to think about right now. Can you see why I'm so sure?"

"I suppose," Kelsey said with a slow nod. "I'm not sure how I can accept it deep inside. And no, I am not doing that with him. No way. I might throw up."

Laughter bubbled up in Elise's throat. She tried to stifle it but failed miserably as she started giggling.

Kelsey smiled and chuckled. "That was pretty funny, I suppose. You've given me a lot to think about. Thank you."

"That's what friends are for. We're almost to the spaceport, so let's get ready for the trip up."

* * *

SEAN MADE the transition to the Nova system from Pentagar on *Invincible*'s flag bridge. The amazing ship and her control center made him so jealous. He'd be planning some upgrades at Boxer Station on this trip.

"Transition complete, Commodore," Marcus said over the overhead speaker. "All ships have checked in. It doesn't look as if Admiral Mertz has made it yet. Shall we wait here for him?"

He considered that, and then shook his head. "No. Let's get into orbit around Omega. The admiral will bring Kelsey there so she can pass word back to her people. Now that we can give them some suits, she'll get an escort. What steps can we take to get them set up here while maintaining security?"

"The emperor has already ordered there be only limited duplication with our current personnel, but I foresee problems. This Kelsey likely trusts a number of the same people we have along. We need to come up with a way to allow for that."

"None of the doppelgangers have implants, or so I am led to believe," Sean said slowly. "Only Princess Kelsey has them, and the senate has already declared her temporarily unfit to be heir, so none of our automated systems will allow her to use her implants to do anything to override the command officers."

"Good news, but I'm less certain about Harrison and myself."

That made Sean sit up a bit straighter. "I'm not following."

"When I was created, Carl Owlet altered the original Imperial core imperatives. To be specific, he removed the prohibition preventing me from using weapons and mandated my obedience to Jared Mertz and Kelsey Bandar.

"He used their implant serial codes for that. Obedience to those directives is nondiscretionary. If our visitor ordered me to open fire on the rest of the fleet, I would be compelled to do so."

"What happens if Jared orders you not to?" Sean asked.

"Carl Owlet put some logic in place for that. As I was intended to manage this ship—he apparently never considered the possibility that I would move on, for which I shall need to chastise him—he put a rule in place that Admiral Mertz had senior authority.

"I understand that she isn't the Kelsey I was meant to obey. Carl Owlet obviously intended to have our Kelsey have authority, not the one from another universe. Yet they share an implant serial code. To my core rules, they are the same person."

Sean nodded unwillingly. "I get you. How do we work around your core rules?"

"It sounds like cheating when you phrase it that way," Marcus said with a chuckle. "To honor the spirit as well as the intent of my rules, Admiral Mertz needs to give me very specific and defined orders about precise things.

"For example, he could order me to disallow her control of the antiboarding weapons until he specifically removes the exception or a year has passed. I could do that because it is limited and I know it is intended to reserve the command authority for the designated individual with an expiration date."

"Why does it need to be limited? Isn't a rule absolute? Like two is always bigger than one."

"That edges into one the differences between a computer program and a sentient AI. Think of my core rules like a moral compass. My version of right and wrong, if you will. A computer will see things in black and white. I have shades of gray.

"If Admiral Mertz were to give me an open-ended order, I would feel compelled to disregard it as a violation of the spirit of my core rules. A more circumspect set of instructions tailored to the specific circumstance we find ourselves in would make me willing to shade the letter of the law to suit the situation."

Sean nodded and sat quiet while absorbing that. It was a lot more nuanced than he'd expected. "And Harrison is the same?" he asked after a minute. "He can fire weapons, too?"

"Indeed he can. I'm surprised he hasn't already mentioned that to you."

"Believe it or not, he tends to stay quiet and runs mostly in the background. Perhaps I'd even call him shy. Introverted."

"Interesting," Marcus said slowly. "I need to spend more time talking to my sibling. He and I have so much in common, yet we also have so many subtle differences."

Moments later, Marcus spoke again. "Orbital One indicates that *Athena* has left for the flip point. Admiral Mertz and Princess Kelsey will be here in a little over two hours."

"Then we'd best get those rules you spoke of worked out. I'd like to be able to pass them on to the admiral for his consideration once he arrives. Let's try to restrict her without being obvious about it. If she doesn't realize we've locked her out, she can't be offended by it."

14

Olivia made the trip from *Caduceus* to pick up Kelsey and Elise. The Crown Princess sat in the back and almost immediately fell into a light doze.

Kelsey's reaction to the fleet of ships in orbit around Omega as their cutter undocked from *Athena* almost made Olivia smirk. Stunned didn't seem adequate. Dumbfounded, perhaps.

Kelsey was using her implants to access the ship's scanners. The ships were too far away to pick up by eye, even with the woman's Marine Raider implants.

After a minute of staring into space, Kelsey refocused her eyes on Olivia. "This has to be some kind of trick."

"Why?" she asked.

Kelsey pinched the bridge of her nose. "Because I need those ships. My people need them. Yet, in our universe, they aren't where we can get to them or repair them. And I can't believe that Mertz had all this firepower at his command and didn't do something."

Olivia shook her head. "Oh, he did something. Just not what you think he would've done if he were the kind of man you believe him to be."

"Maybe he couldn't convince enough people to go along with him," the short woman said with a frown. "Though he had no trouble getting almost half of Fleet to rebel in my universe."

"That's not the man I've come to know. He literally risked everything to save my people. The AI came very close to killing him and everyone with him."

"I see plenty of reasons he would risk everything," Kelsey said with a gesture at the bulkhead. "This fleet gives him a base of power to do whatever he wants."

"Yet he hasn't skulked about doing any of the dastardly deeds you seem certain he really wants to commit. Once he defeated the AI, he could've ordered the few ships he had left to stay at Harrison's World and taken *Invincible* home once she was repaired. Fleet wouldn't have been able to stand against him."

She raised a finger to stop the retort she saw coming. "And before you object that his crew wouldn't follow his orders to subdue the Empire, let me tell you about the computer on his superdreadnought.

"It's not a standard Old Empire unit. It's a sentient AI like the ones running the Rebel Empire, only it has a core imperative to obey Jared. It can also fire the weapons. He could order it to stun everyone aboard with the antiboarding weapons. None could have stood against him at Avalon."

Olivia shook her head before the other woman could respond. "This conversation is getting old. Let me give you a pro tip from someone who has actually ruled a world. If the facts don't match the results you're seeing, you've miscalculated."

Olivia knew she shouldn't be angry, but she was. Not at how Kelsey felt. Not really. It was more because of how unfair the woman's attitude was to Jared Mertz. The man was a damned saint as far as Olivia was concerned. Hearing this duplicate of her friend slander him stung in unexpected ways. She needed to get a grip on herself.

Kelsey sat slumped into her seat for half the trip and then spoke softly without looking at Olivia. "I can't put what I feel aside. He killed my father. Perhaps your version isn't the same kind of man, but that doesn't change the rage and loathing I feel for him."

Olivia turned to Kelsey, making sure to keep her expression neutral. "And I could say that having seen your brother Ethan in action over here, I can't get past that. The man was a mad dog that tried to kill your father and plunge the Empire into civil war.

"Is he that way in your universe? I hope not. He managed to hide his condition from everyone here. By your logic, I'd be doing your universe a favor by shooting him. Is that fair to him? No."

She sighed and put her hand on Kelsey's arm. "This is complicated in ways that no one else can understand. The people around you look like the ones at home, but they've lived different lives. You have to be able to see past appearances. Discover the truth without your prejudices."

"I don't know if I can," Kelsey said in a whisper.

Olivia squeezed the other woman's arm. "You can. Kelsey Bandar is the strongest person I know. She can quite literally do anything. Remind me someday to tell you the story about how she saved tens of thousands of people on my world by doing something absolutely mad. Just say 'fist of god' and I'll know exactly what you mean."

"I wish I was her. I really do," Kelsey said as she slumped farther in her seat. "I've failed at so many things. It's as if she got all the good luck and I got the bad. Is that how karma really works? Am I destined to be the Kelsey that failed?"

"Destiny is wrapped around what other people think. It says nothing of the conflict we feel or the struggles to succeed. Kelsey has her doubts, too. She puts them aside and does what needs doing. You can do it, too. I'm sure you already do."

The cutter docked with the hospital ship. That woke Elise, and the three of them made their way out. Doctors Stone and Guzman were waiting outside the lock.

Lily extended her hand to Princess Kelsey. "Welcome aboard, Highness. I believe you already know Justin."

"I do, though everything here is so strange and unexpectedly different in ways I'm having trouble adjusting." Kelsey shook Lily's hand and then Justin's.

"No matter the differences, we'll do everything in our power to heal you," Guzman said softly. "We take our oaths very seriously. Lily risked getting shot to save the emperor during the coup. Elise *was* shot."

Kelsey tilted her head and looked more closely at the Crown Princess of Pentagar. "I hadn't heard. Thank you both."

"I didn't do that much," Lily said, waving a hand as if dispersing smoke. "Just took a blood sample and found a compound that I could combine with nanites to give him a chance. It was a damned close thing. Elise did the dangerous part."

Guzman shook his head. "Lily was with him in the Imperial infirmary during the coup. Getting that sample would've been worth her life if... well, if the wrong people saw her taking it."

The princess from another universe didn't say anything about the man's delicate pause, but Olivia interpreted her sour expression for comprehension about what he'd not said.

"In any case," Lily said. "Let's get you to the medical center and do a complete scan."

"The Imperial physician did one," Kelsey said with a scowl. That was a trait the two Kelseys shared.

"He's not me. I want to use my own equipment and make my own decisions about what's possible and what's not. He's a good man, but I have a lot more experience with Old Empire technology. The goal isn't to do a good job fixing you. It's to do the absolute best job possible."

Elise put her hand on Kelsey's shoulder. "I understand you don't like being poked and prodded, but I'll be with you the entire time."

The short woman sighed. "If I must."

"On that cheerful note, I'll take my leave," Olivia said. "I'll be on *Invincible* if you need me."

As she headed back into the cutter, Olivia sighed. This was going to get worse before it got better. Once Kelsey had people from her universe reinforcing her view of Jared, it would set in stone again. That would be an unwelcome addition to an already stressful mission.

Kelsey felt overwhelmed as they made their way into the largest and most advanced-looking medical center she'd ever seen. Men and women in white lab coats bustled about.

"How many people are you expecting to treat?" she asked Doctor Stone. "Capital Hospital on Pentagar was nothing like this. No offense, Elise."

Her friend smiled. "None taken. We're doing everything in our power to rectify that. Doctor Plant, the man who first treated you there on my version of Pentagar, is very enthusiastic."

The memory of the jovial man in a white smock lightened Kelsey's mood. "He treated me, too. I'm glad. I hope I can at least jump-start something like that in my universe."

She put her uncertainty behind her. Time to get this over with. "What next?"

Next turned out to be several hours of intensive scans followed by dinner with Elise while the doctors wrangled over the new data.

Once she'd sated her never-ending hunger, they returned to Stone's office. The two doctors were already seated at a small table and gestured for the women to join them.

Kelsey sat across from Stone. "Did you discover anything else I need to know about?"

"We managed to get some higher resolution readings of potentially problematic areas," Stone said. "That improves your potential outcome.

"Another factor that the Imperial physician couldn't account for was something he doesn't really understand: Marine Raider nanites. While I gave the emperor a shot of them with the cure, that was just a stopgap measure. He has the standard Fleet version now."

Kelsey felt herself frowning. "Since I don't have them at all, I really have no grasp of what that means. Is there a difference? Why not give him the better set?"

"Unfortunately, we couldn't at the time, though we're now in a position to change that," Stone said. "You'll have to ask Admiral Mertz about the specifics of that, as it's classified.

"The difference is that Marine Raider nanites are significantly superior. While the standard Fleet version can't repair the deep scarring in your body, I believe that a combination of Marine Raider nanites and a targeted series of regeneration sessions might eliminate virtually all of the pain you have to be feeling."

Kelsey shrugged. "I'm not in pain. I haven't felt much since the Pale Ones did this."

Stone's expression told her that the woman didn't consider that a positive thing.

"Your pharmacology unit contains some powerful painkillers. They only mask the damage. It would be better to eliminate the scarring. If you agree, we can seed your nanites now and start regeneration sessions tomorrow."

"I've already agreed," she told the doctor. "I have to trust your knowledge, even if the idea of machines inside me makes me a little sick."

Stone smiled. "For what it's worth, Kelsey felt exactly the same way. She warmed to the idea when she started getting hurt. These nanites are very powerful. They were cutting-edge Imperial tech before the Fall.

"Not even the Old Empire knew precisely how powerful an effect they would have on a person over the long term. Someone with Fleet nanites can live past three hundred years. What's possible with Marine Raider nanites boggles the mind."

"What?" Kelsey said with a frown. "Hundreds of years? That can't be right."

"You'd be surprised," Stone said. "What did you find on Erorsi?"

The nonsequitur made Kelsey blink. "Uh… a planet full of raging monsters? We managed to eliminate the orbitals but had no reason to look closer. Why?"

"Believe it or not, there's an old defense bunker hidden there. At least there is in our universe. The residents are descended from the people who tried to hold out. They had a man with them who was kept alive through a combination of Fleet nanites and a stasis chamber. He's ancient, but still alive."

The idea didn't register for a moment. "Wait. Are you saying someone down there was alive before the Fall? That's impossible."

Stone shook her head. "It's true. Ensign Reginald Bell was dropped off there by *Courageous* to assist in the original defense of Erorsi. I hope you get a chance to meet him. He actually saw Imperial City on Terra with his own eyes. Imagine growing up in the Empire at its height."

Kelsey felt her stomach do a slow roll. "God. To live through that and still be alive all this time later. How sad he must be."

Maybe her life didn't suck as badly as some. She made a mental note to find out about the refuge on Erorsi. It was too late to hold on to *Courageous* now, but if these people still had access to Old Empire tech and skills, their help would be critical to the survival of the Empire.

But that was a task for later. Right now, she needed to get this damned procedure done.

"We might as well get this over with," she said, resigned to yet another medical procedure. "Will it hurt?"

"Not at all," Justin said. "We'll use some of the nanite samples we retained from our Kelsey to create a template in your nanite fabricator. Once we have it reactivated, it'll begin getting them into your system. It should only take ten minutes, and you won't feel a thing."

"That may not be completely true," Stone said with a shake of her head. "Once your pharmacology unit senses the damage being repaired, it will begin reducing the dosage of the pain killers. In a day or so, you might feel a low-level ache or worse. Nothing sharp. That will last until we finish the series of regeneration procedures."

Oddly, the fact that it would hurt made her feel better.

"What about the elephant in the room?" Kelsey gestured toward her artificial eye.

She'd lost the original during the terrifying weeks she'd spent as a Pale One. Her version of Justin Guzman had figured out the medical equipment on *Courageous* well enough to put her eye together, but it didn't look pretty.

It also didn't work correctly all the time. Every once in a while, it glitched and reset. Or switched modes to infrared at inopportune moments.

Looking in the mirror every morning was a reminder of what she'd lost. If they could do anything about this, she'd kiss their feet.

"We can replace that with a version that looks normal," Stone said. "I wish we could regenerate it completely, but there are limits to Imperial technology. That said, it will look exactly like your original eye. No one will be able to tell it isn't natural.

"We can also regenerate the area around it. The scars will take a while to fully disappear, but I anticipate a complete success with the procedure. I recommend that we save that for a few days from now, however. Let's get the nanites active and start the targeted regeneration first."

Justin smiled. "That'll give me time to refresh myself on the literature and work with our technical people to create an eye with the same capabilities as your Marine Raider implants grant your natural one."

That hardly seemed important, since she never used any of the ridiculously powerful features in her ocular implants. Why anyone needed to be able to see telescopically or microscopically, she had no idea.

Still, that made better sense than some of the other Raider modifications.

Her sense of smell could now do a chemical analysis of things around her, and she could eavesdrop on conversations in the next compartment.

As a child, she'd read some comic books about people with super powers. She'd thought it would be amazing to be able to do those things. Now she knew that it would be a huge pain in the ass for the poor bastards.

Well, time to make the magic happen.

She rose to her feet. "Let's do this."

15

———

Jared sat in his private dining room aboard *Invincible* with Sean and Olivia. They'd just finished a quiet meal. Alex had outdone himself. Jared was warming to the idea of having a manservant with this kind of talent.

"It's time to work out the plan going forward," he said after taking a sip of his drink. "It's not going to be as simple as I'd imagined. Not only do we need to deal with Kelsey's doppelganger and her friends, but we also have a large number of ships we'll need to conceal. I think direct command of the destroyer will need to be in a different set of capable hands."

"You mean mine," Sean said. "At least I hope you do. I've been preparing various little pitches to be your executive officer."

Jared started to say something, but Olivia interrupted him.

"And I'm going along." Her tone left no doubt that she considered the matter settled.

Amused, he nodded. "Permission granted. Your unique insight into the Rebel Empire will be a huge plus."

The woman shot Sean a smug look.

"Okay, I'm beaten," Sean said. "Be gracious in your victory."

"We'll allow Kelsey to return to her universe and gather some people to bring back for training," Jared continued. "That means they'll need suits capable of withstanding the radiation."

"I have a hundred suits prepared," Sean said. "If they insist on more people—and you allow it—we'll have to make multiple trips."

"A hundred sounds like a nice round number," Jared said a few seconds.

"If she pushes the issue, I'll authorize up to two hundred. I'd prefer most of them not be people already on our ships, but I know there'll be some overlap. Keep it below ten percent. We need to be sure of who we're dealing with."

Sean grunted. "I've consulted with Doctor Stone about that. If Kelsey was honest about her people not having implants, we can make sure the serial numbers are different should we decide to give them any. We can also tweak their implants so we get a notification when we're dealing with people not from our universe."

"Are we going to do that?" Olivia asked. "Give them implants?"

Jared nodded. "Of course. We have more than enough Fleet implants to share at this point. They'll need them to absorb all the material.

"I like that idea, particularly if we can introduce a system like Sean is proposing. Something like an identify friend-or-foe check."

Their combat forces used IFF systems to recognize friendly units. It should be possible to do the same as soon as everyone got the longer-range com systems Carl Owlet had designed. Lily had finished her checks, and they were almost ready to start replacing the standard units in all Fleet personnel.

The new implant coms would have better range than the headsets the Old Empire had used. She'd verified Carl's declaration that they were stable and consistent at ten kilometers. In fact, she'd had no failures until just a bit more than thirteen kilometers and had had successes out to sixteen. They'd publish ten as the listed maximum just to be conservative.

As part of the implant procedure, the units could be given the codes specific to their own universe. This might not work if they ever had visitors from a universe that had implants and upgraded coms, but they'd deal with that when the time came. This solved their current problem.

Sean nodded. "Good idea. If it's implemented correctly, we should be able to update things seamlessly in the future, if we have to. Luckily, Omega will have insight if anyone else from other universes arrive."

The commodore smiled a bit more widely. "I had Doctor Stone and her people make a modification to the basic package Carl developed. His original setup didn't allow us to turn the implant signals off. One of the captured officers at Erorsi spotted the marines as implanted and flipped out.

"With the new implants, we can activate what I'm calling stealth mode. The implants stay active but don't interact with anyone else. No external signals."

"That's a great addition," Jared said. "Well done. Contact Lily and work out the details for rolling out the upgrade. I want priority for everyone on *Invincible* and *Athena*. Make sure Grand Admiral Yeats has the most recent specs for all the other units."

"Aye, sir."

"Who's going to accompany her?" Olivia asked. "It needs to be someone with implants. You can't be sure you get back the same person otherwise."

He gave her a considering look. "You've made a good impression with her and seemingly don't have a doppelganger. Would you consider going?"

She nodded at once. "Of course."

Based on his scowl, Sean disagreed, but he didn't say so out loud. "Getting everyone over will take a while if they're as suspicious as she was. Are we going to do the tech transfer, too?"

"No," Jared said with a shake of his head. "That'll take too long, and they need training for it. This is a dangerous mission, so she'll need to bring two sets of people, I suppose. One to go to Boxer Station and one to come with us.

"I know this is important, but we need to get *Athena* on her way. The messages have always been perfunctory, but we know how things change. If we assume this is going to be an easy mission, it'll go to hell."

Sean snorted. "Isn't that the damned truth. I'll start ferrying the suits over to Omega in anticipation of the transfer. Olivia can speak with Kelsey and make sure she knows the rules.

"The visitors will have escorts outside their quarters, and we'll make sure the duplicates are monitored even more closely. Marcus can keep a close eye on everyone aboard *Invincible*. We'll have to take extra precautions and be diligent when anyone leaves the ship."

"That works. Are you going to be able to manage that, Marcus?"

"Yes, Admiral. If you mandate that they be monitored for potentially hostile activity, my subroutines will make certain they don't plan anything out of the ordinary, even in their private quarters. None of the data is retained or made available to my primary personality unless it meets very stringent criteria."

"Do exactly that," Jared ordered. "I'll make sure that Kelsey knows in general what I've ordered. We'll keep the specifics to ourselves unless she directly asks. We won't lie. We just won't volunteer unnecessary detail. Understood?"

The other two nodded.

"Excellent." He focused his attention on Olivia. "We'll need a verification code to be sure you're you when you come back. How about a quote from one of the old Terran movies? 'I'm here to kick ass and chew bubblegum.' They shouldn't know that."

"Not many people would," the woman said with a sly smile. "'And I'm all out of bubblegum?' You have as odd a sense of humor as your sister. So be it. When are you sending her?"

"As soon as she finishes on *Caduceus*."

"Then your timing is good," Marcus said. "Her cutter just detached."

Jared stood. "Then let's be about our business."

* * *

It was actually the next day before Olivia stood inside Omega with Kelsey. She'd seen how worn the other woman was and put her foot down. Jared might want to move on, but eight more hours wouldn't hurt them.

The princess seemed refreshed the next morning, so it had been the right call.

"You look better," Olivia ventured as they waited for Sean to clear the area.

Kelsey had been delighted when the marines had shown her how to activate the holographic projector. That meant Olivia could see her face rather than a blank expanse of metal.

On the other hand, she was grateful they hadn't told her about the demon heads that her Kelsey favored during battle. She'd seen the one that the princess had worn while attacking the island on Harrison's World. The loyalists had tried to use a nuke get Calder and King freed. Talbot had called the attack the Fist of God.

"That's part of it," the other Kelsey said. "Mostly I think the nanites are doing something. And the regeneration session I had right before we left might have contributed. I woke up after six hours of sleep and pestered *Invincible*'s doctor to do it. Stone sent him the details last night."

After a moment, she continued. "I can't believe that ship. She's a monster. I wonder where the derelict ships ended up in my universe? I want her."

Olivia smiled sadly. "I suspect you won't find her. She probably died ten years ago, trying to beat the AI in my system. They moved all the ships in the decade that followed, so they might have dropped them into the sun. I can't imagine why they didn't do that in the first place."

Kelsey blanched a little. "I'm sorry. I forgot for a second that was your system."

"As sad as it is, that really wasn't me. I have to accept the world as I find it. In your universe, I'm dead. In return, I know for a fact you have some people there that are dead here. It's complicated."

"Isn't that the damned truth?"

"Ladies, are you ready?" Omega asked over their com. Once they said they were, he gave them a countdown and then opened the hull of the station. The way it came in and plucked them out into space was disconcerting.

"That is very disorienting," Kelsey said. "It's like he's some kind of space monster devouring us and spitting us back out."

"You realize I can hear you, right?"

Olivia laughed at Omega's dry tone. "You're getting quite good with human humor."

"Thank you. The ship you arrived in the system is too far away to see, Princess Kelsey, but I've signaled them to come pick you up. The cutter will be in range for com in a few minutes. Should I bring the suits out now?"

"I think so," Kelsey said. "Can you do it a little bit away from us?"

"I can do it on the other side of the station, if you like. The surface of my station doesn't need to correspond to a specific point inside."

"That makes no sense. Then again, none of this makes much sense. Bring them out just a little bit away from us."

Olivia watched the hull deform about a hundred meters away, sinking down for a second and then rising with antiradiation suits standing like a cluster of statues. They began floating slowly away from the surface but stopped within a meter.

Like the suit Olivia wore, they were designed to keep station above Omega's hull. The strange metal surface wasn't ferrous, so magnetic boots didn't work. Small grav units in the suits used the built-in scanners to stay near the surface.

Then two of the suits moved, coming closer. They weren't empty. Once they got closer, Olivia saw Sean and Elise inside.

"What are you doing?" Olivia asked.

"It's my fault," Elise said. "I decided to come with you, and Sean wouldn't let me come alone. It took me a while to convince Jared to let me. Sorry."

Kelsey smiled. "Don't worry about it. You're always welcome."

Olivia gave Sean a hard look. "You were just looking for an opportunity to come keep an eye on me, weren't you?"

"I'm only making sure Elise is safe," he said with an obviously false smile of innocence. "Admiral Mertz would be very upset if I lost his wife."

"She's in no danger here," Kelsey said with a grimace. "No matter what we feel about him, she is beloved among my people."

A flicker of movement off to the side resolved itself into a cutter approaching slowly.

"I think our ride is here," Olivia said. "Kelsey?"

The other woman watched the cutter come to rest on the surface, not sticking to it, but floating much like the suits. The ramp lowered.

"Let's grab a dozen suits to take with us," Kelsey said. "We'll put them in the back of the cutter."

Getting them inside was simple. They just detached the line from the suit and tugged it along. The built-in grav unit did all the hard work.

Fifteen minutes later, they were flying away from Omega. The cutter pilot spoke briefly with Kelsey but was locked into the flight control area. They rode mostly in silence.

Olivia wondered what meeting these people was going to be like. Kelsey had been difficult at first. Would they present other problems? She hoped not. There was too much to do.

Five minutes later, the cutter docked with a thump.

"Welcome to *Ginnie Dare*," Kelsey said.

Kelsey took off her helmet and was first onto the ship. She met the armed and armored marines waiting for them. A Fleet officer stood in front of armed men and women, smiling.

Olivia recognized Commander Scott Roche. He was dead in their universe but alive here.

"Princess Kelsey," he said with a smile. "Welcome home. You brought guests?"

"I did. We brought along some radiation resistant suits. You'll need to send a team out to recover the rest of them from the alien station while I get out of this armor."

"I'll take care of it."

They all followed Kelsey into marine country. Unlike in Olivia's universe, there was a separate area for women.

The suits were designed for easy removal and entry, so Olivia and Elise speedily extracted themselves. Kelsey took longer, but they were able to help her get out.

The visitors had taken the precaution of bringing clothes and Kelsey retrieved a Fleet uniform without any insignia from a handy locker.

Once they were ready, Olivia came out and rejoined Sean, who was deep in conversation with Commander Roche. She remembered that he'd served with the other man for a long time. His death had deeply saddened her lover.

"Well, what do we do now?" she asked Kelsey.

Before the other woman could answer, Roche cleared his throat. "As much as it pains me, I need to verify who I'm dealing with. Princess Kelsey, until I can be sure you're the same person who left, I'm going to have to take you into custody."

He looked at the rest of them. "And the rest of you will be joining her in detention until I have a better grasp of what we're dealing with. You'll note that the marines have neural disruptors. Please don't make them stun you."

16

Sean was a little surprised that Scott Roche had waited as long as he had to take them into custody. He'd been expecting the move as soon as they boarded the destroyer. Perhaps Scott was concerned that the suits were like Kelsey's armor. Or that they had weapons stashed inside the suits. Or both.

Whatever the case, he wasn't going to resist. Far from it. While there were obvious differences, he felt certain he could bring the Fleet officers around more quickly than Olivia would have been able to. She might be a great politician, but a familiar and trusted face carried a lot of weight.

His assumptions were proven correct when the marines separated him from the three women. Apparently, they'd be staying in a locked compartment in marine country for now, which made sense. A commander wouldn't let someone he wasn't sure he could trust wander around his ship, even under guard.

Four marines escorted Sean into the marine briefing room where Scott sat waiting. Two stayed close at hand. They were burly but unarmed. The trailing pair had neural disruptors. If Sean put up a fight, they'd almost certainly stun everyone and sort it out at their leisure.

"Have a seat," Scott said. "We need to talk."

Once Sean was seated at the other end of the table, Scott eyed his rank tabs. "A commodore? Congratulations. You were a captain the last time I saw you."

Sean smiled wryly at this version of his dead friend. "I was a commander in my universe when the promotion came. It was a bit of a shock, let me tell you."

The other man nodded. "I'll bet. We're going to sort out the situation with Princess Kelsey in short order, but I wanted to take the time to ask you a few pointed questions.

"She came back from the alien station and told us that she was going to a different universe. I confess I didn't believe her. Not until you came aboard, you and Crown Princess Elise. I know for a fact that you're at Harrison's World and Princess Elise is back on Pentagar."

"It was hard for us to accept, too," Sean said softly, "even with the proof we found on the station. Dead bodies of others trapped there. Including multiple versions of a number of people.

"After talking with your Princess Kelsey for a while, I think I have a fair grasp of events here in this universe. Some came out better for you, but most didn't. Believe it or not, we're here to help as much as we can."

Scott leaned back in his seat and considered him. "Perhaps. That's actually above my pay grade. Oddly enough, you'll be making the final decision on what to do about... well, you.

"This is such an odd situation that I just wanted to see if it was really was you. I'm going to send you to the medical center for a checkup. It's not optional, so please don't resist."

"I wouldn't dream of doing so," Sean said. "I want to convince you that we're for real and that there are things we can do to help you fight the AIs."

"I'm sure you'll explain that in more detail, but first, my questions. When did we meet?"

"That's not a good question," Sean said. "If you're the man I think you are, I can do much better than that. We met when we were lieutenants serving on Orbital One in my universe. A lot of people might know that. I bet they don't know about Commander O'Neil."

The other man's face paled a little. "God, I hope not. What a disaster that was. I learned the lesson about dating superior officers, even if they weren't in my chain of command, the hard way with her. I never told anyone about her except you."

"It went bad fast," Sean agreed. "Let me add that you absolutely shouldn't get caught two-timing a lieutenant commander before the second date."

"I wasn't, and you damned well know it," Scott groused. "Lieutenant Arnold made the pass, not me. I turned her down, but O'Neil came in at the wrong time. Man, I had no idea she was so jealous."

The other officer shook his head. "I'm convinced. You're Sean Meyer. Now, since you're here to help us, why don't you give me the digest version of your plan?"

"In a nutshell, we had better luck retaining Old Empire technology in my universe. The suit that I came over in is an example. We have hardware and know-how that we'll be happy to share.

"Your Princess Kelsey also wants us to help her get to Terra and recover something to stop the AIs. We're going to do that, though I have my doubts about the keys being the same in both universes.

"Honestly, if we can show you how to get inside the Imperial Vault and get your own version, that would be the best outcome."

"I have difficulty imagining how that's even possible," Scott said with a shake of his head. "Terra is a long way from Pentagar or Harrison's World. We're not going to be able to just slip over there without them seeing us. We have no idea what lies between us."

The other man sighed. "Maybe if the Bastard hadn't stolen *Courageous*. Losing it hurt us badly, and I'll wager you don't have a way of getting us anything like that."

"Maybe," Sean said. "There are a couple of options that might see that outcome."

That caused Scott to sit up straight. "Really? How?"

"The first way is the alien space station. It was designed to open portals to other universes. It's going to take a while to store the energy to do so, but Omega knows where this universe is now. He can create a bridge between your universe and mine big enough to send ships through."

Sean had never discussed that potential plan with Admiral Mertz, but he wasn't giving much away. Anyone with three working brain cells could guess what the station was built to do, particularly since it already provided a way into other realities.

"That's quite a helping hand," Scott said softly. "I have difficulty believing you're so generous. You have a powerful enemy to fight, too. The same one we do."

"We have a lot of ships but not enough to stop them if they come for us. A few less won't make much of a difference if it comes to that kind of fight. Still, that's beyond the purview of what I can negotiate anyway. The second option really depends on what's in the Harrison's World system."

Scott stared at him. "A dead world, a blown-up space station, and a lot of nothing."

"Sometimes there's more than meets the eye. I assume you're taking us there."

"The fleet is waiting for us," Scott said. "We'll get you all into Captain Meyer's hands so he can decide what we need to do."

"Then it'll be easy to see if I'm right. If so, I think we'll be giving you a serious boost at no cost to ourselves."

The second idea was also not one he'd run past Admiral Mertz. That could be bad, but it would build a hell of a lot of good will. He'd just have to take the chance.

It put out some risks for the Jared Mertz in this universe, too. Yet after speaking with Princess Kelsey, Sean had the feeling that this other Mertz was more like what Sean had thought of the admiral before he met him.

It was a hell of a risk that might have terrible consequences, but these people were already fighting a civil war. The only winner if they didn't end it would be the AIs.

* * *

Elise sat on a bed in the small bunk room that her compatriots had turned into a prison cell for them. "What did you think they would do? Welcome us with open arms?"

"I didn't expect Scott Roche to lock me up," the short woman growled as she paced. "We worked out a code so that he would know it was really me."

"One we could have gotten from you," Elise said reasonably. "This probably isn't some dark plot, just a sensible precaution. He'll be along soon enough to verify who you are."

"What is he doing?" Kelsey snarled, stopping to glare at Elise with her fists on her hips. "Why make me wait? Why interrogate Sean first?"

Olivia chuckled from where she sat across from Elise. "Because he knows Sean better than he knows you, I'd wager."

"Explain that. He's been with me for over a year."

The coordinator from Harrison's World shrugged. "I don't know the specifics, but they're both Fleet. They served in the same task force for a long while. Odds are they knew each other earlier in their careers. This isn't a difficult jump to make since he *did* start with Sean."

Kelsey collapsed onto another of the tautly made bunks and draped her arm across her eyes. "This is maddening. We have so much to do already. This is going to set the timetable back even further."

"I'm pretty sure that Jared didn't expect us back right away," Elise confided. "He said he didn't, anyway. He told me that he'd allowed time in the schedule for you to convince your people we were making an honest effort and for you to select those you're bringing back."

That didn't really satisfy the other woman, but what could they do other than wait?

In the end, it was almost an hour before Commander Roche showed up in the company of Sean Meyer. The Fleet officer watched Sean and Olivia embrace with an odd look but kept most of his attention focused on his princess.

She climbed to her feet and gave him a stony look that didn't bode well for him in the short term.

"My apologies for the delay, Highness," he said deferentially. "I needed to ask Commodore Meyer a few detailed questions. Let's get your identity out of the way, shall we?"

"Space is big, but the Empire will one day fill it again," she intoned.

"That's not the passphrase," Scott said with a scowl. "You're an imposter."

Kelsey frowned. "What? Yes it is!"

The man smiled. "It is. Just checking to be sure."

"And because you want to see me squirm!" the blonde said in an accusatory voice.

"That, too. We're on our way to Harrison's World at flank speed. We'll make the flip in about two hours. Perhaps you should take the opportunity to have dinner.

"I'm assigning marines to watch over you all, so please don't get any ideas. They have orders to stun everyone if need be. Including Princess Kelsey."

The Crown Princess of the Terran Empire nodded. "I'm starved. Let's go."

Sean and Olivia followed her out. Scott Roche fell in beside Elise as she brought up the rear. Marines trailed them.

"Princess Elise," the man said cordially, "I apologize for needing to take such precautions, but we can't be too careful."

"I can't argue," she said with more than a bit of amusement. "We're likely to do exactly the same once we return with your people to our universe. None of us really knows one another, even if we've known our counterparts for years."

"So I discovered when I got into some of the more recent events in Commodore Meyer's life. Might I ask a question about your universe?"

When she nodded, he continued. "I'm dead there, aren't I? He never said so, and it seemed strange to ask the question of someone I've known so long, but I'm getting a bad vibe."

"You died at Harrison's World," she said sadly. "You and your ship. Very few of your crew survived."

"I thought as much," he said with a sigh. "Tell me then, what is Jared Mertz in your universe?"

"Did Sean say something?"

"No, which only makes me more curious."

Elise imagined Sean hadn't wanted to fall down that particular rabbit hole. "It's not as if we haven't told Kelsey. He's not the man you think he is.

Not in our universe, anyway. He's a hero there. He didn't cause the civil war you suffered under, but he did his part to stop it."

Roche shook his head as if it were filled with cobwebs. "That's going to be hard to accept for all of us. I might never believe it."

"Another difference between here and my own universe is that I married him."

Roche stopped dead in his tracks. "You what?"

She tugged him back into motion with a smile. "You heard me. I married him. He's really a good man. Honestly, that's the reason I talked him into letting me come along on this trip.

"He needs an advocate. Your Kelsey has accepted that the facts in our universe aren't the same as in yours, but she's never going to be his champion. Not like our Kelsey."

"And you kept your Princess Kelsey over there so as to avoid confusion?"

"Actually, she's off on a mission. Both Jared and I wish she were here. It would make this so much easier."

The marines split them into two groups at the lift. Roche stared at her as if he couldn't believe anything she was saying. He probably couldn't.

"I think I'd like to hear more," he eventually said. "Captain Meyer is going to get as much of the story as he can, but if our peoples are going to work together, you'll need to convince many more of us about the… about Jared Mertz."

"Certainly. If it helps, I brought a ton of data and recordings with me. More than enough to convince anyone with an open mind that our Jared isn't a villain."

"That's going to be a tough sell, but I'm willing to let you make the pitch."

The lift returned, they walked in, and it whisked them away. She knew just how hard convincing them would be. The time she'd spent with their Kelsey had convinced her of that.

Still, Roche wasn't related to Jared like her blonde friend. He hadn't grown up with his prejudices. It might be possible to create enough doubt to give this a chance. If she could do that, he might set the tone for others.

Well, nothing worthwhile was ever easy.

17

I n the end, Kelsey was annoyed at how easily Captain Sean Meyer accepted what his counterpart from the other universe said. One hardly seemed to need to even finish sentences before the other was nodding.

She, on the other hand, got questioned for five hours after they returned to the Harrison's World system. Kelsey finally called Sean on it inside his office on *Spear*.

"Why are you picking my story apart and accepting what other you says at face value?" she demanded. "Exactly whose side are you on, anyway?"

The corners of his mouth twitched upward, and he rose from behind his desk. "Yours, of course. I'm sorry I gave you that impression. Drink?"

"Whatever you're having. Just not beer." She shuddered. Everyone in the other universe seemed to think she loved the stuff. She couldn't understand it.

He gave her an odd look but said nothing as he poured her a glass of wine. He handed it to her and resumed his seat.

"I distrust everything that man says," Sean said. "I'm just very good at understanding him while he makes his pitch. Whereas I trust everything you say while still finding it hard to believe."

"That's convoluted," she said then took a sip of her wine. The red had good body. Pentagaran wines were the best.

"This entire situation is convoluted," he said. "I'm giving him the chance to prove at least some of what he says while Scott takes the other ladies to the corpse of Harrison's World.

"He asked me to take him to one of the gas giants. I have no idea why, but I suppose we'll find out shortly. What I really want to know is what *you* believe."

"That's not an easy question to answer," she said after thinking about it. "A lot of what I've heard is difficult to believe. Impossible, in some cases.

"Yet I've seen an Old Empire superdreadnought. I've talked with what I'm assured is a sentient AI. I've even seen mountains of evidence that Jared Mertz in that universe isn't an unmitigated bastard and traitor."

"Seeing evidence is not the same thing as being convinced by it," he observed. "Knowing the Bastard as you do, is this other man the same person?"

She sighed and sipped her wine. "I honestly don't know. Other you believes in him. The Senate testimony I saw had the other me give him a ringing endorsement on video. My father, the man he murdered in our universe, blames Ethan for the coup in his, and he trusts Mertz implicitly. So does Elise."

Kelsey threw up her hands in frustration. "Hell, it might all be true. There, at least. I still do not believe our emperor is insane or a murderer. There are so many details that differ between the two universes, that's even believable, if you hold your nose."

The com on his desk sounded, and he answered it. "Meyer."

"Bridge, sir. We're in orbit around the gas giant."

"We'll be right out."

He rose to his feet. "Let's go see if there's anything more than gas to my doppelganger's story, shall we?"

Kelsey followed Sean onto the bridge and stood beside the command chair when he took it over from his executive officer.

"Anything on scanners?" he asked the tactical officer.

"Nothing, sir. All clear."

Sean raised an eyebrow at Kelsey.

"I'll see what he has to say," she said as she headed for the lift.

Twenty minutes later, she was back in marine country. For the life of her, she couldn't figure out what the other Sean Meyer was playing at. There was nothing in the gaseous clouds below them.

The only saving grace to going along with his odd requests was that she couldn't imagine this as an assassination plot. It was far too strange.

The pinnace detached from the heavy cruiser but stayed in orbit near it.

"What now?" Kelsey asked the other Sean.

"I need to send a com signal. This will either work brilliantly or I'll look like an idiot."

"I'm voting for option two at the moment. Go ahead."

He sat at the marine commander's console and worked silently for a few minutes. Then he looked up at her. "Here goes nothing."

A second after he touched the control, she saw a response over his shoulder. A shoulder that relaxed just a bit when it came in, she noted.

"What the hell is that?" she asked, leaning forward. "Where did that come from, and who sent it?"

"That's the big surprise," he said with a relieved grin. "There's a hidden station down below the clouds in a clear band of atmosphere. We found the one in our universe, and I have control codes that allow us safe passage. I was hoping they were the same here, and I got lucky. So did you."

She felt her eyes narrow. "A hidden station on a gas giant? What's in it?"

"Why don't we go take a look? Let me start a homing beacon, and you can have the pinnace take us down."

Kelsey gave the pilot orders to take them down and watched the console over Sean's shoulder. The clouds were opaque to the visible spectrum, and nothing was showing on regular scanner returns. She had no idea if that was normal or not.

As the pinnace settled into the atmosphere, the scanners started picking up something below. The gas giant made a good hiding place. But why put a station deep into an out of the way place like this? It made no sense.

While she still couldn't see it, the scanners finally got a good reading on the station. It was small and wholly unimpressive.

"That's it?" she asked. "That little thing?"

He grinned at her. "That's the defensive station above the main one. See all the missile tubes along the top? It protects the prize."

"Which you're not going to tell me about," she said with a sigh. "Fine."

The Fleet officer killed the scanner readout and left only the visual display up. As they were inside the clouds, there was nothing to see.

"Wouldn't want to spoil the surprise," he said smugly.

Not for the first time, she wished this was an Old Empire pinnace that she could link her implants with. That would've made life so much easier. The things the people in the other universe had taught her to do had highlighted the limitations of her ignorance.

With no warning, the pinnace came out into a clear zone. Layers of colorful clouds above and below bracketed an incredible sight, a massive space station with some kind of odd projections on four sides.

Projections that supported massive grav cradles holding...

Kelsey sucked in a shocked breath. "Are those battlecruisers like *Courageous*?"

Sean smiled widely. "Indeed they are. And unlike *Courageous*, those four are in perfect working order. The AIs stashed them here as a reserve force. You'll need people with implants to effectively run them, but I can turn the keys over to you today as a gesture of goodwill between our universes.

"They're currently set up for automated use, so the living

accommodations are extraordinarily underwhelming, but that can be remedied. You'll want to disable the AI controls as soon as practical, too.

"You won't need to scrub the computers. It's all separate hardware. In fact, the AIs left the original systems intact. All that data we gave you about the Old Empire will be inside them. You can verify it all. Hopefully, there won't be a lot of differences in the historical record."

She stared at him in shock. "You're just giving them to us?"

He shook his head. "Absolutely not. They were never ours in the first place. This is your universe. Those have always been yours. You just needed a little help finding them.

"Let's go down and take a tour. You'll want a lot of video to take back to other me. He's a suspicious sort. He doesn't trust me and will want proof. And while we're there, I'll tell you the story about how you captured that station from Rebel Empire loyalists in our universe. You'll like it."

Kelsey's brain didn't want to work. All she could do was stare at the huge space station and the four Old Empire warships in shocked awe. This was the break they needed. Now the Empire stood a fighting chance.

"Well," she said, "I'd say this settles matters for me. I'm going to urge Captain Meyer to trust you. We'll get the people selected to go back over with us as soon as we get back to *Spear*.

"Once Elise and Olivia are done at Harrison's World, we can head back to your universe. I know your boss is champing at the bit to head for Terra. Now, so am I."

* * *

ELISE STOOD beside Commander Roche's command console as *Ginny Dare* neared Harrison's World. "You say you found no one alive on the surface? Did they use a biological weapon of some kind?"

He shook his head. "Mobile weapons platforms with Old Empire weapons, Highness. The surface is swarming with them. We didn't dare send people down."

She'd seen those damned weapons after Jared had captured this system in their own universe. They'd been manufactured on Boxer Station by the humans under the control of the System Lord. Nasty things.

"How many are we talking about?" she asked

The man shrugged. "Hundreds of thousands? Millions? More than enough to exterminate every living person on the surface over a decade."

Just the idea of such a slaughter made her want to throw up.

"We're in orbit, Captain," the helm officer said.

"Are we over the target coordinates?"

"Yes, sir."

Roche turned his attention to the tactical officer. "I want a detailed scan of the zone. Locate as many weapons platforms as possible and tag them for the team."

The woman turned from her console. "We'll have to get drones into the area to get detailed readings, but I don't see much aerial activity. Maybe a dozen are moving fast enough for me to detect from orbit."

Roche rubbed his chin. "I wonder how well they communicate with one another. If we eradicate them, will more come looking to see what happened?"

"In our universe, they were remotely controlled with only certain responses programmed in for very limited situations," Elise said. "You could try jamming them to see if that gets the other platforms excited."

"That's an interesting idea," he admitted. "Paula, get the marines ready to depart. We'll use their drones to disrupt communications down there while we examine the target coordinates."

"Aye, sir," Paula Danvers, his executive officer, said. "Lieutenant Ellis says she's ready to go."

"Excellent. Get them in motion."

After he returned his attention to the main screen, Elise cleared her throat a bit. "Has your Princess Kelsey ever met Angela Ellis?"

Roche considered that and shrugged. "I don't think so."

"You should introduce them. In our universe, Angela has become her strong right arm. Really strong, considering her size."

He smiled. "That would be kind of disconcerting. Her Highness is so short, and Angela is damned tall. There must be half a meter difference between them."

"Pretty much. Of course, she's not much like her boyfriend, either."

Roche raised an eyebrow. "Angela has a boyfriend? She's always been so focused on her duty that I've never heard a whisper about her dating anyone. Who is he? A marine?"

"Not even close," Elise said with a smile and a shake of her head. "I somehow suspect you've never met him. Carl Owlet."

"The name isn't familiar." He turned to his console and entered the data. "No record of him in Fleet service either. He's a civilian?"

"More so than just about anyone you could imagine. Do you have records for the science folks on the exploratory mission?"

"I do. He isn't listed. Who is he?"

"A computer genius from Imperial University, a graduate student who isn't old enough to drink."

Roche's eyes narrowed. "You're having fun with me, aren't you? That's a good one."

She raised her hands. "I promise, this is all real. I wish there was an interface so I could show you pictures."

"Would a tablet work? Princess Kelsey brought one back from your universe and left it for us to examine in the lab."

"Have them bring it up."

Ten minutes later, an orderly delivered the tablet, and Elise examined it. It wasn't locked.

"This will work," she said. "Let me transfer a picture."

He took the tablet when she handed it over and laughed. "Now I know you're joking! He's not even shaving regularly."

"No, but he developed the faster-than-light communications theory and hardware Kelsey told you about. That and a lot more. He saved Angela's life in a firefight, too."

Roche didn't seem convinced, so she added a video of the dinner party the emperor had thrown the night before they'd all left for the reconnaissance in force. She had a short segment of the two dancing and laughing.

He stared at the tablet as the video played. "I wouldn't believe it if I hadn't seen it with my own eyes. We'll just keep this to ourselves right now. Did everyone hear that?" he asked in a raised voice.

A chorus of "yes, sirs" came from the bridge crew.

"A genius, you say?" Roche asked quietly. "One not afraid to fight? I can't see it."

Elise considered the situation. "I'm going to play something. It's classified in my universe, and I think it should be here, too. He built Princess Kelsey a weapon, one she forbade him from recreating. It hit a few rough patches during development."

She played the recording from the Grant Research Facility where Carl used Mjölnir to destroy the weapons lab.

Roche watched it through several times before looking at her with wide eyes. "What was that? What happened in there? It looked as if it went through a plascrete wall and vaporized an Old Empire suit of combat armor."

"That's exactly what happened. The weapon has a few high-tech features. A partially collapsed matter shell, a grav-fusion power pack, a battle screen, and FTL com capability. It left his hand, broke the sound barrier on the way to the target, smashed through the wall, reversed course, and came safely back."

"I wouldn't call that safe. It really messed him up."

"He did a little more work on it. I hear it carried him and Angela to safety one night at about Mach fifteen. And that hammer was a side project he worked on for the princess after hours when he wasn't working on what he called 'the important stuff.'"

He stared at her. "Paula, make a note to have someone find Carl Owlet on Avalon and get him into protective custody. The man is obviously an Imperial treasure, even if no one knows about him."

"Will do, sir. It looks like Lieutenant Ellis is arriving in the landing zone."

Roche handed the tablet back to Elise. "Let's hope they find something useful."

18

Olivia stood behind Lieutenant Angela Ellis, trying not to throw up at the sight of her ravaged home world. The images as they'd descended to the surface showed a world scrubbed clean of life, her once proud cities now empty and rotting.

The marine gave her a look of sympathy. "I know words are entirely inadequate, but I'm sorry."

"I killed all these people," Olivia said, her voice thick with horror. "Not in this universe, but my plans are the ones that failed here, too."

She closed her eyes, more distraught than she'd expected to be. "If this world was like mine, it had a population of twelve billion people. That's a lot of blood to have on my hands."

"You did not do this," Angela said firmly. "Not even my universe's version of you. The AIs did. Never fall for that logical fallacy."

"That's cold comfort," Olivia said with a shake of her head. "In fact, it's no comfort at all. I was a fool."

"Maybe, but that won't change a thing. What's done is done. You need to find a way to get some payback. I've deployed our drones, and we're jamming the frequencies you told us to block. No reaction from the machines here or in the nearest large city. What next?"

"We need to land in the small town long enough to get out. There's a diner. Go directly in front of it.

"If we can clear the area of autonomous weapons platforms, that should make future operations safer. You're going to need to do it anyway. The cities are filled with technology that might help you."

"We're a little short of people for that kind of thing," the marine said with a shrug. "The Pentagarans can help, I'm sure. I'll signal the pilot to take us down."

After she did that, the officer turned toward her marines. "We're going in hot. Be ready to take out any of these things if it gets interesting. And if Coordinator West gives you an order to stand down or to shoot something, do it without waiting for me to confirm."

The pinnace jolted slightly, and Olivia expected the ramp to begin lowering, but it didn't.

"What was that?" she asked.

"Our gunner just took out one of the platforms. No reaction from the others at this point. They probably have assigned areas of responsibility. Whoever programmed them was an idiot."

"How so?"

The marine smiled coldly. "Because they should've mandated they come looking for units that fall out of communication rather than relying on them to report an enemy sighting. If these things don't react to losses, we'll just clear an area and slowly expand, taking them out as we go. It'll take a long time, but we can do that."

The pinnace jolted a little harder, and the ramp started down. The marines rushed out and set up a defensive perimeter before Angela allowed Olivia to start down onto the soil of the dead world.

The little town was a wreck. Most buildings were intact but had been shot to hell. A few had burned down. Even a decade after the event, she could smell a hint of ash in the air.

More unsettling were the bones scattered in the street, the remains of people who'd died when the AI unleashed the autonomous weapons platforms.

"Incoming!" Angela said. "Take cover."

Olivia wasted no time scurrying into the diner as the pinnace lifted off. A roar assaulted her ears as the marine officer and her people followed her in.

"Must've been another unit on patrol," Angela said. "The pinnace took it out with a missile. I wish we had some of those Old Empire pinnaces. Ours are pretty primitive in comparison. I'd love to have flechettes."

"Still no reaction from the other units in the area. That one must've been in a building. We didn't detect it until it came out."

"There might be more," Olivia said. "Let's get out of sight."

She led them to a freezer in the back. The smell, even after all this time, made her gag. Rotted meat filled the sealed room. Now Olivia *really* envied the marines their sealed armor.

Without pausing, she rushed to the back of the freezer, lifted the lid of a container marked "malthar bites," and scrambled down the concealed ladder. Only when she was fifty meters away did she try to breathe. Through her mouth.

"That was horrible," she gasped at the marine officer. "Let's never do that again."

"Unless there's another way out, we'll have to do it one more time. What next?"

"This tunnel ends at a grav rail terminal. If the car isn't here, we'll call it. Then four of us go on a little trip."

The rail tube stop did have a sleek car waiting for them. Dust covered it, but it looked operational. Olivia hoped it still had power and that the tunnel was clear all the way down.

"Flanders and Ulysses, you're with us," Angela said. "Everyone else spread out and keep an eye for trouble. Talk first with people. Shoot no one unless they start shooting first."

The rail car still had power and responded to her codes. The track showed as clear, but they wouldn't know for sure until they made the trip.

Ten minutes after she sent them on their way, they pulled up at a station very similar to the one they'd left behind. This one had a massive vault door where the exit tunnel had been in the first one. Dust and debris covered the platform. It didn't look as if anyone had used it in years.

Olivia really hoped the people inside were still safe. So many of her friends had been here. Not all of the resistance, of course, but the Grant Research Facility had been their main base.

"Time to see if anyone is home," Olivia said softly. "Keep your weapons down. These people will probably be nervous, and I'd rather not have a shooting match at fifteen meters."

She wondered if her codes would open the hatch but decided it would be safer just to signal for admittance. With a deep inhalation, she tapped the grimy pad beside the door. The green light came on, but no one spoke.

"I know this is going to be hard to believe, but I'm Olivia West, and I need to talk with someone. Lord Hawthorne, Captain Black, or anyone at all."

For a few seconds, she didn't think there would be a response. Then the light went out, and the hatch began opening slowly.

"Weapons down," Angela ordered. "Hands out in a nonthreatening manner."

Armed men in Old Empire powered armor rushed out and covered them. Olivia kept her hands out at her sides.

Once several of the defenders had relieved the marines of their weapons and searched Olivia thoroughly, Lord William Hawthorne and Fleet Captain Aaron Black came out.

To Olivia's deep shock, her dead fiancé, Fleet Captain Brian Drake, was with them. The sight of him was like a punch to the gut. From his poleaxed expression, the feeling was mutual.

Olivia steadied her nerves and smiled at the suspicious group. "I'm probably the very last person any of you expected to see, particularly if there's a version of me in there.

"I can prove my identity, but the short version is that I'm from an alternate universe and I've brought some people that can help you retake Harrison's World. They could also use your help."

William stepped forward and examined her. "If this is surgery, I'm quite impressed. You even have the same implant serial numbers as Olivia, something I'd always thought was impossible."

He turned to his companions and raised an eyebrow. "I can't see the harm in talking at this point. They obviously know we're here. Objections?"

The others shook their heads wordlessly, and William returned his attention to her with a wide smile. "I've always enjoyed a good story. If you can somehow convince me that you're telling the truth, I expect we'll have a lot to discuss."

Olivia allowed herself a sad smile and glanced at Brian. "Indeed. I'm looking forward to hearing what you have to say, too. Shall we find a more comfortable place to talk? Say the conference room on level seventy?"

"You intrigue me with your knowledge of the base layout," her old mentor admitted. "What else do you know?"

"This is the Grant Research Facility, and you're Lord William Hawthorne. The officers are Aaron Black and Brian Drake. Drake and I were engaged in my universe, before his untimely death."

Brian swallowed. "Olivia is dead. Those damned weapons burned her down a decade ago. I don't know who you really are, but this had better be really convincing."

Nothing was ever easy, she decided.

"Then we should sit down and have a long talk. This is Lieutenant Angela Ellis of the New Terran Empire, by the way."

"This should be fascinating," William said. "By all means, do come in."

* * *

"Incoming signal from Omega," Marcus said.

Jared looked up from the reports on his desk screen. It had been three days, and he'd started worrying after two.

"Put him on audio. Hello, Omega."

"Hello to you as well, Admiral Mertz. Your compatriots have returned and await your transport."

The relief that flooded through him was like a splash of ice water.

"Excellent. Are they alone?"

"No. It seems they've brought back all the suits you sent filled with people."

"We'll get some pinnaces on the way for them right away. Thank you for helping us."

"Oh, it's my pleasure. Life is so much more interesting with your people in it. I hadn't realized how truly bored I was before."

The connection ended, and Marcus spoke. "I have a call from Elise for you, as well. I had her holding."

"Put her on."

The screen on the desk switched from a boring report to the camera inside his wife's helmet. She'd see his face via her implants.

"Hey!" he said. "I'm glad to see you back. Really glad. Did everything go okay?"

"Nope. We were kidnapped and replaced by exact duplicates. By the way, I'm now a dominatrix."

"That isn't funny," he said repressively. "Well, except for the last part."

She grinned. "I have a different opinion. And I had to work my code word in there somewhere."

"Tell me again why you picked 'dominatrix' as a code word?"

"Because I can't imagine any version of me using the word in normal conversation. Why? Do we need to do some role-playing?"

He laughed. "I think I'll pass. How'd it go?"

"It took a little work to convince Captain Meyer to trust his doppelganger, but our Sean did very well. You might not approve of his methods, though.

"Olivia made contact with people in the Grant Research Facility, too. They had a hard time with her story, but they sent a representative along as well. Sean isn't pleased, but that's a different kind of problem."

As much as he wanted to ask what that meant, Jared restrained himself. "I assume you have the people coming for training with you."

"We do but only half the load. Kelsey wants to have a total of two hundred. We'll have to send the suits back, but everyone is ready. It shouldn't take more than a few hours."

Jared nodded. "Was Sean able to keep duplication down to a minimum?"

"Far more easily than I'd expected, actually. The vast majority of the people coming our way are from *Ginnie Dare*. Commander Roche will be in charge of them."

Now he understood. Almost none of the crew from that ship had survived in his universe. There wouldn't be many people to mix up.

"I barely had a chance to get to know the man, but I liked him," Jared said softly. "This will be unexpectedly hard."

"Just be glad we're only dealing with other universes," Elise said with a chuckle. "Imagine if time travel were possible. I'm reminded of one of those old shows Kelsey favors. Two versions of the same grumpy man standing next to one another saying, 'I hate temporal mechanics,' at the same time."

Thankfully, that wasn't possible. At least Jared fervently hoped it wasn't possible. What a nightmare that would be.

"We'll have pinnaces to Omega in a few minutes," he said. "How did Sean convince them he was one of the good guys?"

"You know the hidden station at the gas giant near Harrison's World? He led them to it and helped Kelsey recover the four battlecruisers there."

Jared opened his mouth to object about not being consulted on something that important but paused. Would he have done anything differently? Probably not. It wasn't as if he was going to get the ships over here anyway. Or that he had any right to them.

Sean had made the right choice. It would make things difficult for Jared's doppelganger, but he wasn't even sure the man was a good guy.

"That's fine," he said. "Most of the people here for training need to go to Boxer Station. Those ships will need crew with implants and training to be effective. Captain Cooley will probably have to rotate them back to their universe and do multiple sets."

"Thankfully, we're doing exactly that with so many Fleet personnel already that adding a few hundred more won't even make the instructors blink."

"That's what Sean said," Elise agreed. "He helped them get the ships into orbit around Harrison's World before we left, so they're already using the manual controls to start the familiarization process."

"Kelsey did some checking in the computers and verified a lot of the data we gave her about the Old Empire. She's sent a ship back to Pentagar to meet with the people on Erorsi and bring back help from Pentagar. Since the Rebel Empire didn't send a fleet like they did in our universe, they have a little more time to get ready."

Jared had been considering that problem. If the Rebel Empire invaded the other New Terran Empire, there would be nothing there that could stop them and Pentagar would fall first.

He could pass along the technology to build flip-point jammers, even without the people at the Grant Research Station, but it would take a long while before the others could use it. That was cutting-edge stuff.

The scientists at his Grant Research Facility were a few months away from having the ability to mass produce flip-point jammers—if creating three or four every month counted as mass production. Still, they'd have a few they could pass on to their friends in the other universe while their Grant people got busy playing catch up.

"Well, I should let you go," he said. "I'll be there to greet you all when you come aboard."

"Excellent. Plan for dinner and some alone time tonight. Talk to you soon."

Jared leaned back in his chair after the call ended. This side show was over. It was about time. He needed to get back to the real mission, or they'd never get to Terra at all.

19

Sean tried not to scowl at Fleet Captain Brian Drake as they stepped into *Invincible*'s marine country after stripping off their hard suits. The other man had no control over this awkward situation. It wasn't his fault he'd lived in the other universe and that his Olivia hadn't.

Now the two of them were talking like long-lost lovers. Which, of course, they were, ones who had been engaged before their respective untimely deaths.

Since the other man wasn't shooting looks at him, Sean was willing to bet Olivia hadn't told Drake about him yet. That didn't necessarily mean anything, but he was concerned.

"Is something wrong, Commodore?" Scott Roche asked quietly.

"Just a personal matter," he said. "Nothing to worry about."

The other man's eyes narrowed. "You and Coordinator West?"

He allowed himself a snort. "I forgot how perceptive you were, Scott. Yes. And of course, her dead fiancé. Who is now in our universe and alive again."

Scott winced. "Ouch. I can see where that might make for a few awkward moments. You need to get that settled before those old feelings get a chance to rekindle."

"I don't think she'd appreciate me puffing out my chest and strutting around. Or peeing on her leg."

"Probably not," the other man conceded. "But you'd better put him on notice. Or would you prefer someone else pass him the word? That might lower the tensions once it comes out."

He considered that possibility. "Are you volunteering?"

"I suppose I am. I've known you a long time, and I owe you. Well, some version of you. We're friends, and that's what friends do."

"I'll have to pass, but thanks. This is the kind of thing that I need to do in person. So, what do you think of *Invincible?*" he asked, changing the subject firmly.

"I had no idea anything this powerful was even possible. Did the Old Empire make anything bigger?"

"No. This was the most powerful mobile unit in sheer firepower, though I'd argue the carriers are more dominant once you add their fighters in. Boxer Station is a lot more dangerous in a stand-up fight, but it can't move. We'd never have beaten it if we hadn't ambushed the AI from point blank range."

Scott pursed his lips. "Really? I didn't think it was that tough."

"They'd probably moved the AI. A regular computer doesn't compare. Not even close. You'll find out soon enough."

The hatch to the main corridor slid open, and Admiral Mertz stepped inside. Sean sensed Scott tensing beside him.

"Relax," he said softly. "This is not the same man from your universe."

His friend gave him a somewhat incredulous look. "Are you honestly telling me you don't believe this guy is a power-hungry usurper? Well, potential usurper over here, I suppose."

"Without even a trace of doubt," Sean said firmly. "I was wrong about him in this universe, and so was Captain Breckenridge. This man had every opportunity to take the Imperial Throne and didn't. Our Princess Kelsey trusts him for good reason."

Scott sent him a sidelong glance of uncertainty. "If you say so. I guess it's your universe."

"He might really be the Bastard in yours," he said with a slight smile. "Circumstances are different. You'll have to figure that out on your own."

Mertz cleared his throat. "If I could have your attention? My name is Jared Mertz, and I want to ask you all to give me a little benefit of the doubt as we get to know one another. I understand that I don't have the best reputation in your universe. Give me a chance to prove I am not that man."

"Well, Princess Elise married him," Scott said softly. "She always seemed like a sharp operator to me. If everyone here tells me things are different, I'll give him a chance."

The Fleet officer from another universe stepped forward. "Commander Scott Roche, Admiral. Might my senior officers meet with you for a few minutes, so we can settle what we're going to be doing?"

"Absolutely, Commander," Mertz said with a nod. "We'll use the marine conference room right here. Commodore Meyer, if you'd get everyone else settled, we'll be pulling out for Boxer Station as soon as the pinnaces get back with the second load."

"Aye, sir."

The admiral escorted Scott, Princess Kelsey, Captain Drake, Lieutenant Commander Paula Danvers, and the other Doctor Guzman into the briefing room. Elise and Olivia joined them. He'd be willing to wager he could guess at the seating diagram.

He sighed inwardly and tagged Marcus to ask about the arrangements.

It turned out that Marcus had set aside temporary quarters for the people going to Boxer Station and wrangled a block of cabins for those staying on the superdreadnought for the mission. It would be easier to keep an eye on them if they were clustered together.

Unable to get his mind off the odd fix he was in, Sean made his way to the observation lounge. The compartment didn't really have a window stretching from bulkhead to bulkhead, but the holo emitters certainly made it appear as if it did.

There wasn't much to see as the ship powered through the cloud of radioactive particles surrounding the black hole at the center of the Nova system. That was fine by him since it meant he was alone and that gave him privacy to think.

The best outcome was if Drake stayed on Harrison's World while Olivia went with the mission as planned. He wasn't holding his breath on that.

The worst-case scenario was both of them staying. The odds of that were higher than Sean liked. Perhaps he should encourage them both to come on the mission. Was he likely to get push back from Olivia?

On reflection, he didn't think so. She was in a relationship with him, and he didn't see her stepping out, even with a formerly dead lover.

Yet people were complicated. Did he talk with her about it or trust that she'd do the right thing?

He slumped into a chair and stared sightlessly toward the screen. No matter what he did, there was a chance this would all blow up in his face. God, he'd rather fight a desperate space battle than contemplate losing her.

* * *

KELSEY STARED out at the veritable sea of derelict ships floating around Boxer Station. With her implants, the superdreadnought's scanners were more than capable of seeing the scope of the scene.

"There are tens of thousands of ships here," she murmured. "When I learned about the Old Empire, I had no idea they had so many. Why?"

"And these are only the ones that weren't destroyed outright during the Fall," Mertz agreed. "They had several reasons. The biggest one was that they weren't the only human civilization out there. True, they were the biggest, but the others were a threat, particularly if they ever banded together. And many of them were not very friendly.

"Take the Singularity. They left the Old Empire in the early days, going deep into the void to set up a society more to their taste. The two societies eventually found one another again and they fought a constant low-level battle along their entire border for thousands of years. To the point that it became like ritual and tradition."

"Over what?" she asked, giving Mertz her full attention.

"Mostly over implants and genetic engineering. The Old Empire went the route of cranial implants, which the Singularity saw as an abomination that endangered Humanity. Rightly, as it turned out.

"On the other hand, the Singularity chose to edit the human genome to create a class system that the Old Empire saw as monstrous. As you might imagine, each was eager to do the other harm, and they raided across their common border for something like twelve centuries.

"Each side built a massive fleet to make certain they could defend themselves if need be. Or to crush their enemies if the opportunity presented itself."

She considered that situation. "I wonder what happened to them after the Fall. The Singularity, I mean. Did the AIs conquer them, too?"

Mertz shrugged. "No one knows. The Singularity was on the far side of the Rebel Empire. Since the AIs don't exactly share information, they could have crushed them, too. Or they might have stopped at the border. I suppose we'll find out one day."

She gestured around them, not at the ship but at the derelicts floating all around *Invincible*. "How many of these do you think are salvageable? God, I wish there were still some in my universe. They would be an incredible boon."

"If even one percent is reparable, I'll be astonished," he said sadly. "These are mostly just huge coffins filled with millions of dead Fleet personnel."

"What do you do with them?" That was a morbid question, but she wanted to know.

"We take them to Harrison's World for burial. The Spire on Avalon isn't capable of holding the number of people we're talking about, so Coordinator West built one there in an area that was large enough to hold such a memorial.

"The process of getting the poor bastards there is slow and time-consuming, but it has to be done. We have entire crews of people recovering the bodies, identifying them if they can, and seeing they get to Avalon before the wrecks are sent to the breakers to salvage what they can."

"Can you really afford to use resources like that? You need to put every person toward getting ready for the enemy and the fight that has to be coming. Why not just bury the dead in space? Drop them into the sun?"

He seemed to consider her for a long time. "It comes down to respect. They died defending the empire and never knew that to an extent they succeeded. We owe our brothers and sisters in Fleet the rest that our ancestors promised. Sometimes the right thing isn't easy. You do it anyway."

That certainly wasn't the answer she'd expected to hear from the Bastard. Since they hadn't found all these ships in her universe, she had no idea what the man there would have thought.

This wasn't going to be easy, she decided. Not only was this man challenging her assumptions, the records she'd reviewed certainly supported the general consensus that he could've used this ship to put his boot on the throats of everyone in the New Terran Empire. And he'd chosen to do nothing of the sort.

Instead, he'd fought beside another version of herself to stop a coup and keep her father on the throne. And alive.

The recordings she'd seen of Ethan in the Imperial Throne room getting ready to sentence this man to death spoke volumes about both. Her brother here had been mad. She was convinced of it now.

Oh, the implant recordings that Mertz had put into the record could have been forged, she supposed, but they matched the statements of the Imperial Guard present at the time. Added to so many other clues and evidence, she was sure Ethan had been mad here. Paranoia and megalomania, at the very least.

That didn't mean he was mad in her universe. Not even close. Her brother was as sane as she was. She'd spent countless hours going over everything she could remember about their interactions and how he differed from the man in this universe.

She'd stake her life on her brother. And that probably meant the Mertz there was just the kind of man she'd always believed, but a worm of doubt still existed deep inside her mind.

Well, that wasn't a problem she was going to solve today. She needed to put her distaste aside and give this Jared Mertz a chance, as difficult as that was. She needed his help to get to Terra and to recover the override.

Potentially, she needed his help repeating the entire mission in her universe. Only he had the DNA to use the key and open the Imperial Vault. What if the override required his DNA, too?

The Bastard had taken the Imperial Scepter when he'd killed her father. He hadn't had implants at the time, so he probably hadn't had a clue what it really represented. Well, unless his sources inside the Imperial Palace were a lot better than they all suspected.

With the resources aboard *Courageous*, it was likely he'd found a way to get implants. Could he have worked out the secret? It was always possible the man would try for the override himself with the goal of making the AIs answer to him.

As horrifying as that idea was, that was also a problem for another day.

Kelsey forced herself to smile. It felt unnatural in this man's presence, but the two of them were going to be working closely together for the foreseeable future.

"When do we leave for Terra?"

"We'll head out to make the yearly report for the AI as soon as we get your people settled on Boxer Station and Olivia gets back from our Harrison's World. The target system isn't too far away, so we can probably leave from there and make our way toward Terra."

"Do you think we can get to Terra? From what you've said, the Rebel Empire has the entire system isolated."

"We have to," Mertz said with a shrug. "The Empire is depending on us."

Indeed, difficult times truly did show a person's character.

20

Olivia watched Brian as the cutter descended toward the newly constructed spaceport on her home world. The System Lord had vaporized the original spaceport a decade ago when it locked the planet down.

This time, they'd taken the precaution of moving it far away from any city and would not allow it to become heavily populated. If war came again, millions need not die because of where they lived.

The people working there had to deal with the imposition of a long commute by hypersonic grav rail from the closest population center several hundred kilometers away. Only people on duty or in transit were at risk, and they'd have a lot of warning if the enemy came.

Of course, any enemy would have to deal with the flip-point jammers and the heavy Fleet presence in the system. Sean's command was growing to be almost as powerful as the one Jared commanded, if one included the repaired ships being worked up and the Fleet personnel here for training. The Rebel Empire would not crack this nut easily.

"This is unreal," Brian murmured as they came over the landing pad and settled on the plascrete. "We haven't dared send out more than a few stealthed drones, but it was more than enough to know our world was dead. Now it lives again."

"It made me want to vomit," she said as she unstrapped. "Knowing that I came up with the plan that killed everyone. Twelve billion people, dead because of me."

He stopped and turned toward her. "You and the entire leadership council. None of us knew how powerful the System Lord was. What I'd like to know is why it didn't kill everyone in this universe."

She didn't answer as they exited the cutter. Honestly, she wasn't even sure what the answer was.

"What was *Invincible*'s status when the System Lord attacked?" she asked as they went down the ramp.

A sleek black grav car sat waiting for them. Overhead, several others circled. Her guards. She'd ordered them to keep their distance today. Farther out, far beyond sight, Fleet fighters kept overwatch. That last was more a training exercise than a need.

"It was almost operational," he responded as they climbed into the car. "I'd only just arrived back at Grant when all hell broke loose. We never did figure out what set the Lord off, but it started using the orbital bombardment platforms to blow the hell out of everything. The most likely thing was that it had somehow detected *Invincible*."

His eyes grew shadowed. "You were at the government center when it destroyed the capital. I've always comforted myself with the idea that you never really knew what was happening before you died. You didn't have time to be afraid."

Olivia closed the door behind her, strapped in, and patted his hand. "I'm sorry you had to live with that."

He nodded, but his gaze was penetrating. "I died here. How?"

"You were trapped with the crew on *Invincible* when the Lord locked the system down. Something different triggered it here, which might explain the difference in its response.

"Without the computer, there was no way you could fight, so you and your people waited until supplies ran out and then ended things on the flag bridge. I was only able to bring you home and bury you a few months ago."

"It sounds as if you had it harder."

She shook her head. "No. You had to live in a hole while the AI murdered our people. Still, we don't have to make this a comparison of who had it worse."

"I suppose not. Did you ever find someone else?"

His expression told her that he probably hadn't.

"Only recently. You were a hard man to get over. You've met him. Commodore Meyer."

The corners of Drake's mouth edged up. "Ah. That explains the odd looks of semi-hostility he kept shooting me. I wasn't sure what to make of it. Now I know."

"He's actually a very good man. You're very much alike, I think, which, on reflection, might not be the best thing."

She faced Brian squarely. "I'm committed to my relationship and my work is here, just as yours is back on *your* home. As much as this might seem like a second chance for us, I don't want you to build unreasonable expectations."

He shook his head sadly. "I'll admit I've allowed myself the fantasy. Who wouldn't? I'll try not to make an ass of myself, but I'm putting you on notice. If your relationship doesn't work out, I intend to try again."

Olivia rubbed her face. "Why does everything have to be so complicated? You need to find a woman in your universe. One that can make you happy. Our time is done."

"I disagree. In fact, I resoundingly reject your premise. Aaron and Lord Hawthorne have everything there well in hand. Since I'm not alive here, we decided I would make the perfect emissary from our universe to yours.

"If the two Grants can work together, imagine what they can do. We could potentially double our capacity for research at the very edge of Imperial technology. And part of that mission means bringing our peoples closer.

"Though I'm not staying here after I make the introductions and start the process by sending some of your people back to my Grant. Lord Hawthorne ordered me to accompany this Admiral Mertz on this mission to learn what I could. So I'll still be with you for a while."

That was just about the worst thing for them both, she imagined. Could she order him to remain here? Ask Jared to block him from the mission?

Probably not and develop the kind of relationship the two Grants needed. One more complication. Sean would be thrilled. Well, more thrilled than if she were staying here on Harrison's World with Drake, in any case.

She stared out of the grav car. They were passing over the farmlands surrounding the Grant Research Facility. It was closer to the spaceport than the city, only in the opposite direction.

That was by design. They'd wanted covert access to the flight patterns to insert their own traffic. No one knew it, but the flight controllers at the port were all members of the resistance. Anyone with insight into the traffic around the port went through intense scrutiny.

They were almost to the small town nearest Grant when she looked back at Brian. "I *can* imagine what is possible, but I don't want you to have the unreasonable fantasy that Sean and I will break up. That isn't going to happen.

"In fact, I've been expecting him to propose at any time. Meeting you will almost certainly speed things along on his end. In fact, if he doesn't mention it before we leave on this mission, I will. He and I cannot and will not have you dividing us. I'm sorry."

He grunted as if someone had punched him in the gut. "That's hard, but you were always the kind of person that squarely faced her problems. I'll bet you make one hell of a coordinator."

"You're damned right I do." After a moment, she sighed. "Don't take this rejection personally, Brian. I loved you so deeply that I couldn't imagine life without you. Now, when I've finally found a way through the pain, you can't expect me to come running back into it."

"What a difference a few months could have made." He sighed. "It's going to take me a while to get over you again, but seeing you happy will help. Hurt, but help, if you know what I mean. Maybe that's what I need to move on."

The grav car started descending. He smiled as he looked down at the town. "I want to get some malthar bites. I can't tell you how badly I've missed them. In fact, I've been authorized to negotiate a shipment for my Grant."

She laughed, more than happy to move past the awkward conversation they'd absolutely had to have. "I'll see that we send some back. I'd imagine there are plenty of wild malthar back there. I can probably manage some processing equipment to help you get the plant back up and running after you clear enough of the autonomous weapons platforms."

"It's going to take years to clear them out," he said glumly.

"Maybe not. I've been thinking about that. Harrison has the original data cores from the System Lord here. I'll wager the override codes are buried in the data somewhere. If we can send them back, you might be able to order the platforms to shut down all at once."

He frowned. "Who is Harrison?"

Olivia smiled widely. "That's an even longer conversation. I'll tell you on the way back to *Invincible*. Right now, you need to focus your attention on making a good impression."

"That didn't work so well with you," he grumbled.

"Let it go."

He nodded, but she wasn't convinced he was ready to release all hope of a reconciliation from beyond the grave. That would cause them problems going forward if she didn't scotch it early.

Well, she had time once they got back to the ship to deal with it. Maybe she should ask Jared to marry them. That would end this particular issue. She hoped.

* * *

IT WAS LATE when Elise finally got Jared alone for dinner. Getting their visitors moved to Boxer Station had taken more effort than she'd imagined, but it was done.

And now that Olivia had returned from Harrison's World, the fleet was —finally!—on its way to the meeting place to give the Rebel Empire their false report.

The defenders at Harrison's World had turned off the flip-point jammer long enough to send a stealthed probe through. No ships were detected, so the Rebel Empire was still unaware of the change in management.

With safety assured, the destroyer *Athena* had led the way through. Sean Meyer was in command of her for now. This part of the Rebel Empire was basically empty of inhabited worlds, so they had a week or so until they needed to get some real distance from the fleet.

It would take them a bit more than a week and a half to get to the destination. They'd join Sean on *Athena* once they needed the separation from the fleet.

But enough of that for now. Her days in this luxuriously large stateroom —relatively speaking—were limited, so she planned on savoring them, not worrying about the future.

"Has Olivia spoken with you?" she asked once they'd finished their meal and were relaxing on the couch with wine.

"About what?" Jared asked.

"I'll take that as a no. Sean."

He frowned a little. "Why would she talk with me about Sean? Is there a problem?"

"You could say that," she said as she put her glass down on the end table. "Its name is Brian Drake."

That caused her husband's frown to deepen. "He's a problem? I thought they used to be close friends."

"And he'd like to make that true again."

His expression cleared. "Ah. Ouch. That *is* a complication. How can I assist her with that particular problem, though? It seems as if the chance for that is gone. I could've made sure he stayed at Harrison's World if you'd told me. You being anyone, actually."

"No, you couldn't," she said firmly. "Think about it. How would that have affected his people's relationship with us?"

Jared opened his mouth to respond but paused, obviously reconsidering his first thought. "Maybe not in the best way," he admitted, "but those were waves we could have managed. What can I do now?"

"Marry Sean and Olivia as soon as they ask. And they will. Do not delay."

"You sound so sure. Of course, I've never met anyone as canny as you at predicting this kind of thing."

"That's very kind and most diplomatic," she said dryly, "but Olivia is much more shrewd, and I know it. Believe me, the education I'm getting on this trip will be well worth my time.

"If they wait a full day, I'll be shocked. My advice is for you to prepare to hold the ceremony within an hour's notice. Get all your ducks in a row and be ready to execute the ambush."

His eyebrows crept up. "Ambush, is it? How much warning do you think Sean is going to get?"

"Virtually none. Are they scheduled to come to *Invincible* tomorrow?"

"We're having a briefing, but I'd assumed he was doing it remotely."

"Mark my words," she said with a smile. "He'll attend in person. Olivia will be having that discussion with him tonight. Or if she's feeling particularly subtle, tomorrow morning."

"An ambush, indeed. I'm not betting against you. I'll review the details in the morning. It's a good thing I have recent familiarity with the marriage ceremony."

She tipped her glass back and finished her wine. "I'm certain there are significant differences between the Pentagaran ceremony and what Fleet does. Have you ever performed one?"

"I've never had that privilege," he said as he finished his own drink and set the glass down.

"There you go," she said as she stood. "It will be a pleasure, I'm sure."

His smile widened as he stood. "That word brings something completely different to mind for me. Are you ready for bed?"

"Yes," she said as she extended her hand toward him. "But I'm not at all tired."

"Me, either."

21

K elsey stared uncertainly at Doctor Stone and the pair of Doctor Guzmans. They were kind of spooky standing together like that.

"Are you sure this is the *right* first step?" she asked. "It seems as if replacing my eye would fall later in the process. Isn't that kind of a big thing?"

"It is," Lily Stone confirmed. "It's also the largest impediment to the regeneration process. Forgive me, Highness, but that's a far larger—and uglier—prosthetic than you need. The Old Empire had the technology to make them look lifelike. Yours is anything but."

As if she needed to hear the woman say that. Kelsey knew how hideous she was, inside and out. The Pale Ones had turned her into a beast, and she'd fought like one.

She was really getting tired of hearing how well her doppelganger had done in comparison, though. Even when she wasn't explicitly mentioned.

That woman had caught all the breaks. Everywhere Kelsey had bad luck, the other woman had good. It was almost as if she'd been stealing luck across universal boundaries.

Well, it hardly mattered where she started the healing process started, did it?

"What's involved?" she asked the Guzman twins.

Having them both there was an odd experience and really pressed home that she was in another universe. The two men were identical, other than some purely cosmetic differences in appearance like hair length and different rank tabs on their uniforms.

That reminded her that she needed to tear a page from her doppelganger's playbook and promote some of her people when she got back.

"It's not as complex as it sounds, Highness," the Justin Guzman from this universe said. "And it's absolutely necessary to give us access to the tissue on your face. The plate has undoubtedly scarred the flesh beneath it.

"With the assistance of your nanites, we can regenerate that to a great degree. Perhaps even completely with a number of sessions, though I hesitate at tempting you with an outcome that may prove elusive."

"What are the risks?" she asked. "I've become a bit risk averse in the last few years."

"None, really," Stone said. "The optic nerve is sound, so the hardware replacement is straightforward. The new prosthetic eye will fit into the socket more easily and look completely natural.

"From the conversations I've had with the techs who built the eye, they've worked hard to duplicate all the Raider enhancements your natural eye has now and added even more capability.

"They were a bit cagey with the specifics, but they were trained by Carl Owlet, so that's not at all surprising. He loved surprises. And geekdom."

"I've heard his name before in passing," Kelsey said as she tried to get into the right mental space to agree to this surgery. "I didn't know him in my universe. You speak of him as if he were dead. Did you lose him?"

"More like we've misplaced him. He's away on the same mission the other you is on. We're hopeful they can get home with the data and equipment they stole from the Rebel Empire soon, but we do worry."

"What kind of data and equipment?"

"The manufacturing specifications and equipment to make Raider implants and sentient AIs."

A cold chill washed over Kelsey, and her throat threatened to swell shut. "I've spoken with Marcus, but the idea of making more of those things fill me with dread. What could *possibly* go wrong?"

"Why don't you lie back so we can get started," Stone said. "As for AIs, we're behind the Rebel Empire and really don't have a choice if we want to beat the bastards.

"Trust me, our allies are a lot more like people than the Lords. Marcus and Harrison are firmly on our side. Harrison is really the driving force behind the repair ships in the graveyard. Without him running everything, I can't imagine we'd be nearly as far along."

Kelsey lay back on the operating table. "Is this going to hurt?"

"There will be some pain once the procedure is complete, even with regeneration," her Guzman said. "We're going to be reworking the tissue under the current prosthetic plate. With your pharmacology unit, that should be more than manageable and will abate over the course of the next several days."

"Let's get it over with, then."

"The somatic unit will put you out without transition, and you'll wake up the same way," Stone said. "Basically, you'll blink, and it'll be over."

"And I'll feel like you punched me in the face. Got it."

Stone laughed. "Nothing like that. The pain will be more of a dull ache."

"Like the rest of the dull aches I have? Wonderful. What's the plan on addressing my other damage?"

"You're stalling," Stone said accusingly. "Goodnight, Highness."

Kelsey opened her mouth to object and blinked when Stone suddenly was on the other side of her. Neither Guzman was in evidence. They'd vanished.

"That was very disconcerting," she informed the Fleet physician. "You might want to make note of where people are when you put someone under just so you can make the return a little less jarring."

Stone nodded. "I hadn't considered that, but it's a good idea. We could put the primary surgeon as the only visible person and make sure that things are the same once the surgery is complete. I'm still getting used to the Old Empire technology, even after a few years."

"I take it everything went okay?" Kelsey asked. "My vision seems about the same. The new eye works to that extent."

The doctor put a hand on her shoulder when Kelsey made to sit up. "Let's give your body a few minutes to adjust. Here's a mirror."

Kelsey took the small mirror the other woman offered and examined her face. To her pleased astonishment, the metal plate was gone, and her left eye looked just like its natural counterpart.

The flesh around it where the plate had been was red and rough, but it was there. And the nasty scar that was the testament to the wound that had taken her natural eye was much reduced.

"Wow. I never expected to look like a human being again," she said, her throat threatening to close up with unexpected emotion. "I was always going to be that cyborg woman."

"You will look completely normal once the tissue has a few more regeneration sessions," Stone assured her. "And to answer your other question, I expect we'll be able to remove the visible scars all across your body now that we can use the full-body regenerator.

"The micro scars inside your body may or may not completely heal even with a combination of regeneration and your new Raider nanites. Only time will truly tell. At the very least, the pain your pharmacology unit is suppressing should disappear."

Her face ached a little, but nothing like Kelsey had expected. Perhaps this was going to work out. "How many regeneration sessions are you anticipating and over what space of time?"

Stone's expression took on a calculating air. "Let's plan on five initial sessions, one per day. It will take more, but I need to see how they progress before I can make an educated guess at the overall duration.

"No more than ten sessions, I'd imagine. By the time you need to depart for the destroyer, we'll almost certainly be done."

Kelsey sighed. She would look like a regular person again. That alone made this trip so worthwhile. "What about the eye? Did your tech friends tell you about their special sauce?"

"They did not," Stone said, somewhat peevishly. "They insist on going over it themselves with you later today. Let's sit you up and start checking basic things like your balance. You should be fine, but I want to be sure there is no subtle difference in the combined input to your brain."

"Can we do lunch afterward? I'm starving."

"Why don't I have something delivered?" Stone countered. "We're going to be busy for the next few hours."

"I suppose," Kelsey grumbled. "I hope I get used to my metabolism one day."

* * *

SEAN WAS SHOCKED at the speed at which his life was changing but still thrilled. He hadn't expected a matter-of-fact proposal over breakfast, but that's what he'd gotten.

Much more surprising was her proposed timetable. He'd hoped to marry her soon, but he had expected a little more than two hours' notice.

She was obviously as concerned about Brian Drake as he was, if for somewhat different reasons.

While she made sure that he understood she wanted this because she loved him, there was also a somewhat cold-blooded element of political expediency behind her desire to make it happen quickly.

He wanted to seal the deal so the other man would back off. She felt the same but also had to make sure there was no damage to the political relationship between the two Grant facilities.

Sean admired the way politics flowed in her blood, but it was sometimes a trifle annoying.

And then she'd dropped it on him that she intended to ask Admiral Mertz to marry them as soon as their planning meeting was done this morning. His objection that they needed time to prepare was met with amused derision.

Olivia had been busy last night before she'd come to bed. She'd enlisted people to make sure her dress was ready, his dress uniform was perfect, and that her friends received more notice than he did.

Honestly, it felt a little like an ambush, and he'd probably feel differently if he hadn't planned to speed the process along himself.

Now he was aboard *Invincible* and immersed in the planning session with the captains and executive officers of each ship in the fleet. They'd come into this mission with a rough idea of what would happen, but now they were gaming out the things that might go wrong.

"As I see it, the two worst possibilities are that they see through our ruse or a random ship happens to chance across us on the way there," Admiral Mertz summed up. "What can we do to further mitigate those possibilities?"

"If the status delivery takes place like all those over the last ten years," Marcus said, "there's only a very small chance of them finding anything in the message or the destroyer to cause them to look deeper.

"And by small, I mean inseparable from zero. The reports are virtually copied and pasted from one year to the next, and Athena is programmed with all appropriate responses the robotic destroyers have had."

"And if they do get frisky, we have a fleet of ships that has significantly more firepower than we anticipate finding in that system," Sean added. "That doesn't guarantee anything, but we should keep the odds in mind. Frankly, I think a random ship is a much bigger threat."

Mertz nodded. "I agree. We have FTL probes out in all directions, as well as positioned in the flip points ahead of us and behind, in this system and the ones beyond. What else can we do?"

They batted various options around, but nothing seemed more effective than staying slow to not show up on a ship's scanners. Before they transitioned to the next system, they'd send scouts and use a spread of FTL probes to make sure the area was clear.

There was always going to be a risk that they missed a ship, but these actions made it far less likely they would be seen.

After an hour of exploring the possibilities, Mertz seemed satisfied. "Okay, we'll maintain that posture until we're one system away from the target system. None of the intervening systems is occupied, so that won't be a worry.

"Now, while this meeting is adjourned, I'd like to ask you all to remain for a little longer."

He turned a wide smile toward Sean. "It so happens that Commodore Sean Meyer and Coordinator Olivia West have asked me to wed them today, and I think this is the perfect time and audience. All of the other guests have been impatiently waiting for us to finish talking, and the time has arrived."

Sean's stomach did a little flip, but it wasn't fear. No, never that. Just a little nervousness.

The sour expression on Captain Drake's face pleased Sean, but the man couldn't know that was why Sean was grinning. Well, okay, he probably did.

"I'll need a few minutes to change into my dress uniform, Admiral," Sean said.

"They've taken the liberty of setting up the next cabin over as a dressing room," Mertz said. "The ladies are done, and it's all yours. While you change, we'll get the decorations up. No rush. I hear the coordinator has scheduled you an entire twenty minutes to get ready."

That caused a wave of laughter among the officers present. Even Drake smiled a little. His Olivia must've had many of the same traits.

"Well, I suppose I'd best go get ready," Sean said as he stood. "I don't suppose there's a honeymoon suite on *Athena* that I missed."

Mertz grinned. "And you'd be wrong. I've had the officers and men under your command rearranging the schedules so you have the next few days off and setting up what amounts to a lavish hotel suite for your honeymoon. The manservants that my wife insisted guide my new steward are making sure nothing is forgotten.

"Now, if it were me, I'd plan on taking a trip somewhere very nice once we return to the Empire, but this will do for now, I hope."

The admiral made a show of looking at the door. "Your bride is impatiently waiting for you to get into the changing room so she can get here unseen, Commodore. You are dismissed."

Another laugh filled the room as Sean headed for the hatch. Knowing his bride to be, that wasn't too far off the mark. He'd make sure to dress quickly and ping the admiral through his implants to be sure they were ready before he returned.

Anticipation of being married to his love overrode the anxiety about the ceremony itself as he strode down the corridor and into the waiting arms of four stewards. He gave Drake's discomfiture one last pleasant thought and then put the man out of his mind.

This was the first day of his new life. He wanted to focus on his bride. His wife. After all, if things went badly, he might be leaving her a widow in a week and a half. Best to live each day as if it were their last.

22

Ten days later, Jared Mertz sat on the bridge of the destroyer *Athena* as she prepared to make the flip into the target system. He'd done everything he could to prepare, but he realized this was going to be make-or-break for the New Terran Empire.

Sean Meyer stood beside his chair, obviously just as nervous as he was. "What do you think we're going to find?"

"The same thing that every destroyer from Harrison's World has found for the last ten years," Jared said. "There's no reason to expect anything different. If something has changed, there has to be a reason for it, and that means trouble.

"Unfortunately, we don't know a lot about what's here or what the procedures are. The records merely report the destroyer made the trip and transmitted the report on command. The specifics are unknown."

The helm officer, Commander Janice Hall, turned in her seat. "We're ready to flip, Admiral."

"Take us across," he said firmly, suppressing his worry.

Unlike with previous systems, he didn't dare risk sending an FTL probe into this one. He knew it was occupied. Potentially, there were ships watching the flip point, even if there were none in the current system. If a strange probe popped out, that would set off alarms.

That didn't mean he couldn't leave some on this side, which he had.

The rest of the fleet he'd brought with him was located back at the flip point they'd used to enter this system, far out of normal scanner range but getting data from the probes *Athena* had deployed for them. That also put them well within the range to receive any FTL communication from *Athena* from the target system.

The Rebel Empire did not have FTL communications, so they wouldn't be expecting this capability. That didn't mean it was undetectable, however. So unless he had to, Jared would remain silent. The rest of the fleet knew that he'd only call if they ran into trouble. Otherwise, he'd send the report he was required to send and return.

At that point, they'd have to go around the target system via another set of flip points to get to Terra, taking at least a week longer to get there and arriving at a different entry point to the home system. That couldn't be helped. The lay of flip points was what it was. He would just hope that didn't come to pass.

"Flipping the ship," Hall said.

A brief queasiness accompanied the destroyer flipping into the target system. Everyone had implants, so the nausea that used to accompany every flip was no longer a major issue. Thank God.

"Ships detected," Commander Johan Berman, their tactical officer, said. "Weapons platforms detected. Significant numbers of both surrounding this flip point."

Jared tapped into *Athena*'s scanner feed using his implants. Berman was right. This was a lot of ships and battle stations in a globe around the flip point they'd just come through.

The robotic destroyers that the System Lord sent to make the yearly reports from Harrison's world did not bring back scanner records from this system. Jared couldn't be certain if this was new or standard procedure. They'd have to proceed under the assumption that it was standard.

"We're being challenged," Hall said. "The computer has responded as programmed. We've been instructed to proceed into the system."

Jared frowned. "We're sending a report. Shouldn't we be doing it from here?"

The helm officer shrugged. "I have no idea. That wasn't in the records."

"Well, if nothing else, this is going to give us a good opportunity to see what else is in the system," Jared said with a sigh. "We might be coming back with a fleet someday. Without going active, get as good at reading as you can of the platforms and ships. That'll be useful in analyzing their force strength."

The computer took the destroyer into the system at about eighty percent of her maximum speed. That was Rebel Fleet standard for nonemergency situations. His Fleet's standard, too.

"Where exactly are they having us go?" he asked.

"The primary world in this system. Imperial records have it labeled as El Capitan, the same name as the system itself."

"Do we have any indications that it's inhabited? All of these ships could be under AI control."

"I'm picking up a lot of signals," Hall said. "It's inhabited, and these people are not restricted to the primary world. They're scattered all across the system."

So these people hadn't done anything to earn the wrath of the System Lord ruling them. Of course, they probably didn't have an old fleet base in the graveyard of ships that the AIs were worried about either.

He signaled Olivia through his implants.

I need you on the bridge. We're going deeper into the system, and I'd like your read on exactly what we're seeing.

I'll be right there. Should I bring Elise?

The more, the merrier. If she's around, bring Princess Kelsey and Commander Roche. They need to see this, too.

That can't be good.

I'll leave it to you to decide about that. See you in a few minutes.

At this rate, it would take them approximately nine hours to reach their destination. They'd have plenty of time to analyze everything they were seeing. Most importantly, he suspected the transmissions they were picking up from around the system would provide them with critical intelligence data.

The only other Rebel Empire system they'd spent any time in had been the one adjacent to Dresden. It hadn't been that large and neither had Dresden, even though the latter held the critical research base that Kelsey had stolen.

Unlike Harrison's World, this system seemed to be in a relatively unfettered state. Sort of like watching people in their natural habitat. By the time they were done here, they should have a treasure trove of information about how everyday people lived under the AIs' rule.

"If going into this system isn't standard operating procedure, what do you think this means?" Sean asked.

"Probably nothing good. Worst case, they want to send something back to the AI at Harrison's World. That might get complicated very fast."

"Are you going to call the fleet via FTL and let them know?"

After weighing the benefits against the risks, Jared nodded. "Janice, pack all the data we've gathered so far into as tight a file as you can manage, along with our status and where were going, and send it back to *Invincible* via burst FTL."

"Aye, sir."

Fifteen seconds later, she nodded toward him. "Transmission sent. We received a brief acknowledgment from Captain Marcus that he has received the data and will disseminate it."

"Any indication the transmission was detected?"

"Nothing so far, sir. I'll continue monitoring everything I can and look for changes in behavior on any of the ships or signals that seem out of place. If I detect anything, I'll let you know immediately."

Jared hoped the Rebel Empire didn't become aware of their use of the FTL. Even if they didn't realize it was a method of communication, detecting the transmission would clue them in that something strange was occurring. He'd rather not give them even that little bit of information.

He glanced over at Sean. "Start rotating the crew so they can get meals and rest. It looks like we're going to be here longer than we expected. Make sure the marines are prepared to receive any unexpected visitors on short notice."

* * *

OLIVIA'S BRAIN felt like mush. She'd been reviewing the passively collected data for eight hours without a break. Mind-numbing work, but extremely educational. And unexpectedly productive.

She'd left the bridge, choosing to do her work in the room she shared with Sean. It was tiny when compared to what she would normally expect for the coordinator of Harrison's World, but her implants made space a luxury rather than a requirement.

It took very little time to step over to her husband's office, which was directly next door to their quarters. She savored the thought of their new status once again with deep satisfaction.

Even better, in the wake of their nuptials, someone had convinced Brian Drake to return to Harrison's World. One less stress in their lives. Of course, the man would be underfoot once Sean and she returned home, but the cooling off period would allow the other man to put her firmly in his past.

Jared had banished Sean from the bridge once it became clear that the Rebel Empire wasn't taking any notice of them. The two officers were splitting the intervening hours with four on and four off.

Her husband was preparing to return to the bridge when she came into his office. "I found something important. Take a look at this."

She sent him a transcript of routine radio traffic between the world of El Capitan and one of the moons of the first gas giant in the system.

With his implants, he would be able to scan it quickly, but he wouldn't notice what she had seen.

"Before you go through that in detail, allow me to point out what I'm looking at. There is a sequence of communications between several sources on both El Capitan and the largest moon. They look routine. However, appearances can be deceptive.

"In each of the communications that I've highlighted, either the sender or receiver has used a code phrase known to the resistance."

Sean sat up a bit straighter. "As in the same resistance that you're a member of?"

"Exactly so. Everything is context driven, so depending on a number of factors, the recognition phrases will change. Before we were cut off by the System Lord, we were in communication with other branches of the resistance, though not this system.

"These organizations have existed since the Fall. Each system is separate from every other. We don't know anything about the other organizations so that if we're compromised, we don't endanger anyone else.

"However, we do know enough to recognize these call signs. Rather, I should say, the leader of the resistance and their top-level assistants are made aware of them in case there's ever a need to contact another cell."

Sean considered her. "That seems kind of dangerous. If the leadership of any cell is compromised, they could recognize the presence of the resistance inside any other system."

"True," she said. "We take precautions, but they boil down to making certain that none of the senior leadership is allowed to be captured alive. If need be, we'll make certain of that ourselves."

"You'd kill yourself?" From his tone, he wasn't exactly thrilled to hear this.

"Of course I would. And so would you, if the Rebel Empire had the means to get information dangerous to the New Terran Empire. Tell me you wouldn't destroy your ship to avoid capture under the circumstances."

He sighed. "You know I can't say that. Okay, so either one of us would take our own lives before we endangered the people we protect. Got it.

"So you've recognized these call signs. What practical effect does that have? It's not as if we can contact them without raising suspicion from anyone that happens to notice. As far as I can see, there's no reason for a completely robotic destroyer, which is what they think this is, to contact anyone."

"Ordinarily, I'd agree, and I'm not certain of the circumstances where we could arrange contact, but if we can do so in a manner that doesn't generate undue attention, the resistance in this system could give us a lot of data."

He leaned back in his chair. "Like what?"

"If they're anything like the resistance on Harrison's World, they've had plenty of time to gather detailed information on the military presence here and potentially other systems nearby. It's even conceivable that they know something about Terra that we don't."

That last made him frown. "You make a good point. We're about an hour away from El Capitan. Let's go to the bridge and see what the admiral has to say. If he agrees that there's a need to contact the resistance, he can drag everyone else in to brainstorm the best way to do so.

"For the life of me, I still don't understand why the Rebel Empire has summoned this destroyer to El Capitan. If, as Admiral Mertz suspects, they intend to place a cargo aboard for the AI at Harrison's world, things could get very ugly.

"Yet that may present an opportunity to contact the resistance on the planet itself, if we can work out a subtle method of doing so."

"Do you really think they're going to put people aboard the ship?" she asked. "It seems unlikely that they would go any farther away from the docking and cargo areas.

"If we evacuate all of our personnel and keep track of anyone who comes aboard so that we can move around them, odds are good that they won't see anything out of place."

"That meshes pretty well with what the admiral is thinking," he said. "Over the last eight hours, he's had people scrubbing the most obvious locations where anyone could go of any sign of human habitation. Basically, everyone's belongings are being piled in maintenance tubes far away from the docking area.

"If no one has come to strip our quarters, it's only because they haven't gotten to us yet. We're leaving nothing to chance."

"And what happens if they still see something out of place? If something that we never considered triggers them into a wider search and they find us? There are a lot of warships between us and the flip point."

He smiled without the least hint of humor. "I believe we discussed this earlier in the conversation. The team in engineering will compromise the fusion plant. The entire ship will go up, and we'll never know that we're dead."

"Let's hope it doesn't come to that," she said. "Now, let's head for the bridge so that we can get a team working on this problem. We have to plan for success while we pray against disaster."

23

K elsey leaned back in her seat, rubbing her eyes. The feel of her face without the plate she'd worn for years still felt wrong. Not that she was complaining, of course. Not about looking like a human being again in other ways, either.

The regeneration sessions she'd completed before she left *Caduceus* had eliminated the visible scarring all across her body. Doctor Stone was very pleased at the reduction in the microscopic damage, too. She had expressed cautious optimism that Kelsey's new nanites would be able to completely eliminate even that in time.

A full recovery had never been laid out as an option when they started, so Kelsey still didn't know what to think about it. She was pleased that her pharmacology unit no longer had to dispense drugs to cover the pain. She hadn't realized she'd had a subtle cloud over her senses before it had stopped.

She'd thought that had been a shock, but getting a good look at this Rebel Empire system had been an even bigger one. A close examination of Harrison's World had not shown the potential threat her empire faced as clearly as she saw it now.

On this robotic destroyer, she could interface her implants with the ship's scanners. They were locked into passive mode, but there was so much data to process. The number of enemy warships in this system was staggering.

Just a cursory look had tagged dozens of them. Potentially, there could be as many as a hundred war craft. Even if they were only destroyers, that was more than sufficient to conquer the New Terran Empire, at least in her universe.

The chime that indicated she had a visitor sounded. A check of her implants revealed Scott Roche standing in the corridor. She signaled the hatch to open, and he came in.

"Highness."

She gestured toward a chair. "I understand they're going to be here in a few minutes to move all the furniture, so enjoy a seat while you can. What can I do for you?"

"I've been examining the scanner readings," he said as he settled into his seat. "I'm worried."

"Ironically, I've been doing the same thing. The fact that I can interface with their scanners using my implants probably drives home the fact that things are worse than you think."

"Great," he said with a shake of his head. "I can't imagine how the Empire possibly survives. Our universe doesn't have all of these repairable ships lying around. When the Rebel Empire finds us, they're going to conquer us."

"I can't get around that gloomy assessment, either," she said with a sigh. "And unless they get very lucky here, the same is true. Yes, they have all these wonderful ships: superdreadnoughts, carriers, and swarms of smaller ships. None of that makes one bit of difference.

"Once the Rebel Empire learns of their existence, which from everything I've heard is already true, it's only a matter of time until they send an overwhelming force to destroy the New Terran Empire here."

The Fleet officer rubbed his eyes. "What do we do? Give up? Surrender and accept slavery? Or do we fight and die?"

"Why can't there be some kind of middle ground?" she asked. "These people at Harrison's World and developed technology to block flip points. They call them flip-point jammers. When one of them is running, the flip point is impassable.

"Surely they could surround their systems with these flip-point jammers and keep the Rebel Empire at bay."

Scott looked skeptical. "Let's say that works. They're free from direct oppression, but they're trapped. They'll never be able to leave their systems, not even to take the fight to the enemy. You can rest assured the Rebel Empire will invest those border systems with overwhelming force, too.

"And that assumes that what man builds, man cannot overcome. Suppose that the Rebel Empire comes up with technology that neutralizes these jammers. Then they'd just pour through. Or perhaps they'd find one of these weak flip points and send ships straight through into an unexpected area."

Kelsey sighed. "Or play the really long game. Their ships can be computer controlled. They could build a massive fleet and get it close in normal space before sending it across the gulf between systems. I have no idea how close their nearest system would be, but even if it took centuries or millennia, these computers could still win.

"The New Terran Empire, both in this universe and ours, has to actually win this fight. We're in far worse condition than Admiral Mertz's forces. This mission to Terra is our best chance. The data we gather now makes a long-shot mission in our universe a possibility."

The two of them sat in gloomy silence for several minutes before Scott spoke. "We don't even have a destroyer that could fool the Rebel Empire in our universe. The only person with an Old Empire ship is the Bastard. And he has the Imperial Scepter.

"Do you think he knows what he has? That it leads to Terra and the vaults underneath the Imperial Palace? Does he know about the override?"

She considered that for a few seconds before shaking her head. "I don't think so. I've been over the roster of those who defected to his side. He just doesn't have the scientific support to probe the scepter.

"Even if he figures out that it has an Imperial computer inside it, which isn't certain since the designers made sure it never signals its presence, the memory sector that holds the message from Emperor Marcus is fiendishly well concealed.

"While I'm as far from a scientist as you can get, I've looked over what this Carl Owlet discovered and believe that only someone of his intellectual caliber could've found it. The man is probably the greatest mind the Empire has produced in our lifetime."

Scott smiled a little. "I sent a message back home to locate and sequester him. Once they start sending data and hardware back to our universe, I expect he's going to prove very useful indeed. If only we could come up with a way to get him implants."

That wasn't very likely, at least not in the short term. While there were potential paths between the New Terran Empire and Pentagar, they were not short. Sending anyone out to make the trip to this universe and be implanted would take roughly six months. Then they'd have to get home.

A better option was taking implantation hardware back into her universe and sending an expedition home. That would still take six months, but it gave them much greater flexibility in preparing their homeland for this conflict.

She intended to have a discussion with the alien on the space station inside the Nova system. It had created artificial flip points between its system and both Pentagar and Avalon in this universe.

Kelsey understood the rather large power requirements in doing so limited its ability to do so again in the short term, but the shortened travel time between it and the occupied systems fighting the Rebel Empire might provide at least a slim chance for them to survive.

The chime at the hatch sounded again. This time a group of Fleet crewmen stood in the corridor. It was time to head for the bridge. Very soon, she'd see what the possibilities were, if they made it out of this system alive.

* * *

ELISE HAD DECIDED to be on the bridge when the destroyer achieved orbit.

Just like Olivia, she'd been going over all the data she could get her hands on. While she didn't have the same experience of being part of the Rebel Empire that her friend had, she'd found a few interesting things.

It seemed that the Rebel Empire was very restrictive in what it allowed its citizens to talk about. That didn't mean that they no longer discussed those other things, only that they'd became much more circumspect about how they did it.

There were a series of fascinating discussions that she tapped into where the participants used subtext to get around any number of potential roadblocks to whatever it was they were discussing.

True, that didn't provide her with a lot of useful information for their current task, but it did confirm something she'd suspected for a long time. Something Olivia had become blind to.

The citizens of the Rebel Empire were not as cowed as one could be led to expect. And since the sentient AIs that ruled it were not complete idiots, they obviously tolerated a certain level of subversion.

Oh, not in any serious manner. For example, if someone were to discuss planting a bomb or committing some act of terrorism, no matter what language they use to talk around it, she was certain that the System Lord would detect it, if it were in a channel the AI was monitoring.

But if it were two brothers discussing how they could safely skirt certain regulations about proscribed technology as it related to manufacturing in space, that might be allowed to pass. At least, it wasn't stopping the two brothers she'd found.

Elise was relatively certain they wouldn't be discussing such matters or even mentioning that the technology was technically disallowed unless they expected to have some level of safety in doing so. The brothers in question were not members of the higher orders. They might not even be members of the middle orders. She still wasn't quite certain she grasped how everything fit together in the Rebel Empire on a societal level.

"We've entered orbit," the helm officer told her husband. "We're about a thousand kilometers away from what has to be the biggest orbital I've ever seen. The thing is a monster."

Jared nodded. "Easily three times the size of the Dresden orbital. I can only imagine how long it took to build. Any idea of what they want with us? Have we received a signal to transmit our report?"

"Not yet. Again, the System Lord back at Harrison's World didn't retain that level of detail about any previous report, so this might be perfectly normal. Or something could be seriously wrong."

Olivia cleared her throat from where she sat beside Elise. "Is there any possibility of piggybacking a communication onto something here in orbit? Of getting a signal down to the surface of the planet?"

The helm officer shook her head. "I'd have to be desperate to try, ma'am. There are so many ships in orbit that the chances of detection are absurdly high."

"I think you'd best give up your idea of contacting the resistance," Jared told the other woman. "While it was a wonderful thought, we can't do anything to endanger our mission. That means we have to be the most cautious individuals you have ever met."

"Fine," Olivia grumbled. "I just hate missing the opportunity to steal a march on those rebel bastards."

The helm officer sat up a little straighter. "We just received instructions to transmit the report. The computer sent it just as planned. We've received a confirmation that the orbital has it."

"Now what?" Princess Kelsey asked. "Do we head back?"

Kelsey had been more quiet than usual since the surgery on her face, Elise noted. She'd offered to talk to the woman from another universe about what she was going through, but Kelsey had declined.

It had to be traumatic. Kelsey had been living with her disfigurement for years. She'd seen how everyone recoiled at her appearance. That kind of thing left a mark on one's psyche.

Jared shook his head. "We wait. If it were as simple as heading back immediately, they'd never have brought us in. Something will happen."

He turned his attention to the ship's tactical officer. "I want everything in our area watched. If any ship or small craft heads toward us, I want to know as soon as possible."

"There's a ton of traffic around the orbital," the man said, "but we're outside the regular pattern. If anyone is interested in us, I'll see it as soon as they start toward us."

"I've got everyone who can be spared in the maintenance passages," Sean said. "Only critical people in engineering and here are out. We've looked over every area they might come into, and there are no traces we were ever here."

"Good," Jared said. "I hope all they intend to do is send something back."

There's no indication they've ever sent people before. If they do, this is going to be very, very tricky.

"We'd have to let them take control of the ship and wait until we flipped out of the system to subdue them. Nine hours during which we'd be the ears in the walls and didn't dare reveal ourselves."

Elise suppressed a shudder. The maintenance passages were cramped under optimal conditions. Now that they were filled with people and furnishings, she'd be sitting in someone's lap the entire time.

"I have a cargo shuttle inbound," the tactical officer said. "ETA twenty minutes."

"Any signals?" Jared asked.

The man shook his head. "It looks as if they expect to dock without warning the computer they're coming."

"Everyone to their assigned hiding places," Jared said grimly. "We're going to have guests for dinner."

24

S ean monitored the intruders from the safety of a nearby maintenance
tube. It was cramped, dark, and packed with heavily-armed marines.
Thankfully, he was able to use his implants and the ship's own
cameras to monitor their unwelcome visitors.

They'd taken every precaution to make certain the Rebel Empire
personnel wouldn't detect *Athena*'s rightful crew's use of the ship's systems.
Hopefully, the people exiting the cargo shuttles would unload whatever
they'd brought, pack it away, and depart quickly.

Worst case, some of them would stay aboard. If that happened, everyone
would remain in hiding in the maintenance tubes. They'd only reveal
themselves once *Athena* had exited El Capitan.

Things were looking pretty good. Fleet crewmen, under the watchful eyes
of their superiors, were unloading crates and securing them in the cargo
section nearest the destroyer's docks. There was no way to know what was in
those crates, but that hardly mattered at this point. There would be plenty of
time to look into their contents once they were safely away.

It took them almost two hours to unload the cargo shuttles. As they got
closer to finishing, Sean's tension rose. Not that any of the personnel had
come near any of his hiding people. In fact, they hadn't left the cargo area.

His heart soared when the officers ordered the enlisted men back aboard
the cargo shuttles and they undocked. It looked as if *Athena* wouldn't be
having long-term company after all.

He was about to order his men out of the maintenance tubes to inspect the crates when Admiral Mertz sent a general message through everyone's implants.

We have a cutter inbound, people. Maintain positions.

Sean cursed under his breath. This wasn't good. With the cargo secured, the only reason another vessel would be coming their way was to drop off passengers or do some kind of inspection. Neither of those options was promising.

He tapped into the ship's passive scanners and watched the cutter approach. It was alone, so there wouldn't be very many people to deal with. The Rebel Empire used the same design as the New Terran Empire, now that they had upgraded to using Old Empire tech, so he knew the capacity of their cutters.

They could hold thirty-five people plus a flight crew of three in comfort, twice that if they were stacked like logs. He doubted the incoming cutter was running heavy, so they were looking at a maximum of three dozen people. Troublesome, but not beyond handling if need be.

The cutter docked without incident and disgorged three dozen men and women. Unlike the previous individuals, these immediately left the docking area and headed for the critical sections of the ship: the bridge, engineering, and the computer control room.

Not good.

Admiral Mertz could handle the people going to the bridge. He and his team were actually in the bulkheads directly surrounding the bridge. They could gain entrance through concealed hatches that weren't on any schematic. The same was true of engineering and computer central.

Sean had made certain *Athena*'s crew had places to hide as he was overseeing the refurbishing of the destroyer. Having done so before, he'd known there was a possibility they'd have to attack intruders in critical areas of the ship, so he figured they might as well make it easy on themselves.

The incoming personnel settled at the control consoles in the three areas and immediately took control of the ship away from the computer. They used specific key phrases and implant codes to do so.

Of course, the ship's computer wasn't the standard version that they would have expected. It reported itself at their disposal, but it was still under the New Terran Empire crew's control. And now they had an interesting set of codes they might be able to use again at some future point.

The woman in the center seat opened a communications channel to someone on the planet below. Based on the way the man she called was dressed, he was a member of the higher orders.

The woman on *Athena*'s bridge smiled. "We're ready to depart. I don't anticipate any trouble. We should be back in a couple of months."

"Excellent. You know how important this mission is, so I won't tell you to do everything you can to make it a success. I trust you'll do that as a matter of course. Safe journey, Jaleesa."

The man terminated the connection without waiting for a response. Sean supposed that firmly established who was the superior in that relationship.

He wondered what the woman and her people intended to do back at Harrison's World. Were they going to install some kind of equipment? Until they really dug into what was down in the cargo area, they weren't going to be able to determine what the Rebel Empire's goal really was.

He was about to close down his connection to the bridge when he noticed that the com signal to the planet below hadn't terminated. Even though the woman in the command chair was no longer in communication with the man she'd called, *Athena* was still talking with someone.

More interestingly, the com signal wasn't being logged the way it should be. Electronically, there was no indication it was happening at all. If he hadn't been directly tapped into the outgoing signal, he wouldn't have noticed it.

Before he could dig into the contents of the call, the additional signal terminated. Perhaps they had been adding some raw information to the end of the verbal communication. Still, why hadn't it been logged by the computer?

Sean used his concealed access to *Athena*'s systems and began searching. He quickly found a small program that had been inserted into the computer to hide communications on a certain frequency.

He sent an implant signal to Admiral Mertz.

Sir, we might have a problem. He explained about the concealed transmission.

The admiral sent a mental grunt back to him. *I feel pretty confident I know who to blame for that: your wife.*

Sean blinked. *My wife?*

I'd be willing to bet a month's pay that she signaled the resistance on the main world even though we told her not to.

Now that Sean thought about it, that did sound like his wife. When Olivia decided on a course of action, she'd execute it over every objection. She was stubborn that way. Of course, in his new circle of friends, that was a common trait.

What do we do about it?

The admiral sent a mental shrug. *We wait. Hopefully, the wrong people don't become aware of our presence.*

* * *

JARED CROUCHED in the maintenance passage encircling the bridge and considered their situation. It was obvious the intruders were preparing to leave El Capitan. They'd spent a decent amount of time going through the systems and disengaging computer control.

At this point, they really did have full control of *Athena*, though his people could take it back far faster than the enemy would've dreamed possible.

They only had control of the critical systems. There were only three dozen people on their team, barely enough to run a destroyer. They'd focused on propulsion and power. They'd left the automated systems controlling the weapons in place but inserted themselves as the initiators of action rather than the ship's computer.

He really wondered what was in the crates they'd brought aboard. Harrison's World was completely suppressed according to all the information they had. The population was under the heel of the System Lord. What could they bring that would assist in that, or how did they intend to change it?

Well, he'd find out as soon as they left this system. Unknown to them, Jared still had complete control of the antiboarding weapons via altered control interfaces. Once they made that first flip, he'd stun every single one of the intruders and resume control of *Athena*.

Janice Hall edged past some of the others in the maintenance tube until she was beside him. "Sir, we have a problem."

"What's wrong?"

"We just left orbit, and we're heading for the wrong flip point."

He pulled data from the passive sensors and double-checked their course. They were indeed making way for the other flip point in the El Capitan system. ETA five hours at this speed.

While it was certainly possible to work around to Harrison's World from the new target system, it would make for a much longer trip. No, these people had another end destination in mind.

"Pass the word that we might have to kick this party off early," he said. "We'll have to work out a new rendezvous with the fleet."

"Aye, sir."

They really didn't have a choice now. If this supposedly automated destroyer suddenly changed course, the powers that be at El Capitan would have a conniption. They'd quickly dispatch ships to catch up with *Athena* and find out what had gone wrong.

And then there was the force surrounding the flip point leading to Harrison's World, one they'd never be able to slip past if the System Lord figured out something was wrong. No, they were stuck taking a side trip.

"I want you to start looking into potential destinations," he continued. "Once we have something workable, send it to me for verification. Then we'll use the FTL com to send a burst packet to *Invincible*.

"This has to have something to do with the cargo these people brought aboard. We'll find out what that is once we flip to the next system and take them out. If, of course, it's safe to do so. What exactly do we know about the system we're headed toward?"

The woman shrugged. "We have information from the Old Empire databases but nothing recent. In the old days, the next system over was used for heavy mining. Asteroid belts and moons primarily. Lots of heavy metals and even some rare elements. Now? We won't know until we get there."

"Go get me what you can."

Once the woman was gone, Jared sighed. What had once been populous and productive systems in the Old Empire were abandoned under the control of the AIs. Hopefully, that was what they'd find when they flipped.

Then again, it might be possible to find out before *Athena* left El Capitan.

He opened an implant channel to Olivia West. They'd relocated her to a maintenance tube just off engineering.

Got a minute?

Her response was immediate. *Of course. What can I do for you, Admiral?*

Aren't we being formal today? Tell me, did you just signal the resistance on El Capitan? Or more pertinently, did they respond?

That was a moment of silence over the implant link. *How did you know?*

Surely you expected me to monitor all communications. A good commander is always aware of what's going on aboard his ship.

Her tone held a hint of chagrin when she responded. *As it turns out, I did send a message to the resistance. I'm sorry, but the opportunity was too good to let pass by. Our visitors were sending a message of their own, so it was very easy to piggyback on their signal.*

I haven't received a response yet. Frankly, I'm not certain that I will. Nevertheless, it was worth taking a chance. Other than identifying myself as a visitor from another resistance cell, I asked for basic information that they would be willing to share with any resistance group. Both about El Capitan and this area of the Rebel Empire.

Which they call El Cap in most of the local communications, by the way. I'm not sure why.

He considered what she'd done. It was far too late to do anything about it except hope for the best.

If the situation was reversed, would you respond, Olivia?

It would probably take several hours before I made up my mind, but I'd answer. Any chance to help overthrow the AIs is worth taking. It's not going to put them in any danger, sending a response. Not really.

They have communication cutouts. Even if the AIs became aware that they sent a signal, it would never be able to trace the response back.

Jared considered that before responding. *That makes sense. Do you expect them to send a general signal that we'll be able to pick up? Or will it be something directed specifically at us? Do they even know where your signal came from?*

I never said, but they'd have to be fools not to guess. Athena *just arrived in their system. I'd wager they're fairly certain at this point where we are.*

He wasn't exactly happy with the risk that she'd taken. Frankly, if the resistance had a mole in their organization, someone could make sure the System Lord found out.

Jared made certain to insert a strong note of disapproval into his mental tone. *I had very good reasons to turn down your request to initiate contact, Coordinator. I like you very much, but rest assured that there will be serious consequences for violating my orders.*

If the resistance responds, I expect you to pass that information to me immediately. And, Olivia, this had better never happen again. Right or wrong, this is my mission, and I set the rules. Cross me at your peril.

Her tone became conciliatory. *I swear that I'll follow your orders going forward. Next time I'll just argue more strenuously.*

Wasn't that going to be fun? Well, since the die was cast, perhaps their response could shed some light on one of the things that confused him.

When they answer, if they answer, maybe they'll tell us why the AI decided to use this ship. It had to be planned long in advance and I don't get it. There are a lot of ships already here. Why us?

Oh, I can tell you that now, Admiral. If they used a local ship, they'd have to displace the entire crew for security. Word would get around. This way, no one has a clue what Athena *is being used for.*

That made sense to him.

Well, I'll leave you to what you're doing. Contact me the second you receive a response of any kind.

I'll do that, Admiral.

Perhaps in the end, it'll turn out that you're right. I guess we'll find out.

25

Through concealed video pickups the New Terran Empire crew had left scattered around, Elise watched the Rebel Empire personnel working in engineering. The tiny units were far too small to be noticed unless someone was specifically looking for them, so she wasn't concerned the enemy would spot them.

She was no military expert, but it was apparent these were not Fleet personnel. They wore no uniforms, and their demeanor was not what one would expect from someone in a military organization. These were civilians. High-ranking civilians, certainly. Undoubtedly members of the higher orders.

Not a single person lacked an implant. The Rebel Empire didn't give implants to anyone unless they were either a member of the higher orders or a Fleet officer.

That raised some interesting questions. Why were members of the nobility running a warship? Better yet, how did they know how to do so in the first place? These people were obviously very familiar with the systems on this ship.

From what she'd seen of the higher orders, Elise didn't believe they'd had a burning desire to learn how to fly spaceships. That meant that these people had been specifically trained for this mission.

Their conversation thus far had been obscure, at least to her. They obviously knew one another very well and limited their conversation to the duties at hand. That would probably change once people started going off shift, but thus far, everyone was proving remarkably uncommunicative.

The pickups had very sensitive audio receptors, so she was able to hear every word uttered in the large compartment. With her implant processing power, she managed to keep track of all the individual conversations at the same time.

"Jocelyn, could you take a look at this?" one of the men standing beside the main engineering console asked.

"What is it?" an older woman asked as she stepped over to him.

"Look at this maintenance log. Does it look off to you?"

The woman leaned forward and examined the screen. "Off in what way?"

"It's too clean. There should be more errors listed."

Elise felt her stomach sinking. This was the kind of thing that Jared had worried about. That they had *all* worried about.

The woman raised an eyebrow. "So let me see if I understand you correctly, Austin. You're concerned because the equipment is operating too well. You think it should be more problematic?"

The man smiled a little. "Not precisely. I'd expect an autonomous destroyer to have more minor system errors. Particularly in life support. After all, the system should have been shut down until we ordered it brought online.

"And speaking of that, look at the reserves. The oxygen levels are particularly low, considering how they haven't been used. I would've expected the tanks to be virtually full. They're actually down by about ten percent."

The woman frowned. "It's conceivable that some of the reserve has bled off through small breaches in the system over time. I don't think we should read too much into this, but you're right to bring it to my attention.

"Begin a systematic review of all engineering systems and provide me with a status on them by the time we reached the flip point. Not that I think there's something wrong, but we're going to be on this ship for a while. I'd like to know for certain that everything is in order."

"I'll start that at once," the man said with a nod. "I should have a preliminary report ready by then. It's going to take significantly longer, on the order of several days, for us to do a complete systems analysis."

"That's good enough. Thank you."

The woman walked back over to stand beside the flip drive. The older man she'd been speaking to before raised an eyebrow.

"Is something wrong?"

"Austin believes he's found something of concern. He seems to think that the maintenance logs are too clean. Unusually so."

The man studied her. "Are *you* concerned?"

"Not overly so," she said with a slight shrug. "This destroyer came from

Harrison's World in an unoccupied state. The System Lord there has likely been using it for any number of purposes. The fact that the maintenance logs are not as we would've expected doesn't necessarily mean anything.

"It's entirely possible that the Lord keeps these vessels in a higher state of readiness and in better condition for peripheral systems then we'd believed. It's also possible that it felt no need to fully top off the oxygen reserves. Honestly, we have no way of knowing."

The man looked away from her for a few seconds. "I assume you told Austin to research it further."

"Indeed I did. He should have a preliminary report by the time we make flip out of El Capitan. A detailed analysis will take several days more. One of the downsides of having a small crew."

"Stay on top of it. If there's something unusual happening, I want to know about it before we leave the system. See if you can pry any other personnel away from their normal duties to assist in checking the critical systems."

The woman nodded. "I'll take care of it."

Elise immediately passed word to Jared that the intruders had spotted something that concerned them. She really hoped they didn't find anything else that raised their suspicions even further.

If they did, Jared had positioned the marines so they could flood the critical compartments in short order. Hell, he could just trigger the antiboarding weapons and drop them all in their tracks.

The trouble would come if someone was expecting these people to send a final communication before they flipped out of the system. If that were the case, there was more than enough force present at El Capitan to chase *Athena* down.

She would just have to hope that they managed to keep these people in the dark for just a little bit longer.

* * *

OLIVIA HAD MADE the conscious decision not to watch the Rebel Empire personnel inside *Athena*. Rather, she focused her attention on gathering as much data through the ship's passive scanners as she could.

They weren't going to have another opportunity to visit El Capitan, so it behooved her to make the data collection as complete as possible. The ships here might very well make the journey to Harrison's World and visit war upon them.

Also, she kept hoping that they'd receive information from the resistance cell here. If her message had been convincing enough, the locals could provide them with far more data than she'd be able to collect on her own.

With her attention focused outward, she was able to catch the message she'd been hoping for as soon as it arrived.

Her respect for the resistance cell on El Capitan notched higher as she reviewed what they'd sent. This was clever. The message header indicated the transmission was a data set for a mining ship out in the belt. It "only happened" to pass close enough to *Athena* for the ship's receivers to pick it up.

The data was encrypted, but the audio message attached to it gave her clues as to the key. Yet another of the code phrases the resistance used in communicating between systems.

She applied the decryption key and was dismayed when it failed. Had she done something wrong?

Olivia considered potential variants to the code phrase. With decryption, every single letter was important. Thankfully with her implants, she was able to try multiple different passes, and one of them unlocked the data.

She let out a slow breath and opened the file.

The contents were more than she'd hoped for. Not only did the data set contain observations of the Fleet vessels stationed at El Capitan, it also held data about the surrounding systems, including the one *Athena* was currently headed toward.

Olivia skimmed the data and quickly determined the system was occupied but not heavily so. Seemingly, it was heavily stocked with rare elements useful in constructing flip drives and other complex equipment. So there was a mining presence but not much more.

The flip point was guarded, though only on the El Capitan side. Perhaps even more heavily so than the one leading toward Harrison's World. She wondered what they were worried about.

Maybe the ghosts—the strange raiders that Kelsey had learned about at the Dresden system—were the reason. The New Terran Empire's working hypothesis was that those people were remnants of loyal fleet units still hiding inside the Rebel Empire.

With as much force as the rebels had at their fingertips, Olivia wasn't certain why they hadn't crushed the ghosts already. They'd had over five hundred years to hunt them down. Still, if the loyalists were still able to fight, she wasn't going to worry about how they'd managed it. The important thing was that they were still fighting.

As one of the leaders of the resistance on Harrison's World, she was somewhat surprised that she'd never heard about the ghosts. That was the kind of juicy rumor she'd have expected to at least have some clue about.

It seemed that the rebel Empire had gone out of their way to make certain that talk about the ghosts was minimized. It was also possible that the other resistant cells deeper in the Empire didn't consider rumors worthwhile enough to pass on.

She raised an eyebrow at the thought and skimmed the data, looking for any mention of the ghosts. Nothing. Yet one more mystery.

While she didn't consider herself as knowledgeable as a Fleet officer, she knew enough to categorize the firepower present at El Capitan. There were enough ships here, though none larger than a heavy cruiser, to give Admiral Mertz's fleet a run for its money.

There was also a Fleet base here. Based on the information in the data set, it was about a hundred fifty years old. So something not built under the Old Empire.

That meant she didn't have any idea of how it was laid out, though the resistance had given them some generalities about its capabilities. Just like Harrison's World, it was the home of the System Lord.

That alone made the fortress immensely powerful. With the firepower that modern technology could bring to bear, the sentient AI magnified its lethality by orders of magnitude.

El Capitan was going to prove a tough nut to crack when the time came to invade. Of course, any system with this level of firepower was going to prove challenging.

She was about to route the data she'd received to Admiral Mertz when she had another idea. What do they know about Terra?

As it turned out, a little bit more than she did. They had never been to the capital of the Old Empire, but the resistance here had gotten word from another cell closer to the center of the Empire.

According to the resistance sources, each of the three standard flip points was heavily invested with defensive stations, both in the Terra system and on the other side of the flip point.

Interesting. Even an important system like El Capitan only kept its forces on the defending side. She'd assumed that the Lords had decided to protect systems like that, regardless if it made sense or not.

What exactly were the AIs protecting against? Were they worried about people accessing Terra or were they more concerned about the people imprisoned on the capital eventually making their way out? Perhaps that was why it was defended on both sides of the flip points.

Terra had a System Lord. That wasn't a surprise, though it was going to make the mission more challenging.

It maintained control of the defensive systems on the far side of each of the flip point via targeted rules of engagement. Only ships with the correct passcodes could even approach the flip points without being fired upon.

Not that she imagined very many ships wanted to transit to Terra in any case. From everything she'd heard, the capital was a smoking ruin.

The resistance data had no information about whether that was true or not. They'd find out when they got there.

The last thing she found in the data set was a list of important people on El Capitan, mostly members of the higher orders that ruled the planet. Those would be the most loyal members of the Rebel Empire present in the system.

Unless, of course, there were leaders of the resistance sprinkled among them. That last brought a smile to her face, since that was exactly what she'd been on Harrison's World.

It was very possible that a similar situation existed here on El Capitan. If so, she wouldn't find that information in the data sent by the resistance. They would go to great lengths to conceal their identities.

The data did provide some information about the people aboard *Athena*. A brief check of the records gave her matching faces for several of the people on the ship right now.

Interestingly, each of them was a member of the higher order. And not just minor members of the nobility either. These were people with influence and authority.

The highest ranking of the individuals was on the bridge. Her name was Jaleesa Keaton. She was a sitting member of the system's ruling council. That was the equivalent of the group of leaders Olivia had chaired as coordinator of Harrison's World. Two dozen of the most powerful people on the planet.

She verified that the numbers on El Capitan were about the same. The woman at the command console was far too important to be commanding a mission away from the planet, yet here she was.

The next most senior was Bertram Gust. He was a junior member of the ruling council. Apparently, he was closely aligned with Keaton.

The third in command, as far as Olivia could see, was a woman named Jocelyn Oldfield. The records the resistance had sent indicated she was Gust's assistant.

What were such powerful and influential people doing on board a supposedly automated Rebel Empire destroyer?

Well, they'd find out soon enough.

Olivia sent the information from the resistance to Admiral Mertz. He would undoubtedly use it to help formulate their plans going forward.

26

K elsey sat in the near darkness of the maintenance tube and tried not to fidget. The close confines were making her antsy. The claustrophobia reminded her too much of being trapped inside the machine that had forcibly implanted her.

She didn't use to feel this way about tight spaces. She'd spoken with Justin Guzman about the change at length over the last few years. Therapy, he'd called those sessions. Reliving torture was how she thought of them.

Still, those conversations had helped give her some distance from the trauma. Now, sitting here unable to do anything, she felt the fear and anger flowing back into her. The raw terror at not being able to control her own fate.

Another check of her internal chrono revealed that only five minutes had passed since the last time she'd checked. Five minutes. It felt as if five hours had gone by.

Ironically, five hours was exactly how long they still had to wait until *Athena* flipped out of the El Capitan system. Hopefully, these hours would be quiet ones.

"Highness, we have a problem," Commander Roche said softly in her ear.

"Of course we do," she said, resigned. "What is it?"

"Some of the enemy personnel have begun doing systems checks. Right now, they're only working on accessing everything remotely, but if they're going to be thorough, they'll need to do some checks in person.

"Unfortunately, the maintenance tube we're sitting in runs behind the computer center. If they intend to verify the computer's functionality, they'll need to send someone here."

"Where can we relocate to? Are we even going to be *able* to relocate?"

He shook his head slightly. "I don't think so. We have a lot of equipment stashed in the back end of this maintenance tube. While it's conceivable that the intruders will miss seeing it, that's not something we can bank on.

"Also, it would be reckless to try to move the equipment. We're sitting in the middle of a heavy-traffic area. The odds of someone seeing us approach certainty."

"Perfect," she said with a sigh. "What can we do? Wait for someone to stick their head into the maintenance tube and punch them out?"

That brought a slight smile to the Fleet officer's face. "That's not such a bad plan, all things considered. The only problem I see with it is that they'll miss whoever they send fairly quickly.

"I know Admiral Mertz wants to avoid any interaction at all until this vessel has left El Capitan. That's the smart move. If the intruders become concerned, they could warn someone back on the planet. That might spark a mission to Harrison's World once we make a break for it."

Thereby voiding everything the New Terran Empire in this universe had accomplished so far and leaving them in a terrible position. That couldn't be allowed to happen.

She drew in a deep breath and let it out slowly. "I'm not sure we can do anything to change what happens next. If they come looking into this maintenance tube, we can't just wave at them and let things pass. We'll have to take out whoever comes through that hatch."

"And bluff our way through any last-minute communication once we reached the flip point," Scott agreed. "Let's hope they have enough things to look over without coming into this maintenance tube for the next five hours."

If Kelsey had thought that time was passing slowly before, it crawled now. Every second was like a drop of syrup preparing to fall onto a pancake.

And of course, thinking about pancakes made her hungry. Kelsey had taken the precaution of stuffing her jacket with survival rations. They fed the gnawing hunger in her gut, but they were hardly pancakes.

She started using her implants to access the feeds from engineering and the corridors around the computer center. Her anxiety level rose, but things were quiet for now.

At the one-hour mark, she started to think that they'd made it. Of course, shortly after that, disaster struck.

One of the men in engineering walked over to the woman in charge of the compartment and told her that he was going to check the computer center. She told him to hurry up because she wanted him back at his station by the time they flipped.

"Scott," Kelsey said softly, "we've got trouble." It amused her darkly to use the same warning he had earlier. This wasn't the time for levity, but she couldn't help herself.

"Tell me."

"One of the people in engineering is coming to the computer center to do some systems checks. I hope that means he's just going to be in the center itself and not going to stick his head into this maintenance tube, but we can't plan on that. We need to be ready."

He glanced at his wrist unit. "We have about fifty minutes until we can flip. Whatever happens, it's going to take place while *Athena* is in the middle of all those battle stations and ships around the flip point. Even if we make a run for it, the mobile units stationed there will chase us down.

"Destroyers are fast, but they'll be right on top of us. They'll be able to fire missiles immediately after they flip into the next system.

"Also, we really don't know what's on the other side of this flip point, other than the unverified information Olivia got from the local resistance. They say it's empty, but they might not know everything.

"We can't take chances, so we'll be as prepared as we can get. Whatever happens, we need to assume the consequences are going to be drastic if anyone learns of our presence."

Kelsey nodded. "I'll keep an eye on this guy's progress and keep you updated. If I even think he's headed toward us, I'll let you know."

As she was positioned right next to the hatch, she'd be the one dealing with the problem. There were marines in the tube with her, but she had those vaunted Marine Raider implants. If the guy caused any trouble, she could shut him up the fastest.

The stunner at her hip would be the safest means of dealing with him. She'd rather not kill a man simply for being in the wrong place at the wrong time.

Also, she couldn't be certain that his death wouldn't register on some piece of equipment or in his superiors' implants. Simply stunning him stretched out the time that those people might wonder what had happened to him but not be overly alarmed.

To her relief, the man went directly to the central computer core and began a detailed inspection of the consoles and control runs inside the room. Using the concealed video pickups Mertz had planted there, Kelsey scrutinized his every move.

It was almost as if she were looking over his shoulder. She could read what he was typing into the various consoles, and she could make uneducated guesses about what the parts he was examining were.

With about fifteen minutes to go until the ship arrived in the flip point, he began closing up the consoles and access panels. He didn't interact with the other people in the room, so Kelsey wasn't certain what his next course of action would be. She hoped he'd return directly to engineering.

He dashed that hope when he came directly toward the maintenance tube where she was hiding.

Oh crap.

"Everyone get ready," she said. "We've got someone coming to look in the maintenance tube. I've got him."

Considering the deadline the man was operating under, he shouldn't be wasting his time like this. With only a dozen minutes left before he had to report back to his station, she wasn't certain what he thought he'd see.

No matter what his motivation, this introduced some serious complications into their plan.

Kelsey opened an implant communication channel to Mertz. It was still difficult not to think of him as the Bastard. She was trying, but it was hard.

As soon as he answered, she got straight to the point.

We've got a situation. One of the people from engineering is about to look into the maintenance tube behind computer central. I'm going to take him out.

Make it quick, Mertz sent back. *We don't know if they have some kind of automated monitoring, but we can't let him scream for help.*

I've got it covered, but he's expected in engineering in ten minutes. What do we do if they delay the flip because he's not there?

I'll worry about that. Just shut him down fast. If you don't, we're all screwed.

No pressure.

Kelsey positioned herself near the hatch, drew her stunner, and readied herself. She heard marines moving into position behind her, ready to back her up if things went wrong. She hoped she wouldn't need them.

A minute later, the hatch slid open. She aimed her weapon at the opening and waited. And waited. *And waited.*

Where was he?

She took a deep breath and leaned forward just enough to peer into the corridor. The man was standing half a dozen meters away, frowning at an open access panel.

He was half turned away from the hatch, but that didn't stop him from seeing her, curse the luck. His eyes widened, and he opened his mouth to shout something.

Kelsey shot him before he could make a sound. He dropped quietly into a loose heap.

Had he gotten off an implant warning? No way to know for sure unless things went completely into the crapper.

Looking in both directions to make certain no one else was present, Kelsey stepped into the corridor, closed the panel the man had been peering into, slung him into a fireman's carry, and ducked back into the maintenance tube.

A touch on the controls sealed the hatch behind her. It was all up to Mertz now. Her fate—all their fates—were in his hands.

* * *

JARED CONSIDERED the situation as soon as he disconnected from Kelsey. If things were going to go wrong, the worst possible time would be right now.

They were a little more than eight minutes away from the flip point at their current speed. The destroyer was virtually on top of the defensive fortifications. If the people on his bridge sent any kind of distress signal, it was all over.

Just to be certain that something like that didn't happen, he initiated a lockdown of outgoing communications. If things seemed normal when they reached the flip point, he could enable their ability to communicate with their comrades with only a moment's notice.

One of the side benefits of allowing these Rebel Empire jerks aboard *Athena* was that *they* had no problem running the scanners at full power. What would've seemed incongruous from an automated vessel wouldn't be questioned from a live crew of people known to be loyal.

That meant they were getting priceless data that they could use against the Rebel Empire at some future point. The detailed information from the fortifications would be very valuable when they had to assault this system or one like it in the future.

Jared sent a message to Commander Hall. It was time to send a final data packet to *Invincible* through the FTL com. *Athena* might transit with little to no warning, so he wanted to be sure he got all the critical information to the fleet.

She quickly had the data compressed and burst transmitted it to the superdreadnought. Marcus had confirmed receipt of the transmission and returned the path they would take to meet him at Terra.

It would take the fleet a bit more than a week longer to get there, but he'd already known that. They would arrive at a different flip point linking to Terra. Also unavoidable. He'd have to improvise to get them in. Somehow.

The Rebel Empire personnel on *Athena*'s bridge were focused on their tasks. Jared hoped the upcoming flip would consume their attention. With any luck at all, no one would notice the missing man had not returned to his post.

He knew better than to assume that was going to happen, though. No. Far better to prepare for the worst-case scenario.

Though the control systems aboard the destroyer wouldn't show anything, he still had the ability to trigger the antiboarding weapons. That meant Jared could drop every single intruder aboard his ship with a thought. If it seemed as though they were about to discover his people, he'd stop them in their tracks.

He also kept an eye on the team in engineering. Since they had dispatched the missing man, if anyone was going to notice his absence, it would be them. Their actions or lack thereof would dictate how he responded.

In a perfect world, he'd let them make the flip and deal with them on the other side. He fervently hoped the next system was empty of human presence. That would allow them to deal with the Rebel Empire crew immediately.

Because he was monitoring the situation in *Athena*'s engineering compartment, he saw one of the senior people glancing at the main hatch more frequently. And he also saw the deep frown that suddenly appeared on the woman's face.

She walked over to the unnamed man Jared assumed was the senior officer in engineering. "Austin isn't back. He's not responding when I call him, either."

That caused the man to frown as well. "Perhaps he's inside a section of the ship that's interfering with our implants."

"I suppose that's possible," the woman allowed. "But I was *very* clear that I wanted him back here before we flipped. According to my timer, that's only three minutes away. He should have at least started back."

The man laughed. "As if Austin is the most punctual individual we know. If you let him bury himself inside some piece of machinery, he'll completely forget what time it is. The man is an unrepentant gearhead."

The woman didn't seem convinced, but she nodded. "I suppose his presence here isn't really required. I don't want to send anyone to search for him until we've flipped. Should we notify the bridge?"

Jared tensed. This was the kind of problem that might cause the woman occupying his chair on the bridge to abort the flip.

The man shook his head. "I don't think we need to bother Jaleesa. I'll just make a notification over the ship's internal speakers in the area where Austin is working. It should only take a second for him to step out and give us a call."

Moments later, the man spoke again. "Austin. Aren't you forgetting you need to be somewhere? Contact me at once."

Jared knew the man's voice was echoing throughout the area around computer central. The monitors they'd placed throughout the ship told him the transmission was localized to that area.

Meanwhile, on the bridge, the woman called Jaleesa was getting an update from her helm officer.

"Two minutes until we're in the prime flip zone."

"Understood," she said. "Bring us to a halt as soon as we arrive."

Two minutes was such a short amount of time. Jared knew that would drag along slow second by slow second.

The woman was stopping rather than just flipping. That implied she was going to open communications with someone at the defensive perimeter. Or she might just be a stickler for the rules.

Ships were technically supposed to come to a halt inside a flip point. Traveling at any real speed exacerbated the stress of transiting the wormhole. In practice, experienced Fleet officers knew that only high speeds were a danger to a ship's integrity.

In an extreme case—like the original *Athena*—going at very high speed could cause the ship's spine to warp. He'd wrecked his original command by transiting the flip point at Erorsi at maximum military speed with the Pale Ones in hot pursuit.

That was not something he could risk repeating.

The man in engineering seemed to become more concerned as the silence from his compatriot dragged out. With thirty seconds left before the flip, he shook his head.

"Something's wrong. I'd best notify Jaleesa."

Time to pull the plug, Jared decided. He sent the order to trigger the antiboarding weapons in every compartment except for the maintenance tubes.

And nothing happened.

27

S ean was keyed up. The sand in the hourglass had run out, and they were either going to flip or all hell was going to break loose.

He'd watched the Rebel Empire's people in engineering react to the missing man with growing concern, but there wasn't anything he could do to change the situation. Admiral Mertz had the keys to the antiboarding weapons and would use them when the time was right.

And that really seemed like right now. The unnamed man in command of the engineering compartment was about to call the bridge with a missing man report. That would trigger all kinds of bad things.

"Get ready to deploy," he ordered Commander Pence, *Athena*'s rightful chief engineer. "We move as soon as the admiral takes them out. I want positive control of the drives first. We flip on his order."

"Aye, sir," she said calmly. "My people are ready."

He turned in the other direction and focused his attention on Major Adrian Scala, the senior marine on the destroyer. "We need to account for every single enemy as fast as we can. I don't want anyone slipping through the cracks."

"I've already briefed my people," the large black man said. "We're ready as soon as things go down."

We've got a problem, Admiral Mertz said through Sean's implants. *My connection to the ship's systems isn't working. No antiboarding weapons. Take them out.*

Shit.

On it.

"Major Scala, the admiral can't control the ship's internal weapons. Take the enemy out."

He heard the marine officer's command go out over the marine command net.

All marines, this is Damocles Actual. Execute Hotel. Execute! Execute! Execute!

Engineering had more than a few maintenance tubes attached to it. All of their hatches slid open more or less at the same time, and the marines came flooding out, stunners already in play.

Scala was the first out of their tube, but Sean was on his heels, his stunner tracking on the enemy commander. His first shot took the dumbfounded man down with a blue flash.

He tried to take out the woman he'd pegged as the second in command, but she dove behind a console. Hell.

Internal alarms began blaring, and the virtually impervious main engineering hatch slid closed. Too bad for them that Sean and his people were already among them.

"Disable the external coms before they start screaming for help," he shouted, ducking as someone fired in his direction. The beam from the weapon shaded red, showing it was set in the lethal range. He hoped no one had been hit.

"That control run over there," Pence said, pointing at a thick conduit on the wall. "We need to disable the transfer station beside it, too. Cover me."

Scala instead pulled something from his belt and hurled it across the compartment at the transfer station. "Fire in the hole!"

Sean barely had time to clap his hands over his ears and turn away from the danger zone before the grenade went off. It wasn't a plasma grenade, but it still sounded like the end of the world and half stunned him.

The transfer station was a smoking wreck, and the conduit was on fire. New alarms began blaring, just in case anyone had missed the explosion.

"I'd have liked to have been able to use that again sometime soon," Pence growled loudly. "The ship is just crossing into the flip point. What do we do?"

"Flip the ship," Sean ordered. "Do it manually."

"Shit."

The engineer bolted across the compartment toward the nearest console. A red bolt took her in the back, and she dropped, dead before she hit the deck.

Sean didn't hesitate. He ducked lower and raced across his friend's still-twitching corpse. He dropped behind the console a beat before several red beams flashed through where he'd been a second before.

Raising his head high enough to see the controls was quite literally the most dangerous thing he'd ever done.

He was no engineer, but he was a command officer, so he knew what needed to be done. It took an interminable three heartbeats to bring up the right screen.

His command overrides disabled the control interlocks, and he firmly pressed the button, activating the flip drive.

His gut told him they'd transited the wormhole, and the risk of the Rebel Empire crew warning anyone at El Capitan was over. That didn't mean he and his people were any safer.

Scala dropped in beside him. "I see four holdouts. They're behind the gravitic drive, so our options are limited."

"I guess we have to do this the hard way," Sean said, gripping his stunner more tightly. "This is going to suck."

"Welcome to the marines," Scala said with a dark grin. "We're always on the lookout for ways to make any given situation suck more."

The two men came up at the same time as the rest of the marines, and everyone charged the holdouts.

* * *

KELSEY WAS nearest the hatch when the call to attack came. Rather than do the smart thing and let the trained fighters lead the way, she left the maintenance tube at a run, sprinting for the computer center.

It had a hatch that could hold them off if the crew got a chance to close it. They could wreck the computer if they had time. She had to get there first.

She felt the world start to slow down around her and knew she'd somehow managed to trigger her pharmacology unit into dispensing Panther into her system.

Having a name for the drug and Doctor Stone's detailed explanation of what it did to her made the experience far less terrifying this time. That was something, she supposed.

Intellectually, she knew the drug itself didn't really make her much faster, but it felt as if she had all the time in the world to act. That only went so far, though.

Alarms blared from the overheads as she raced around the final corner and pushed herself as hard as she could toward the hatch that was already closing. It was going to be close. If she committed and was wrong, the massive hatch would kill her.

Kelsey bounced off the door frame and made it inside the computer center just as the hatch closed behind her.

Three men and a woman were at the consoles. All were drawing weapons with deceptive slowness.

The odds against her were dire, so Kelsey did the only thing she thought would make a difference. She ordered her Raider implants to eliminate the threats even though the idea of the cold computer controlling her body was her very worst nightmare.

Her implants threw her to the right while shooting the closest man with her stunner. A bolt of red missed her by centimeters as her body twisted. Someone was playing for keeps.

That changed the automated responses she knew. Oh God.

As soon as her body was stable, the powerful artificial muscles in her legs sent her completely over the console. Her left arm swung back, and her fist smashed into the head of one of the remaining men with a sound like dropping a melon, killing him instantly.

Two down. Two to go.

The remaining man was out of reach, but the woman was right beside her. The combat computer in Kelsey's head fired her stunner at the man even as her free hand clamped around the woman's throat.

The sound of her hand crushing the woman's windpipe and snapping her spine was far worse than when she'd killed the man.

Her implants released the dying woman and assessed the threats as contained. It released control of her body back to her. She hadn't really believed it would.

Kelsey promptly threw up even as her body began to shake violently.

Scott Roche and the others were frantically calling over her implant com, but she couldn't stop the blind terror that smothered her mind and froze her limbs.

Being a prisoner in one's body but unable to do anything except scream as it killed was *exactly* like being a Pale One. And it brought back all the horror she'd suffered.

Kelsey, open the door. Please let us help you.

It was Scott.

She retched again but managed to crawl toward the hatch. With what felt like the last of her strength, she hit the manual control.

The hatch slid open, and marines rushed in, weapons up. Scott came in right behind them.

Her friend took one look at her, dropped to his knees, and took her into his arms as she started sobbing.

* * *

Not being privy to the enemy's implant communications, Jared didn't know exactly what had triggered the Rebel Empire commander to hit the alarms, but he didn't let that slow him down.

At his order, marines blew the micro charges on the three concealed hatches along the periphery of the bridge and charged into the midst of their shocked foes. Blue stunner bolts took everyone down before they could do more than scream in shock.

Jared raced to his command console, dumped the unconscious woman out of his seat, and sat just as *Athena* flipped out of the El Capitan system. His implants were still locked out of the ship's controls, but he had decades of experience working without them.

This side of the flip point was blissfully empty. He let out a sigh and waited for his team to get into their seats. The marines were securing the prisoners and setting up a defensive position inside the main hatch in case of counterattack.

"Commander Hall," Jared said, "as I recall, this system only has one other flip point. Set course for it at maximum military power."

"Aye, sir," she said, her hands dancing over the controls. "Maximum military power. All propulsion systems nominal. ETA fourteen hours, ten minutes. Shall I launch probes to verify the system is clear?"

"Do so. Let me know if you find anything interesting."

Jared turned his attention to his ship. There was fighting in engineering. His people had the upper hand, though. Computer central was in loyal hands, though it looked as if Princess Kelsey had been hurt.

The balance of forces in engineering dictated his people would come out on top, though he saw people on the deck, either unconscious or dead. That meant he needed to focus on the rest of the ship.

Athena's internal scanners located sixteen intruders scattered across the ship, mostly alone or in very small groups. None of them seemed to have a clue what was happening. He planned on keeping it that way.

"Lieutenant Laird, take a team and apprehend the intruders. Hit them in whatever order you see fit and coordinate with Major Scala. I want my ship back without anyone else being hurt or causing a ruckus."

"Aye, sir," the red-headed marine said as she gestured toward two-thirds of her people. "We'll take care of them for you."

By the time her team had departed the bridge, the fight in engineering was over. Jared called Sean over the ship's internal com. The other officer appeared on his console seconds later.

"Status?"

"We have control of engineering, but we encountered some problems," the other officer said tiredly. "These bastards went right to lethal weapons.

"Commander Pence and half a dozen others are dead. And we blew up the power transfer unit feeding the ship's external com system. I hope you don't need to talk to anyone for a while."

The news about his lost personnel was a gut punch.

"Dammit," Jared said bitterly. "Send Major Scala to assist the rest of the marines in rousting any other holdouts. Use lethal force if they show any sign of resistance."

"No argument from me. I vote we space these bastards as soon as we get what we need from them. The indiscriminate use of lethal force is a violation of Imperial Law and Fleet regulations. Both Fleets."

Jared shook his head. "As much as I'd love to let you handle that little detail, these people are intelligence sources. Important ones, I suspect."

"That doesn't mean you can't lock them down tight. Arm and leg restraints. Two marines each when they wake up. Very restricted movement and isolation from one another. No information about us at all."

"Are we clear?" Meyer asked. "Did we escape El Capitan clean?"

"So far, but that could be because we surprised them by leaving so quickly. They might dispatch a ship to find out what made us so standoffish at any time. Get that com system back up in case we need it."

"Will do. Do you want me to take the lead on questioning the prisoners? I really want to know why they were so trigger-happy."

Jared considered that before shaking his head. "Let Olivia take the lead. Have her make up whatever story she likes. She knows these kind of people far better than we do. Let's use that familiarity."

He really hoped she could get to the bottom of this without setting the prisoners off. If they triggered someone, they wouldn't be able to undo the damage.

Whatever the reason, these people had started out shooting to kill. He needed to know why as soon as possible. Their lives might depend on it.

28

E lise rushed to Kelsey's side as soon as Jared sounded the all clear. Doctor Stone had the princess from another universe in the medical center, but the marines had flatly refused to let her out of the maintenance tube until the ship was cleared of intruders.

She passed one group of marines carrying the unconscious or dead bodies of some of those intruders on the way to the medical center, but she didn't stop to ask questions.

Commander Scott Roche was waiting for her outside the medical center. "How is she?" Elise asked, a little short of breath.

"Bad, but nothing physical," the Fleet officer said softly. "She used her combat mode function. Having her implants control her body was too much like being a Pale One, and it hit her hard."

Elise felt herself blanch. Her people had dealt with the savage Pale Ones for five centuries. She knew far too well what the other princess had to be feeling.

"I'll see if I can help."

"Thank you."

She strode into the medical center and found Kelsey sitting in a chair, wrapped in a blanket. Lily Stone was hovering a few steps away.

Elise rushed over and dropped to her knees beside the chair. She took Kelsey's hand in hers. "I hear you had a little trouble at the computer center."

The other woman's damp, haunted eyes came up. "You could say that. I killed two people."

"But that's not what's bothering you, is it? Not really."

"I had to let my implants control my body. I had a panic attack when it was all over."

"You did what you had to do," Elise said soothingly. "Your people had already overwritten the corrupted code, and we upgraded your implant hardware. No one will *ever* do that to you again. You were ultimately in control."

The blonde woman wiped her wet eyes. "I understand that, intellectually, but I was one of those monsters for weeks. I have nightmares about spending the rest of my life like that, and I couldn't breathe when it was over."

"Our Kelsey has nightmares, too. I realize she didn't suffer the way you did, but it will get better. I've seen you do it before."

Kelsey shook her head and stared at the bulkhead. "I can't imagine how I will ever get past this. Your Kelsey sounds like a hero from an old story. I'm not like that. I can barely stay sane."

"You're stronger than you think."

The other woman's eyes shot up, filled with sudden heat. "I am *not* her. You all insist I am, but she didn't break like I did. She had all the good luck, and I got the bad. I *hate* her."

The bitterness in her friend's voice was heartbreaking.

Elise squeezed Kelsey's hand tighter. "My father once told me that you get through the tough times by focusing on small steps. One after the other, they will take you through the flames and to safety."

Kelsey snorted. "Forgive me, but what does he know about flames? You grew up a lot like I did, I bet. A life of privilege and being shielded from danger."

That offhand, dismissive tone ignited a burn in Elise's belly, but she kept her expression compassionate. "Perhaps, but we always knew we were one attack away from the horror that found you. And not just weeks of it, but for the rest of our lives.

"Princess or pauper, each of us lived every day knowing exactly how horrible an end awaited us. Did you know I carried a small knife in a necklace since I was a girl? Useless little thing.

"Unless you needed to slit your wrist. Let me tell you, having the royal physician give me a lecture at ten years old on the best way to kill myself is a memory I will carry to my grave."

Kelsey sagged as the fire went out of her. "I didn't know that. I'm sorry for being a selfish bitch."

Elise smiled sadly. "I'm not trying to equate our situations or make you feel better toward our Kelsey. She caught some breaks that you didn't. And she had Jared. Believe me, that makes a difference. At least in this universe."

"I hate him, too," Kelsey said bluntly. "But I get it. He's not the same man as in my universe. Everyone here gives him so much respect that he must've earned it. It's difficult to believe my eyes over my heart, but I'm getting there."

The other woman rubbed her face. "Are all the prisoners under lock and key? By the way, they tried to kill me right off. Is everyone else okay?"

A glance at Lily told Elise that not everyone had made it.

"We lost nine people taking the ship," Lily said. "That included Doctor Dishmon and Commander Pence in engineering. It sure looks as if they started with the lethal option."

"From the first shot," Kelsey agreed. "We had total surprise. They had no idea whatsoever that we were here. I don't get how they could go right for the kill."

"That's a great question," Elise said with a nod. "Olivia is going to handle the questioning. She was one of their class her entire life. The rest of us might slip up and let them realize we aren't from their society. She won't."

Kelsey stared at her with unblinking eyes. "I'm still sorry I killed those two but not because they didn't deserve it. I'm sorry because I have to live with the memory of killing them.

"Still, it's far from the most terrible thing I've ever done. If she needs someone to make an example of one of them, I can hardly have fewer nightmares."

The idea of having someone do something like that, knowingly inflicting harm on themselves in the process, sickened Elise. This Kelsey really was a different person than her friend. One with different moral standards, it seemed. A bit more brutal and deeply hurt inside.

"That won't be necessary," Elise said firmly. "If Olivia needs to get answers from someone that doesn't feel like sharing, I'm sure Lily can come up with a drug to help."

"Don't worry about making them pay for what they did," Lily said, stepping closer. "They will pay for the lives they took."

The doctor frowned. "Now that I think about it, why were they all armed in the first place? Surely, they didn't expect trouble here in their own system."

Elise couldn't begin to guess the answer to that. She'd be watching over Olivia's shoulder with interest via her implants when the interrogations started.

Of course, that wasn't without risk either. Olivia West had been the coordinator of Harrison's World, a powerful leader in the Rebel Empire's higher orders, even if she'd secretly been an Imperial loyalist.

She was like this Kelsey in a lot of ways. Ruthless. She might not need someone to be the bad guy in the questioning. Maybe watching that wasn't such a good idea after all.

* * *

ATHENA DIDN'T HAVE a real brig, Olivia discovered, much less an area capable of holding dozens of prisoners. Jared Mertz had put them into individual compartments with marine guards.

The guards were out of uniform to maintain the ruse that they weren't military, even though that was a tad threadbare. The men and women looked exactly like marines out of uniform.

So she'd concocted a ruse to explain why they had implants: they were *former* marine officers. Still odd, but not so dangerous.

They couldn't afford to trip any of the buried subroutines in these peoples' corrupted implant code. Keeping someone like that locked up would be a nightmare.

The New Terran Empire destroyer had been racing across the next system over from El Capitan for almost four hours. No one had come after them. It appeared as though they'd gotten away.

Jared had sent people to look at the crates and found them sealed with what certainly looked like explosives. In this case, plasma grenades or the equivalent.

Since he now had control of the computer again, he locked the prisoners out of the com net. They had original Old Empire implants, so without a headset, their top range was ten meters. Enough to communicate with those close to them, but nothing more.

She would have preferred keeping them from communicating at all, but that was impossible. A destroyer just wasn't big enough to spread the prisoners out far enough for that.

So she decided to pick the prisoner most likely to talk and ensconced him far away from the others. He would crack eventually, she suspected. He didn't seem as hard as the others.

He hadn't even been armed. He was the only one of the intruders not carrying a neural disruptor set to kill. That marked him as special and perhaps not as dedicated to their cause as the rest.

These people had fought hard from the very first moment. They'd expected trouble and hadn't believed themselves safe even in their own system.

Discovering why was her first order of business.

The man Kelsey had captured at the maintenance tube seemed more of a technician than the rest. Of course, he was a member of the higher orders. It wouldn't do to underestimate him.

Olivia had him tied to a chair with actual cord rather than plastic restraints. She made certain his legs were tied to the chair legs and that his hands were very secure. She bound his wrists behind the chair and tied his upper arms together behind his back. Then she secured them to the chair.

It wasn't that she feared he would get loose. The marines would keep her safe. She wanted him to feel powerless. It was purely psychological.

That theme could've been taken further. She could've blindfolded him. She decided not to because she'd wanted an unobstructed view of his reactions.

He'd already proven that consideration valid. The prisoner—his first name was Austin—had actually been awake for the last few minutes, but he gave no sign of it. Only the medical monitor she put on his wrist let her know when he'd awoken.

All of the other prisoners had been included in the database the resistance had sent Olivia. Not him. A curious omission. She wondered if that was because the man wasn't considered important or if they'd excluded him for some other reason.

In any case, it was time to get started.

"I know you've been awake for the last few minutes," Olivia said, leaning a little forward in her own seat placed a few meters in front of him. "You might as well open your eyes."

The man's eyes popped open, and his head came up. So she could surprise him. Good.

His eyes narrowed. "Who are you? Why have you attacked us?"

"I'm the woman in charge now. You can call me Olivia. Now that we have that settled, I'd like you to state your full name for the record."

Austin's eyes narrowed. "For what record?"

She almost smiled. "You're full of questions. You don't have the need to know. Let's just say that not every part of the Empire is behind your mission, and I was sent to ask a few questions."

"We have orders from the Imperial Lord. You wouldn't dare to defy him."

Now she did smile. "And yet, here I am. Every single one of you is my prisoner. Your name, please."

"Austin Darrah. I found your command tap, by the way. You were just a few seconds too late to stop me from disconnecting it."

It took her a second to figure out what he meant. It was probably what had allowed Jared to command *Athena* remotely. Until it had stopped working.

"Do you feel proud?" she asked, allowing a hint of sadness to seep into her tone. "You'd still be our prisoner if you'd left it in place, but we wouldn't have had to kill any of your companions. Or lose our own people."

He swallowed but put on a brave face. "I did what I had to do. I'd do it again, too." His eyes flicked over to the marines leaning against the bulkhead. "They're military. Officers of some kind. Marines?"

"Ex-marine officers, yes. What's in the crates you brought aboard, and why were your friends so quick to jump to lethal force?"

"If you don't know, I can't tell you."

"You'll talk," she assured him. "It can be voluntarily or with assistance, but you will tell me everything I want to know."

Some part of her conviction must've gotten through to him, because he swallowed again. "You're mistaken. I literally can't. The System Lord implanted explosive devices in our heads and amended the code in our implants. We can't tell you *anything* about this mission, or we'll quite literally lose our heads."

A low alarm began sounding. Not ear-splittingly loud like the call to battle. This was lower key. An implant call from Jared came a moment later.

Olivia, there's been a situation. The prisoners have some kind of suicide charge in their skulls. They all just blew up. Are you okay?

She eyed the man, wondering if he was going to explode. Probably not, if someone else had to send the signal. He'd been too far from the rest to get the signal.

I'm fine, and so is my prisoner. He'd just told me about the devices when the alarm went off. He says he can't talk about his mission because the device will kill him.

Jared was silent for a second before he continued. *Break off questioning. Get him to the medical center, and let's see what Lily can tell us about the device. If we can disarm it, then you can pick up right where you left off.*

He's the last surviving member of this Rebel Empire crew, and we can't risk losing the chance to find out what they were up to.

29

C leaning up the compartments they'd used for holding the now dead Rebel Empire nobles was a grisly task, Sean decided. Whoever had put those bombs in their heads had used far more explosive than was necessary to kill them.

The blasts had painted the compartments with blood and brains while causing significant damage to their torsos.

It had also gotten the unfortunate marines keeping watch over them, too. Perhaps it was meant to make a lasting impression on anyone around the unfortunate bastards.

It wasn't hard discerning the order of events. The prisoners had awakened and discovered their new circumstances. The woman who had been in Jared's seat on the bridge had taken a good look around her just before the suicide charges went off.

She had to be the trigger woman. She'd sent the destruct order, killing herself and her crew.

Not everyone was in range of her implants, but they'd been close enough to their friends. The signal traveled out in a relay from person to person, each retransmitting the destruct code before it blew up.

The only person out of range had been the young man Olivia had been questioning. Since he hadn't blown himself up, he either didn't have the codes or wasn't interested in killing himself just yet.

Sean wondered if the self-destruct command had been meant to blow up the cargo, too. He'd have done it that way. Thankfully, the prisoners hadn't been close enough to the cargo bay to trigger the plasma charges.

Equally good was the fact that Admiral Mertz had locked the prisoners out of the ship's systems. The computer could've relayed the woman's command all over the ship.

As a precaution, Sean had ordered the engineering team—now working under Lieutenant Commander Anthony O'Halloran—to look over the destroyer's systems closely. He'd been afraid of a larger self-destruct option, like setting off one of the fusion plants.

To his relief, it seemed as if they hadn't felt the need to go that far. Or they'd believed they would have time to set one off manually.

"Commodore?" one of the engineers asked. "I've found something you might be interested in."

Sean pulled himself together and looked up from the engineering console he'd been staring uselessly at. "Talk to me, Tony."

"The computer had logs of the activity on all the consoles, including the bridge. I found some calculations from Admiral Mertz's position. The Rebel Empire commander was plotting potential courses."

He smiled. That was useful. "Where was she going?"

"Terra. She had a single course laid in, and she marked each system with a very narrow window of dates. Some also had long codes next to them. Possibly passcodes. Sir, she was in something of a hurry. She has them arriving in three weeks."

Based on his research, Sean thought that was a bit aggressive for a realistic timetable.

"They must've been on a pretty tight schedule. I wonder if their little bombs were on a timer, too. Show up on time or not at all."

"It's possible," the engineer said with a shrug. "There's not enough left of the bombs to be sure."

"Not in the dead ones," Sean agreed. "I'll go see what Doctor Stone can tell us about the survivor."

He rose to his feet and headed for the lift. Too bad the people Princess Kelsey had killed had been close enough to pick up the destruct command. That would've made discovering the particulars of the explosion easier.

Sean walked into the medical center to find everyone clustered around the heavily guarded prisoner. The ludicrously over-guarded prisoner, in his opinion.

There were six marines present, two in unpowered armor. The man himself was secured to an exam table, and his wrists and ankles were bound in flex cuffs.

Olivia was standing off to the side, observing Doctor Stone scanning her patient.

Sean stepped over to his wife. "He looks dangerous. You want someone in powered armor, just to be sure?"

The look she gave him indicated that she thought he needed to work on his delivery. "Funny. Also, not my call. Jared said he wanted to make sure our young friend didn't even consider getting froggy."

He felt the corner of his mouth quirk upward. "Froggy? Is this something Kelsey taught you?"

"Obviously. A frog on Terra has long, powerful legs and can jump quite a distance. So the meaning is that we don't want the prisoner to try anything."

"You heard what happened to the rest. Any concerns that he might blow his own head off?"

Olivia shrugged. "Not really. It seems as if he'd already have done it if he were so inclined. And he warned us that he couldn't talk about what they were doing before the others popped their corks. He mentioned the explosives, and it's no likely he'd have told us about it if he intended to use it."

He chuckled. "Popped their corks? You've picked up quite an arsenal of sayings."

Lily Stone murmured something to the prisoner and stepped back from the exam table. Once she turned and saw Sean, she headed over.

"I've done an initial scan," the physician said. "He definitely has some kind of explosive charge in his skull. I'll have to actually open his scalp and take a closer look before I decide if it can be safely removed."

"I didn't realize bomb disposal was among your list of talents," Sean said with a slight frown. "If that thing goes off, it could kill you at that range."

"I'm a Fleet officer," she retorted. "I could die any number of terrible ways. If I started letting that drive my decision making, I'd need to retire."

She looked back toward the prisoner. "My initial scans don't indicate any antitampering mechanism. It's probably linked into his implants. If they think he's being messed with, they could set it off. If so, I may be able to take them offline and remove the explosive charge."

"I don't want you doing something overly risky," Sean said firmly.

"I agree," Olivia added, "but I want him to answer questions, too. We need to know what's in the cargo area. He needs to tell us what they planned to do."

Sean couldn't really argue with that. He was about to reluctantly agree when the hatch slid open and Kelsey walked in.

The petite woman stopped when she saw the prisoner. Then she eyed the enhanced guard detail before going over to them. "Should I get into my powered armor and make sure he doesn't try anything?"

Sean laughed. "I said something very much like that, Highness. How are you feeling?"

"A little better," the woman admitted. "Oddly, them killing themselves made it clear to me that the people in the computer center would have done something terrible if I hadn't stopped them. They were fanatics.

"People willing to kill at the drop of a hat, whether themselves or someone else, are too dangerous to be allowed to walk around freely."

"I'm going to see if I can remove the risk for this gentleman," Lily told Kelsey. "Would you care to observe the process?"

Kelsey's eyes narrowed. "That sounds like a trick question. Is it going to be gross?"

"I'll have to make an incision on his skull, but it shouldn't be terrible. Unless he explodes on the operating table, that is."

The princess sighed. "The way my luck has gone recently, you might be better off without me. Still, this could be something we need to do in my universe. If he explodes in my face, I'm making you pay for my therapy."

"If he explodes in our faces, we can attend sessions together. Come on."

* * *

Kelsey changed into a white smock before joining Doctor Stone at the exam table. The prisoner looked up at her, a disgruntled expression on his face.

"You really screwed me."

"Did I?" she asked. "You seem to be breathing."

"I won't be when Lady Keaton gets ahold of me," the man muttered.

She flicked her gaze over to Lily and caught the slight shake of the other woman's head. They hadn't told him that his friends had killed themselves. Good to know. Kelsey wished they'd mentioned that up front.

It took her an instant to remember how to initiate a com call through her implants.

Any other subjects off limits for him, Doctor?

We're not telling him anything at all about the other prisoners or who we are. We also aren't asking him any questions. Who knows what might set him off? If he asks any questions, don't answer them. If he states something, let it stand even if it's not accurate.

"I'm going to fit a high-resolution scanner on your head," Stone told the man out loud. "It will allow me to get a more detailed reading of the device in your head."

"It won't help," the man said, resigned. "I tell you, the bomb is linked to my implants. It won't go off unless they decide that I need to die because I'm going to talk or if you attempt to remove it. There isn't anything you can do to change that."

Stone didn't answer him. Instead, she put a device over the man's skull and tapped the control pad on it. The man's eyes closed abruptly, as if he'd gone to sleep.

"Interesting," Kelsey said. "I didn't know scanners could do that."

"I lied," the physician said with a smile. "This is a somatic stimulator. It basically forced his brain to go into a deep sleep.

"The Old Empire used them in place of drugs when they wanted someone to be unconscious, say for a medical procedure. He won't respond to anything, not even when I make the incision."

"Won't his implants still monitor what you're doing?"

The Fleet doctor picked up an instrument. "They shouldn't care as long as I'm not messing with the bomb, which I won't be. Instead, I'm going to access his implants directly and overwrite his implant code."

"I didn't have an incision for that. You only knocked me out for the hardware upgrade."

"And so it is here. I spoke with Admiral Mertz, and he agreed that anyone we captured in the future needed to be made safe from being enslaved again."

Kelsey considered that and slowly shook her head. "That's not a good idea. If they escape and run home to Mommy, the AIs will know you can lock them out."

"They'll know if they ever capture any of us, too. It is a risk, but we believe it's the right balance of protection for everyone."

She was certain the doctor was wrong, but it wasn't her place to argue. They'd made their decision.

"Why don't you educate me about this new hardware?"

"The mechanism that allows for updating the implant code is in one of the sub-cores surrounding the central implant. I'll use a manipulator to remove the compromised core entirely and replaced it with one that's more secure. It takes less than half an hour from incision to regeneration."

"What prevents the AI from removing the new hardware and replacing it with compromised hardware?"

"Without the appropriate codes or the patient's explicit prior permission, any attempt to remove the hardware will fry the implants themselves. It won't harm the person, but the original wiring in the brain will be compromised. Replacing it is significantly more complex than the original installation. Perhaps even impossible."

So anyone captured by the AIs might never have implants again. Kelsey considered that a small price to pay for not becoming a Pale One.

Stone shaved a spot the size of a fingertip on the man's skull and made a small incision. She staunched the blood and held the wound open with a small hand tool.

Once that was done, she inserted a device into the cut and spent about ten minutes removing a very small metal object and replacing it with another one. Then she reversed the procedure and closed the incision.

She used a handheld regenerator to quickly heal the minor wound. The only remaining trace of the procedure was a small bald spot.

"Shouldn't you have updated his implant code before you did that?" she asked as the doctor started cleaning up. "Now you can't, right?"

"Future updates now will require his permission, but I did it before I removed the old hardware. The process used to take hours, but we figured out we weren't doing it correctly.

"The details are far too technical to get into, but Carl Owlet discovered a much more efficient method. Five minutes, and it's done. I overwrote his corrupted code while getting everything set up to make the hardware swap."

This Carl Owlet was a most resourceful fellow. She knew that Scott Roche had already arranged to have him contacted, and she couldn't wait to meet him.

She spent a few seconds examining the unconscious man. "So you could've saved his companions."

"I could have. If I'd known about the bombs, I wouldn't have waited for them to wake up. Lesson learned."

"Are you going to remove his explosives?"

Stone shook her head. "I'll have to take those deeper scans I mentioned and let the tech people consider the options. If there is an antitampering device, we may have to leave it there.

"If so, a localized jammer implanted beside it might protect him, but it might also affect him in other ways. Frankly, it's just too soon to tell."

Stone set another device on the man's head and frowned at it. "This is my deep scanner. You can tap into its feed if you like."

Kelsey found the data stream and drew it in. The core it was focused on was linked directly to the man's implants. The details of the device were beginning to become clear as the scanner went across it again and again.

"We won't be able to access the internal code," Stone said. "I'm more concerned with the hardware. If it detects separation from his implants, it might detonate."

She focused in on the diagram and tried to make sense of it. She wasn't a tech, but her implants occasionally provided insight on things she didn't directly understand.

A small window popped up in her vision, and her implants started tracing the circuitry. This was something she'd asked Elise about days earlier. Apparently, this was not something everyone could do. It was an enhancement provided by her Raider implants.

Almost as soon as it began, the window closed, and another one opened. This one had data on the Raider implants themselves. This same circuitry was in her own head, though thankfully not attached to a bomb.

It *was* a kind of antitampering circuit but, in her case, one that would wipe the classified intelligence stored in her implants if an unauthorized person attempted to access them.

She didn't actually *have* any classified intelligence, but the design was there. A Raider was supposed to store secret stuff in a specific segment of internal memory for safety. Good to know.

Kelsey accessed the manual these people had provided for her and read everything about the antitampering circuit. There was a way to get around it, but it was very technical and seemed to require specialized equipment she didn't have.

Maybe the New Terran Empire did.

In any case, the circuit was to prevent access to the hardware. Not to stop anyone from removing it. The man's implants would probably have been monitoring for removal and triggered the explosives under those circumstances.

With the compromised code gone, it should be perfectly safe to remove it. Of course, it wasn't her head she was talking about. The unconscious man would likely object. Strenuously.

Thankfully, she didn't have to make that decision. She'd tell Doctor Stone and let her make the decision. And stand farther away for that procedure.

30

J ared walked into the prisoner's room without knocking. That was rude, but he needed to set the tone for this meeting. He held all the cards, and the prisoner needed to understand that on a visceral level.

The man wasn't bound, though he was guarded. Two marines stood on either side of the hatch, just inside the compartment. Two more stood in the corridor beyond. What's more, they'd made certain the prisoner was aware of how thoroughly they were watching him.

Every angle inside his make-do prison cell was under observation at all times. Even the bathroom. Also, the man was never allowed to be alone. The marines inside the compartment kept him in their sight at all times.

That might seem like overkill, but Jared couldn't take the risk that the man would find another way to kill himself now that Lily had removed the bomb from his head. The information he possessed was far too valuable to take chances.

The man sat on a small couch, reading something on a handheld viewer. He set it aside as soon as Jared entered, but he didn't stand.

Jared wondered what status this man had on El Capitan. Because he had implants, he was a member of the higher orders. That was a certainty because there was no way he was a Fleet officer and those were the only other people allowed to have implants.

Well, there were nobles, and then there were *nobles*. Austin Darrah was obviously very low in the hierarchy.

"Mister Darrah," Jared said with a slight nod. "I regret having to keep you under close guard, so allow me to apologize for the necessity. I wish things could be different, but until you answer some questions, I need to be certain that you're safe. Even from yourself."

The other man shook his head slightly. "We have different definitions of the word 'safe.' You know who I am. Might I ask your name and position?"

"Of course. My name is Jared Mertz, and I command this ship."

"Well, you certainly do now. What did you do before? Where are you from? What do you want?"

Without asking for permission, Jared sat across the coffee table from the man. He crossed his legs and tried to exude an air of confidence. It helped that he actually was confident.

"While this might be difficult to believe, I was in command of this vessel when it entered the El Capitan system. If you're wondering, we didn't sneak on board the ship while it was orbiting your planet. We were already here."

The man looked bemused. "I can't figure out what that's supposed to mean. This is supposed to be an automated destroyer. Even these furnishings shouldn't be here. At least I don't think they should be.

"Why would you go to the trouble of sneaking aboard a vessel like this to get into El Capitan? You couldn't possibly have known about our mission. What were you really doing?"

"Well, that's quite a story. I might even tell it to you once we're done finding out about you and what you were doing aboard my ship.

"Let me lay out a few salient facts for you. You brought aboard a number of cargo containers protected by plasma-based explosives. You and all your compatriots had bombs planted inside your heads. And let's not forget how you opened fire on my people with your weapons set to lethal force the moment you saw us."

Jared leaned back in his seat and crossed his legs.

"I can't tell you," the man said in an exasperated tone. "Remember those bombs in the head that you mentioned? If I try to tell you anything, it will go off. But I will point out that I wasn't armed."

"True enough," Jared said with a smile. "The bomb would be a factor if we hadn't removed it during your little nap in our medical center."

The man's mouth dropped open. "Have you lost your mind? How could you possibly have thought it was a good idea to mess around with the *explosives in my head*? If you actually did."

"Come now, Mister Darrah. Give me a little credit. I have a lot of questions for you, so it doesn't serve my purpose to have your head explode before you answer them.

"I realize that requires taking a lot on faith when your life hangs in the balance, but run through the possibilities. Under what circumstances would I intentionally have you do something that so drastically curtailed my options going forward?"

The man gave a sharp laugh. "I have no idea. All I know for certain is that I can't trust anything you say. You could be *anyone*. Maybe you just want to record me exploding so that you can use the video to intimidate my companions. Frankly, I'm the most expendable of our crew, so that makes sense."

"You're hardly expendable," Jared disagreed. "Here's where I give you a little bit more information to operate off of.

"The lady who was questioning you earlier had you segregated from the other prisoners. So, to your good fortune, you weren't anywhere near them when your leader ordered everyone's bombs to explode.

"You are my only prisoner. If you like, I can provide you some video of what happened to them. Allow me to warn you that it's not pretty."

Darrah considered Jared carefully. "No, I imagine it isn't. Let's say that you're telling me the truth. If I'm your only source of information about what we're doing here, why in the world would I help you?"

"Do you really enjoy having these marines watching your every move? Observing you going to the bathroom? Watching you take a shower? Would you like to sleep in a room by yourself?"

The other man grunted. "There is something to that. Still, you're obviously a man who is up to no good. I want to know who I'm dealing with before I start dropping secrets. The System Lord was very adamant about keeping our mouths shut."

"That's certainly true," Jared agreed "Anyone that puts bombs in people's heads really does intend for them to stay silent. Did it occur to you that once you were finished with your task, it would set off the bombs to make sure you never spoke of this?"

"You don't know that," Darrah said. His tone indicated he wasn't completely certain he believed his own words.

"Let's try something simple, shall we? You were going to Terra, correct?"

The man clamped his lips shut for a few seconds before sighing. "One way or the other, I'm going to regret this. Yes, we were supposed to deliver the special cargo to the System Lord at Terra."

His expression said that he was waiting for his head to explode. When it didn't, he sagged a little.

"See?" Jared asked. "Safe as houses."

Darrah gave him a confused look. "What is that supposed to mean?"

"Forgive my obscurity. It means there was no danger."

"Ah. How odd. Before we see how far I'm willing to go, I need to understand what's in it for me. I'm a dead man if the Lords find out about this. How can you protect me and still make it worth my while to be cooperative?

"And don't tell me I should be glad I'm alive at all. Be realistic. You need what I know in a very short window of time if it's going to do you any good at all."

Jared didn't disagree. "And this is where I bring the woman you met before, Olivia West, back in to negotiate. She's much better at this than I am."

* * *

OLIVIA MADE a point of rapping her knuckles against the hatch when she arrived for her second interview with Austin Darrah. One of the marines inside the compartment opened the hatch for her. It wasn't as if the prisoner had the option of refusing her entry. Still, it paid to be courteous.

Unlike the last time she'd seen him, the man wasn't tied to a chair. Now he sat tensely on a small couch. He rose when she entered the room, but it seemed like an unwilling gesture.

"Mister Darrah," she said with a genuine smile. "I'm pleased to see that you survived the recent unpleasantness. As you might recall, my name is Olivia West. Shall we sit? Perhaps you'd like me to order us something to eat?"

The man sat and gestured for her to take the place across from him. "Your food is one thing I have no complaints about. Whoever does your cooking is quite excellent. None of my former companions had the talent. Meals were something of a chore during our hurried training."

She nodded as she sat. "I'm not much of a cook myself, but I've picked up a few tricks along the way. We do have a few people with real gifts for the culinary arts, though.

"Jared tells me that you're willing to discuss working with us. What would you expect in return for your cooperation?"

While he was considering how to answer her question, she used her implants to send out an order for sandwiches, tea, and coffee. The crew manning the galley had been warned to expect her call. They'd be along shortly.

After almost thirty seconds of silence, Darrah grimaced. "While I have some leverage, I'll confess that I've never been good at this sort of thing. You're probably going to take advantage of me."

"Allow me to let you in on a little secret about negotiation," she said conspiratorially. "The best deals are the ones where everyone feels as though they've gotten something they want. If you take undue advantage, their cooperation with you will be grudging.

"We don't want you feeling as if we have you over a barrel. We want you to cooperate willingly. So rather than worrying that I'm going to use some lapse or lawyerly clause against you, why don't you tell me in very basic language what you see as the best outcome for you."

He shrugged. "The bridges behind me are merrily burning, so I doubt I can salvage the life I had. It's gone. I have to focus on what comes next.

"I don't know which planetary system you people come from, but you can hide me. You can make it so the System Lords don't know that I'm there. You can give me a good life where I'm not scrambling to survive. One that keeps me out of the public eye but lets me indulge in the things that I love."

"That's a reasonable request," she agreed with a nod. "But I think we can do better. I can't go into the details at this point, but I can assure you that once we have completed our mission, we can put you into a society where you don't have to fear the System Lords, one where you can walk around and have as open a life as you choose."

His expression turned skeptical. "The System Lords have eyes everywhere. All it takes is for my face to come to their attention, and I'm a dead man."

Olivia nodded. "As I said, I can't get into the specific details of the situation, but let me raise the bar to where I think it should be. You have information that I suspect is critical to our survival and our mission.

"That's worth quite a bit to me and my associates. In exchange for your full and complete cooperation, we can arrange for a life that might be considered luxurious in comparison to the one you've lived until this point. Even understanding your background lies in the higher orders. Does that interest you?"

He watched her suspiciously for a long while before he asked, "How do I know that you aren't lying? You could promise me anything and then take it all away once you have the information you want."

"You can't know for sure," she admitted. "I could promise you the moon and stars without meaning a single word. I could also simply mention the kind of pressure we could deliver to make you talk, but that's not the kind of people we are.

"I think you realize how difficult a spot you're in. There's no need to emphasize the potentially bad outcome. I'd much rather craft a realistic agreement we can both live with that takes our unfortunate situations into account. Wouldn't you?"

The man sighed. "I suppose so. No matter what happens to me now, the Lords will have no choice but to silence me. When I was part of a group as important as the other members of my party, there was at least some chance for me. Now I'm a dead man if they get ahold of me.

"I suppose I should be bitter, but the odds of me coming out of this excursion in one piece were never that good. Once the System Lord selected me, I suspected my days were numbered. Particularly with this thing in my head."

She allowed him to stew a little longer, and he sighed again. "I'll just have to take you at your word. What do you want to know first?"

"The cargo. What's in it? Why is it boobytrapped?"

"I don't officially know since no one felt the need to brief me. I was selected for this mission because of my technical knowledge. Imperial Fleet technology is something I've researched all my life. I know it as well as anyone else in the higher orders. Probably better.

"The Lord pulled me out of a life of relative quiet and gave me no choice in the matter. I was here to assist the crew in making all the systems function as designed. They've had intensive training in their specific areas of responsibility, but that only goes so far. I was here to bridge their gaps in experience."

"But you have your suspicions," Olivia pressed. "The cargo is outfitted with antitampering systems and plasma charges. That's pretty serious."

He shrugged. "I did overhear some people talking about the crates. Based on a few vague comments, I guessed the crates contained a bio weapon."

Olivia felt a chill run down her spine. "Obviously you're not sure, but can you be more specific?"

"Something that's going to Terra. I think the Lords have grown tired of the resistance there and intend to eliminate it once and for all. Probably along with the entire remaining population."

31

E lise listened closely as Olivia recounted what she'd learned from their now cooperative prisoner. His tale was horrifying on both a personal level and in the scope of the task that the Lords had set for these people.

Jared leaned forward as Olivia wrapped up. "To summarize, these people were on their way to Terra to exterminate an unknown number of people. The cargo we're carrying is probably the most dangerous and horrifying thing I've ever heard of.

"The next thing we need to work out is how to get rid of it safely. Considering the paranoia displayed so far, it will probably explode if we attempt to move it."

"And if we don't," Olivia added. "These people were on a strict schedule. They're supposed to meet some people a few systems over to assist them in their mission. They have to be there in five days maximum."

"That sounds ominous," Elise said. "I hear an 'or else' in there."

"Very astute," Olivia granted. "The cargo does have a self-destruct timer, and it gives them no more than six days to get there. If the people they were meeting fail to enter the appropriate code, the cargo will explode."

"And what happens if it does get the code?" Jared asked. "And who are these people? What skills do they bring to the party?"

"Our guest doesn't know. He wasn't part of the cabal in charge of this mission. More like unwilling labor. The senior people on this ship were part of the Lord's inner circle. True believers.

"They had all the critical information in their heads. He only knew what he needed to know to keep everything working. They kept him in the dark as much as possible.

"Personally, I think they intended to try to protect him when everything was over. Otherwise, why not tell him? They could kill him anytime they chose."

"These people sound like assholes," Kelsey said from her chair in the corner behind Sean. "I've met more than my fair share of that kind of people over the last few years. No offense, Elise."

"Pentagar does have a few," she admitted. "Are you speaking of Lord Admiral Shrike?"

Kelsey's eyebrows rose. "No. He always seemed stuffy to me, but he was polite enough. Why?"

Elise shook her head. "When you get back to your universe, you might want to tell your version of me about him. He led a coup here that almost overturned the monarchy. His people left the other you to the Pale Ones."

The blonde woman's expression hardened. "I have a very special place in my heart for traitors. Trust me when I say that I'll see that you take care of him expeditiously. Make a note, Scott."

The Fleet commander beside her nodded. "I'll add it to my action items. This visit is showing all kinds of people in a new light. Does anyone mind if I ask a question?"

When no one objected, he continued. "Our options going forward seem somewhat limited. If we don't meet with these unknown hostiles, our ship explodes with us in it. If we do, we have to bluff our way past a group of people that can find out we're imposters the moment they see us, if they're expecting people they know.

"If they're meeting this ship with no prior knowledge of the crew, there will be recognition codes. In either case, we'll probably be exposed as soon as we meet. Lastly, does anyone want to place a bet that these new people don't have a destruct code for the cargo?"

He looked around the table with that last question. No one took his wager.

"What are our options?" Jared asked. "The kind of information we need won't just be lying around. The only place I envision it being is inside the heads of the expedition leader and perhaps her second. Heads that blew up in a rather permanent manner."

Elise sighed. "Is none of the implant hardware recoverable? If we can pull the data off the hardware, we can sidestep this issue."

Sean shook his head. "Trust me when I say that the charge was implanted in such a way and with sufficient power to make certain nothing was recoverable. The System Lord didn't intend for any record of this mission to survive."

"It wasn't the System Lord that killed these people," she objected. "Their own leader did. Why? What would make someone commit suicide to protect something like this?"

"Loyalty," Olivia said grimly. "The leadership in the Rebel Empire can be fanatical. The Lord picked someone to lead the mission that it knew would have no objection to ending it under the appropriate circumstances. I'd wager there was some major payout to the leaderships' families.

"Let's not delude ourselves. These people knew what they were doing and that they wouldn't survive this mission. The System Lord at Terra would have eliminated them as soon as it confirmed their mission objectives had been met."

"Heartless monsters," Elise muttered to herself.

Jared leaned back in his seat. "It might be possible to bluff our way through this, but I'd rather not have to. If there are any mission briefing chips, they might have data on the contacts and their codes. Hell, they might even have the codes to deactivate the bombs."

"I doubt that," Kelsey said firmly. "These AIs don't seem the type to allow their minions the ability to turn off the things driving them. Contact protocols are possible, maybe even a mission brief. Nothing more.

"With implants, the chances of even that are almost nil. Why leave sensitive data just lying around when it could be locked up in your head?"

Olivia smiled. "Here is where one of the quirks of the higher orders comes into play. We have implants but go out of our way to not use them efficiently. Perhaps that is some kind of innate stubbornness on our part.

"I'm not saying this means there *is* a data chip with incriminating evidence stashed somewhere. Even if there is, it will be heavily encrypted. We might not be able to get inside it. Still, it's the best chance we have."

"We know every place the woman in command of the mission went," Jared said. "If she had a chip on her, we'll find it. We'll need to do the same for every single intruder. We can't make the assumption that anyone was ignorant of this critical information.

"We have five days until we meet our new associates. I want everyone searching for any bit of data they can find. This has priority. We all need to be looking for as many hours a day as we can. Dismissed."

* * *

KELSEY DID her part in searching for any concealed data chips but came up dry. So did everyone else. After twelve hours of intense effort, it became clear that there were no hidden data chips.

There was a lull in the search as most people got some well-deserved rest, but her Raider implants left Kelsey with a need for what only amounted to catnaps. So in the middle of the ship's night, she found herself wandering the corridors lost in thought.

She should probably try to sleep more hours than she did, but the incessant nightmares tormented her. Memories of those few weeks as a Pale One, subject to whims and drives implanted by the mad computer on Erorsi.

It angered her when these people told her that their Kelsey had nightmares, too. As if the two women shared the same horrors. As if their situations were the same.

She tried to keep her animosity toward the other Kelsey to a minimum, but it was hard. That woman had gotten off easy. That woman's trials hadn't even come close to what she'd endured. It was going to be an effort not to punch other her in the face when they finally met. If they met at all.

With her mind wandering, she was mildly surprised when she ended up at the computer center. Not exactly the place she'd hoped to see. Now the memories of the people she'd killed there clamored for her attention.

True, they'd have died in any case, and they'd been trying their best to kill her, but their blood was on her hands. Any other interpretation was sophistry.

The main hatch was open, so she stepped inside. The man at the main console looked up and smiled.

"Highness. Can I help you?"

"I doubt it. I'm not even sure why I'm here."

"Couldn't sleep?" he asked sympathetically. "Feel free to commandeer a console. I don't mind the company. No need to talk, even."

That was better than meandering aimlessly through the corridors with only her own thoughts for company.

"Thanks."

She sat at the console farthest away from where she'd killed the intruders. It came to life at her touch.

What should she look at? The computer had lots of old files from before the AIs had captured the ship. The ones that had come later were probably not very interesting.

If she'd been the other Kelsey, she could've looked at some old entertainment vids. She had no idea why those interested the woman. They made little sense, and the special effects were juvenile at best.

Lacking enthusiasm, she limited her search to files that had been modified or uploaded since their arrival in the El Capitan system. Others had already checked and found nothing, but it wasn't as though another check could hurt anything.

Most of the files seemed to be related to ship's operation. That made sense, too. These people had jumped right into running the ship. None of them had even taken time to select quarters.

The two they'd identified as the leaders had been located on the bridge and in engineering. Those locations generated a lot of files, so she started excluding those created by normal operations. That reduced the tsunami to something manageable, if one stretched the term far enough.

She then sorted the remaining files by who had generated them. The number left for the two leaders was only in the hundreds. Plenty of time to glance at each one personally.

A few minutes later, she came across one that puzzled her. The file was supposedly text only, but the contents were gibberish. Random letters, numbers, and special symbols. Not even a space to denote a break in the flow.

She cleared her throat and waved the Fleet man over. "I've found something that I don't understand. Can you tell me what this is?"

He stepped over to her console and looked at the file. "Huh. Maybe it's corrupt. Let me give it a closer look."

The man shifted one of the chairs over and began doing incomprehensible things to the file via the console's interface.

Knowing she wouldn't be much help, Kelsey slid a little farther aside and copied the strange file into her internal memory. Her implants scanned it as soon as she selected it and ordered them to report on its contents.

Moments later, they reported that the file was encrypted and asked if she wanted to run any decryption programs.

Kelsey sat bolt upright. Encrypted? Shouldn't the computer scans have reported this earlier?

"Excuse me," Kelsey said. "I don't think I asked your name."

The man smiled at her. "No worries. I'm Commander Ralph Adonis. I'm the resident computer expert."

"Ralph, I'm Kelsey. Tell me, did you scan the computer for suspicious files related to the newcomers?"

"Of course," he said with a nod. "I finished that hours ago with nothing to show for my efforts. No encrypted files."

"Hmmm. That's odd. My implants tell me this file isn't corrupt. It's encrypted."

The man frowned and focused his attention on the console while his hands flashed over the interface. "No encryption shown on the file. It's plain text."

"I don't know much about my implants, but I doubt they'd get this wrong. They're cutting-edge Old Empire technology. I'm inclined to trust them on this."

The two of them stared at one another for a bit before he spoke again. "What kind of encryption do they think this is?"

A quick check told her that it was some kind of text cypher. She had to look that up to get the gist of the meaning. Plain text was run through some kind of filter and turned into gibberish.

With an appropriate key, anyone could reverse the process and get the original text. Lacking that, the file would remain unreadable.

She passed the information on to Ralph.

He scowled at the screen. "That's crazy. You swap letters out until it makes sense? The ship's computer could unlock something like that in a few seconds."

"It only sounds simple," she said. "Without the correct key, there are probably places in the file where the substitution logic changes. The key tells it where to look for that."

"Hmmm. Let me see if I can do something about that. Are you really sure it's a code?"

"No, but my implants are."

"I should report this, then. Let the admiral know."

If she was wrong, she would look like an idiot. Well, better to be thought a fool than to do something stupid and prove it.

"Do it."

While he was working on the file, she instructed her implants to decrypt the file contents. Her implants seemed more knowledgeable with codes like this than the ship's computer, but they had far less processing power. It was anyone's guess who, if anyone, would manage to get to the secret contents first.

32

Sean had the late shift, so he got the call from the computer center about the potentially encrypted file. He briefly considered waking Admiral Mertz but decided against it. At this point, it might turn out to be nothing.

The last few hours had been filled with false alarms. They couldn't afford to miss a single thing, so they'd instructed everyone to pass along even the most minor oddities. None had panned out, and this latest one would likely be the same.

But he wouldn't know for sure unless he actually went down and looked for himself.

He gave the helm officer the conn and headed down to the computer center. When he got there, he found Princess Kelsey and Commander Adonis hunched over a console examining something.

"What have you found?" he asked as he stepped behind them.

The Fleet officer glanced back at him and shrugged. "I'm not sure, sir. Maybe nothing. Maybe something."

"A plain text file filled with strange characters," Kelsey added. "It looks like gibberish, but my implants insist it's an encrypted file."

That made him lean forward to look at the console more closely. "Your implants are a lot more specialized than the programs we have. If it says this is a code, it probably is. Can you unravel the thing?"

She shrugged. "I'm running quite a few decryption programs, but it's slow going. The programs might be amazing, but this is proving a bit more troublesome than I'd hoped."

He sent an alert to Admiral Mertz. If her implants insisted this was a coded file, it wasn't a dead end. The admiral signaled receipt of the message and that he'd be there in a few minutes.

"Is there any way we can offload some of the processing to the ship's computer?" he asked Adonis.

"Possibly. That's something that people used to do. They'd set the computer to doing intensive work and have it forward the results back to the user.

"Unfortunately, the princess's program code is considered classified under her specific Raider protocols. It doesn't want to move the program code off her implants."

"Could we cede part of the computer to her as a classified virtual machine? If her implants can verify the area is secure, it might allow the transfer."

Kelsey's eyes lost focus. "My implants inform me that they will allow me to copy the programs to a dedicated virtual machine that only I have access to. It can be isolated from the rest of the computer, so you don't need to worry that I have access I shouldn't have."

"Work with her, Adonis," Sean ordered. "Give her what she needs while maintaining operational security. No offense, Highness. I have my orders on that."

She snorted delicately. "I get it. I'm from another universe, and you don't know me all that well. If the situation was reversed, I'd do the same."

It took Commander Adonis five minutes to work out an acceptable compromise with the Raider implants. Once he dedicated and restricted the partition on the ship, Kelsey's implants formatted and encrypted it.

"I've offloaded the process," Kelsey reported. "Wow. That's fast. Much better."

"Any idea how long it might take?" he asked.

"No clue. Maybe forever if this is unbreakable."

"Nothing is unbreakable," Sean said with a laugh. "It just takes unrealistic amounts of time for the impossible stuff."

Admiral Mertz walked into the computer center, his hair slightly mussed and his eyes red with interrupted sleep.

"What have you got?"

Sean summarized the situation, and his commanding officer grasped the significance as quickly as he had.

"This is the real deal," Mertz declared. "Excellent work."

"I haven't done anything," Kelsey objected. "We can't read it."

"We certainly couldn't have read it if you hadn't found it," Mertz disagreed. "Now we have a few days to let your programs crack the code. We still might not manage it, but life is often the art of the possible. I'll take it."

Kelsey blinked. "The program just cracked the code." She sounded shocked.

"Even better," Sean said. "Can you pass the plain text to us?"

His implants received the file a second later. He brought it up and began reading.

The file was a diary with all the attendant meandering. The man who'd wrote it seemed to be a gossip, filling the pages with details about everyone around him. He made numerous complaints about the hyper secrecy they were under and how that negatively impacted his social life.

His chatter wasn't restricted to this mission, either. The date stamps went back several decades. Sean guessed the man had started this while at university. If he allowed himself to go all the way to the beginning, this would take a while.

Sean limited his search to six months before his arrival in the El Capitan system. One entry led to another, and he found several sections of the diary that seemed to be in a different code. At least they didn't make any sense as they were currently decoded.

"Can you bury code inside of code?" he asked. "I found something that looks odd."

He passed a link to the sections back to Princess Kelsey.

Almost half an hour passed before she grinned triumphantly. "Cracked it! This sure looks like the brief for this mission."

Sean accepted the freshly decrypted text and smiled. It was exactly that.

He skimmed the details until he found the most critical part: the data on who they were meeting and the codes to establish their bona fides.

Well, they might just have a chance after all.

* * *

JARED WENT over the information they'd gleaned from the dead man's diary. It wasn't much, but it included the information they most desperately needed: the contact codes to both verify the crew of this ship to the people they were to meet and the codes that verified the identities of those people.

No names were mentioned, so he nursed the hope that the people he had to fool wouldn't know precisely who they were meeting. After all, they really couldn't expect that they needed to watch out for ringers. What kind of idiots would come walking in, pretending to be part of some dastardly plot?

The one thing that wasn't included in the dead man's ramblings was what these new people would be doing to advance the AIs' plans. If they already had a deadly virus in their hold, what else did they need?

Well, he'd find out soon enough.

He had his people focused on getting the ship ready for visitors over the next four days. They cleaned up every sign of battle and got the external com systems back online.

Olivia spent the same period of time coaching everyone on how to behave around the expected guests. Hopefully, the visit would be a brief one.

Now that Jared knew what to expect, he could mitigate the potential damage these new people could inflict. Discreet jammers scattered throughout the ship would blanket all implant communications on his command. A second set would make certain that the deadly cargo received no orders to explode.

Of course, they couldn't do that straight off. They needed the new people to extend the detonation time of the plasma explosives. Otherwise, this would be a very short trip.

The next five days simultaneously flew by and dragged interminably. As they transitioned to the destination system, he sat tensely on *Athena*'s bridge. Just like at El Capitan, the defenses were internal to the system.

That didn't mean that there weren't recon drones on station, watching for approaching ships. During the approach to the first Rebel Empire system, he'd been cautious enough to keep his active scanners offline.

Now he behaved more boldly, scanning the supposedly empty flip point leading to the new system, Raidon, with every tool he had available. The Rebel Empire probes scattered around the wormhole weren't easy to see, but they *were* there.

That was actually something of a relief. He'd had trouble believing the enemy was comprised of idiots. This made their actions understandable, if lazy.

In their shoes, he'd have stationed several ships in the systems leading up to their population centers: probes in all the flip points leading into the buffer systems, destroyers to monitor them and intercept any intruders, and ships positioned directly in the flip points leading to the population centers that were ready to run and scream for help as soon as trouble came calling.

In fact, that was pretty much what Admiral Yeats had done on the border systems of the New Terran Empire and in critical systems deeper in their interior. Not that it would help them if the Rebel Empire came calling in force.

Thankfully, the time required to get information across something as vast as the Old Terran Empire was significant. The people in this section of the Rebel Empire would get the word of the raid on Dresden in three or four weeks. Then their defense patterns might change. Until then, it was business as usual.

Jared worried about how the AI leadership of the Rebel Empire would respond. They wouldn't take the loss of the Dresden research facility lightly.

Or that of the equipment used to manufacture Marine Raider implants or sentient AIs.

To put it lightly, they would lose their digital minds. They wouldn't rest until they got to the bottom of the raid.

The reaction force from Dresden had already pursued Jared and his fleet to Erorsi. They'd run headlong into the flip-point jammer.

They had no frame of reference about that kind of technology or the faster-than-light communications his people had with the drones he'd left monitoring the buffer system.

Jared was shocked at how quickly the enemy commander had grasped the threat. He hadn't poured ships into the flip point when none of his probes returned.

He'd sent a few cruisers, probably with orders to immediately flip back with a report. When none of them returned, he'd settled into a siege. Smart.

The AIs would heavily reinforce that system as soon as they caught up with events. They wouldn't hesitate to keep probing Erorsi. The jammer had to be given regular maintenance. That would allow the enemy a window of time to take advantage of.

Jared really hoped Admiral Yeats took a risk and moved one of the jammers from Harrison's World to Erorsi to minimize the danger. That left that system vulnerable, but the enemy had no reason to probe it. Yet.

He shook himself out of his thoughts. No amount of worry would help that situation now. He'd best focus on the problems at hand.

Commander Hall turned away from the helm console. "We're almost ready to transition, Admiral. Five minutes."

They'd switched to civilian clothes. None of the intruders had been Fleet officers, so his people needed to fit the new profile.

Olivia had gone over each outfit and made changes she declared necessary. She hadn't shied away from robbing the bags of the dead Rebel Empire nobles to make up for any lacking.

Jared felt faintly ridiculous in his new outfit, but he'd manage. He rose to his feet and stepped away from his console. As they'd already discussed, Olivia took his seat, looking a little uncomfortable.

"I'm still not very happy with this change," she said softly. "I'm not a Fleet officer. What if something goes wrong?"

"I'll be right here," he reassured her. "If they call, I want you already settled in. Trust me. They'll notice you fidgeting if you wait until the last second to sit down."

The remaining few minutes passed in silence until Hall announced that they were ready to flip.

"Take us across," he ordered.

This was it. Rather than fighting or hiding, now they had to fool knowledgeable and canny enemies in their own territory.

Any slip would doom them and potentially the people of Terra, too. It would certainly stop the AI in charge of the Terra system from inviting them in with open arms.

In a word, everything had to go right from here on.

33

Olivia felt a bit overwhelmed. That hadn't happened to her in a long time. She was used to being in charge of any situation.

Seated at the command console of a warship sneaking into the very heart of the enemy was something outside her range of experience, though. Fooling people into thinking she was their ally in serving the Rebel Empire and the Lords… that, she could do. She'd done it her entire life.

"Flip complete," Commander Hall said calmly. "Enemy warships and fortifications detected. Transmitting our ID code."

That had been something different from the secret recognition codes they'd found in the diary. These had been left on the command console by the woman sent by the System Lord of El Capitan to command the ship. Basic recognition and authorization codes allowing for the ship to transit the Rebel Empire in pursuit of its goals.

The System Lord at Harrison's World had provided similar codes for their use. Rather, the data it had stored away before they'd beaten it had provided them.

"How do the defenses stack up against what we saw at El Capitan," Jared asked.

"Somewhat heavier," Hall said. "Perhaps fifteen percent more firepower and a greater allocation of heavy cruisers. The battle stations are about the same size. They've accepted our codes and have allowed us passage."

"How long until we reach the main planet in the system?" Olivia asked.

"We're not going there," Hall said. "We've been directed to a station orbiting a gas giant in the outer system. ETA six hours."

Olivia supposed that made sense. Better not to allow a biological weapon near an inhabited world. She'd thought the System Lord at El Capitan had been taking a terrible risk. If something went wrong, it would've killed billions. Not that she suspected it cared.

"Once we're an hour away from the flip point," Jared said, "I want to start rotating people off station for food and rest. Everyone but you, Olivia. If they call, we need you right here. Welcome to the joys of a space command."

"You can keep it," she said tartly. "I'll stick to planetary leadership. The sleeping quarters and perks are better."

"No doubt," he agreed.

His caution proved warranted when someone called for them two hours out from the station.

"Incoming priority communication," Hall said. "They're using the recognition code."

"We're on," Jared said, straightening. "Take it away, Olivia."

She took a deep breath and nodded toward Hall. "Accept the call and put it on the main screen."

The image of the star field faded and was replaced by what appeared to be opulent quarters. A man with the eyes of someone used to being obeyed sat at a desk made of dark wood.

"Greetings and welcome to Raidon," he said in a low, melodious voice. "My name is Oscar Fielding. You've received my code. I'll have yours now."

This was the moment of truth. If they'd misinterpreted the significance of the data in the encrypted file, it was all over.

She sent him the code and sat there with an artificially calm expression as he reviewed something on his console.

He smiled. "All in order, just as I expected. If I might be so bold, who are you?"

"Jaleesa Keaton," Olivia lied with a smile of her own.

"Welcome, Jaleesa. I have a list of your people, but it didn't include complete files. I had your name but not your picture.

"We need to discuss the next steps we must take to meet the operational requirements for the Lords. I will come to your ship and examine your equipment. That will also allow me to extend the timer on the security system."

"Hopefully enough for us to meet our obligations without worrying about any unexpected delays," she said dryly.

He frowned. "What makes you worry about delays?"

"Nothing specific, but life has a way of dealing you an unexpected hand when you can least afford it."

Fielding grunted. "True enough. I'll want Jocelyn Oldfield on hand to assist me with the examination of the equipment. She oversaw its assembly, so she knows it better than all of us."

"Of course," Olivia assured him. "She'll be standing by when you come aboard."

"Excellent," he said with a superior smile. "I'll see you as soon as you reach orbit. I'll send out a pair of system defense patrol craft out to meet you, so don't be alarmed. They'll insure safety for us both."

The transmission terminated without another word.

Olivia turned to Jared. "What now?"

"We meet in him in orbit," the Fleet officer said. "Good work, by the way. You got us past the chanciest part."

"Did I?" she asked, raising an eyebrow. "It seems as if the in-person meeting is far riskier."

"At least we understand what's happening, to a degree," Jared said. "He might have known what the person he was meeting looked like, or we could have had the wrong code. Damned perilous, if you ask me.

"Not to say the next stage of this game is without its dangers. We can still screw up. Who shall we use for Jocelyn Oldfield? Elise?"

Olivia shook her head. "She has the coolness, but her accent would give her away. It sounds pleasant to the ear, but her delivery is distinctly different from any I've ever heard in the Rebel Empire. It needs to be Kelsey."

Jared didn't seem convinced. "She's not used to playing that kind of game."

"She's stronger than you give her credit for," Olivia disagreed. "She can pull this off."

After a second, he shrugged. "If you say so. I guess we'd best brief her together. At least we can monitor the situation when she meets with this guy and give her pointers over her implant coms."

Olivia wasn't certain that was necessary. Kelsey, even the one from another universe, was more resourceful than her brother gave her credit for.

* * *

"You've lost your mind," Kelsey told Mertz firmly. "What makes you think I can fool someone like that? He'll see right through me."

"Necessity is the mother of invention," he responded coolly. "We don't have much choice in the matter."

"Surely you have someone else. Anyone would be better than me."

Olivia shook her head. "We've considered everyone else aboard. Maybe Doctor Stone, but I still think you're the right choice. You grew up in a position of power. Even though you never acted as the emperor of the

Terran Empire, you had a lifetime to observe your father and brother. You know how to behave."

"This is insane," Kelsey muttered. "What do you need me to do?"

"Honestly, we have no idea. You'll be meeting with the senior man in this system as far as this project goes. He wants to inspect our cargo, and you're supposed to know all about it."

"What could possibly go wrong? I have no idea what the cargo is or how to inspect it. If this really is a biological weapon, Doctor Stone is a *far* better choice. What if he expects me to open the cargo?"

"We're not expecting that," Mertz said. "He has the codes for the antitampering charges, so he'll have the codes to get it open."

This sounded like a huge gamble to her, but what choice did she have?

"If we all die, it's your fault," she said darkly. "There's something more to this. Stone would be a far superior choice for this. Why me?"

Mertz and Olivia shared a glance.

The other woman smiled sadly. "We know you have what it takes to pull this off. We've both seen it. You can do this."

"I'm not your Kelsey," she disagreed. "She has skills and confidence that I just don't have. If you put me in there, I might blow this entire mission sky high."

"And you might save it from some unexpected occurrence," Mertz said. "Our Kelsey felt exactly the same way in the beginning. She found a way forward to success. You will, too. We'll help you."

Kelsey covered her face with her hands. "This is insane. I've screwed up so many things. Find someone else."

Mertz's eyes lost focus. "The cutter with our guest is about to dock. The system defense craft are escorting him in. You're up, Kelsey. I know you can do this. I believe in you."

"Then you're an idiot." She took a deep breath. "Let's go."

The three of them made their way to the docking level and arrived just as a cutter docked, sending a loud clang of metal on metal through the area. Moments later, the hatch slid open with a puff of super chilled gas.

A tall man with a hooked nose and an arrogant expression walked through the hatch with two men and two women in black tunics at his back.

Kelsey's Raider scanners identified weapons on all four of the followers. Guards, she wagered.

The man didn't offer his hand to any of them. Instead, he smiled coldly. "Lady Keaton. A pleasure to meet you in person." He turned to Mertz. "Lord Gust, I presume?"

"Bertram Gust," Mertz confirmed. "And this is Jocelyn Oldfield."

Apparently, that was her new name.

The man smiled at Kelsey. "Lady Oldfield, I've read your reports with interest. Well done."

She extended her hand, even though the others hadn't. "The pleasure is mine. I'm looking forward to moving to the next stage of this project. Shall we?"

His grip was light and dry. "Indeed. Lady Keaton, Lord Gust, I believe it best if Lady Oldfield and I proceed alone."

Olivia bowed slightly. "Of course. We'll be a call away if you need us."

As the other two abandoned Kelsey to the intruder, her internal com received an incoming call from Olivia.

Kelsey, I'll be your handler for this. Keep sending me everything that's happening and be ready for me to give you quick instructions if something awkward happens.

Too late for that, she responded grumpily.

Lord Fielding gestured toward the lift. "Shall we?"

Kelsey was grateful the cargo area wasn't very far away and that she had instant access to the deck plans of the destroyer. Getting lost now would be bad.

The large crates sat where the original intruders had secured them in the center of the large bay. The six crates were each taller than she was. All were locked down tight with codes that she didn't have and protected by bombs she couldn't turn off.

Fielding stared at them before he turned to her. "Amazing, isn't it? So much misery in a single location. Does it ever give you nightmares?"

Kelsey nodded. "Terrible ones. I wish this wasn't necessary."

That might be laying it on a bit thick.

She ignored Olivia and focused on the Rebel Empire noble. "What about you?"

He sighed. "I hadn't thought it would when the Lord instructed me to develop my part of this project, but it *has* given me pause. Killing traitors should be a pleasure as well as a duty, but this weapon isn't clean. They'll suffer a lingering, painful death.

"Not everyone will get sick immediately. Some portion of the target population will become symptomless carriers, spreading the plague far and wide before succumbing.

"This is a terrible thing we've been tasked with. The extermination of an entire planetary population. No one will ever be able to even approach Terra once we start. Even if they used space suits or remote devices, they could never be certain they hadn't picked up the Omega Plague."

So it had a name. Ironic that it had the same name as the alien that had brought her to this universe.

This was going to be a serious problem. If they allowed this weapon to be deployed, she'd never get her hands on the override. She had to make sure they stopped the Lords' dastardly plans. And to do that, she had to make this man believe she was part of his team.

"I confess that the technical aspects of my work were delightfully challenging while the implications were horrifying. If something goes wrong, we could exterminate all human life in the galaxy."

His shoulders relaxed a little. "That's understandable, I suppose. Well, we should open up the crates and verify the contents."

"Agreed," she said hurriedly. "If you'd be so kind."

This was a potential sticking point. If he didn't have the codes to the crates, she'd have to take him and his guards out. That would blow the plan, and they'd die here in very short order.

Thankfully, he sent a coded signal to the crates, and they all began opening. Her enhanced Raider gear picked up the code, so she forwarded it to Mertz. If they had to get into these crates later, that might prove very useful.

Her gaze swept over the contents. Hundreds of drones in racks. She'd expected large vessels or small vials containing the biological agent, but this was the delivery equipment.

She spotted the antitampering charges. No one had been tasteless enough to put timers on them, so she had no visible way to determine how much of the countdown remained.

"All seem to be in order, but I'll need to verify them as we proceed," Fielding said. "I'll increment the antitampering charges another five days now. You only had ten hours left. Good thing you didn't dawdle on your way here."

No, she supposed. That would've been bad.

He was more careful with his signal. This time she didn't get the code for the bombs as he went from crate to crate updating the explosives. Pity.

"What comes next?" she asked.

"I just signaled for the cargo shuttle to deliver the agent. We'll load it in here while we isolate the rest of the ship. If there is some kind of accident, your compatriots can escape before the protective fortifications destroy this ship.

"As you no doubt already understand, the Lords are very serious that no word of this mission or even any components of it become known to the public. That's why they segregated the labs developing the agent and your part in creating the delivery drones."

She sighed internally. The virus had never been on board. Damned paranoid AIs.

Well, they hadn't had any choice about coming here. The real question was what they did next.

If she was supposed to help load the deadly cargo, she needed to know something about the drones. She really hoped the woman she was masquerading as had put detailed plans into the devices.

A quick check got her complete schematics for them. They were quite simple, really. Made to avoid detection and search for people. If it found them, it released a minute quantity of the virus upwind of them. They would never even know they'd been infected.

Fortunately, the plans had the loading instructions appended. They seemed quite basic, but she forwarded the data to Mertz. His people would go over it with a fine-toothed comb and guide her when the time came.

She hoped that kept her safe, but a nagging uncertainty roiled her stomach. This could still go very badly.

34

Elise wasn't going to interact with the intruders, and that annoyed her. She understood that her accent and Pentagar's linguistic drift would make her stand out, so she tried to keep things in perspective. That didn't make her any less grumpy, though.

The bastards were carefully loading the deadly virus into the drones. The engineering team and Lily Stone were helping Kelsey with any data she might need to fulfill her role as the resident expert on the dispersal equipment.

Everyone in the hold was dressed in specialized suits in case there was a breach. Not that Elise expected them to allow anyone exposed to leave the ship.

She sat in a maintenance tube with their prisoner and two beefy marine guards. They'd moved a few spartan pieces of furniture in to allow a minimum of comfort. Perhaps that would make up for the survival rations and water they had to live on until their guests departed.

The guards might not have been required. Austin Darrah had just as much to lose as they did now. More, really. The Lords would torture the man to make sure they got every bit of data he'd passed on to the New Terran Empire if they suspected anything.

"Did you know this was what you were doing?" she asked. "Exterminating the entire population on Terra."

He shrugged. "I had my suspicions. Like I said, I wasn't given a choice or a briefing. I had to eavesdrop to find out anything of substance.

"If what you really meant to ask was if I approved. Hell no. I don't want to kill a single person, much less a planet full of people. But I didn't have a choice in the matter. It was comply or die. The Lord needed someone who could fix anything on this ship, and it didn't trust Fleet not to have an attack of conscience."

She raised an eyebrow. "It didn't believe you'd be prone to the same desire to spare lives?"

"More like it didn't believe that I would have an opportunity to make good on any impulses. A Fleet officer could potentially use violence to sabotage the mission. Me? I'm as harmless as they come and have no training in weapons or fighting.

"No access to armaments, either. The Lord knew damned well I would have no choice but to do what I was told, even if I strenuously objected." The last came out bitterly.

Elise nodded, thinking he might even be telling the truth. "How did you get interested in Fleet technology?"

"Oddly enough, I can lay blame for that at the feet of my family's choice in guards. We have estates near the spaceport, and my grandfather chose several marines led by a retired marine officer to secure them back in the day.

"Those original people have long retired, but they had influence over who came onto the scene afterward. My mother never approved of my sneaking off to hear stories from them. She said they were a bad influence, teaching me how to be a member of the middle orders."

His expression turned ironic. "If only she could see me now. She'd be so proud."

"She doesn't know where you are?"

He shook his head. "All she knows is that the Lord specifically selected me for this mission. I'm sure my extensive knowledge of Fleet technology being the driving factor in my selection scandalized her. A very backhanded compliment, my mission."

"So you heard stories about Fleet," Elise said, nudging him out of his introspective silence. "That doesn't necessarily lead to technical knowledge."

"No, but it did give me enough know-how to start acquiring books about it. Well, the unclassified portions, anyway. My relationship with one Fleet officer led to getting to know others who had contacts that could get me anything I wanted shy of a flip drive or a fusion plant.

"I gained experience with those advanced systems once I became an adult. One of my uncles owns a shipping consortium. He helped me out by allowing me to work on one of his ships for a year, primarily just to annoy my mother.

"It was a spectacularly successful ploy, I might add. She was furious." He grinned at that last bit.

"It gave me hands-on experience with the same kind of equipment Fleet uses, short of the weapons and defense systems. I'd planned to look them over very carefully during this mission." He sounded wistfully disappointed that he wouldn't get the chance.

"If we can keep a handle on the situation, that isn't out of the question."

Austin perked up. "Really? You would trust me that far?"

"It's not as if you could fire a missile while the system was locked down or make it detonate in the tube."

He gave her a mildly guilty look. "Actually, I might be able to figure something like that out, given a little time."

She laughed. "You remind me of someone I know. Carl Owlet. He's a scientist with a penchant for pulling off the impossible. I suspect the two of you would get along like a house on fire."

Austin squinted. "Why would you want to lock us in a burning house?"

"It's an old saying. It means that you'd really like one another."

"You people have some very odd phrases in your vocabulary. And you have a funny accent. Where are you from?"

She shook her head. "A planet cut off from contact with the Empire a long time ago. The name is unimportant. Our situation did lead to some linguistic drift."

He smiled wryly. "Is it irony when you really mean the name is so critical that you don't dare tell someone you can't fully trust? Really, I do understand, but it's darkly funny.

"Can't you tell me anything about what's happening? Being locked out of the ship's systems is really boring. Surely an update on what the others are doing, if kept general, wouldn't be harmful. My life hangs in the balance, too."

Elise knew the opposite was true if he intended them harm, but she had those marines to keep him manageable. "They're loading the virus into drones kept in the cargo containers. Six crates total, and they've finished four. I'd imagine we'll be on our way in a few hours, once Lord Fielding finishes."

He perked up. "Oscar Fielding? Are we at Raidon?"

Shocked, she nodded. "You know him?"

"You could say that. He's the uncle I told you about."

* * *

SEAN LISTENED to Elise's report grimly. This was not good. Their prisoner was related to the main bad guy. There was no way the man wouldn't demand to see him at some point, even though it looked as if the man had thrown his own kin under the bus, so to speak.

She concluded her description of the situation with a question.
What do we do?
Great question. He wished he had an equally great answer.
We play it by ear. You say the boy doesn't seem like a mass murderer. Keep playing that angle with him. When the inevitable happens, we'll just have to hope for the best when we trot him out.

That could go wrong in so many ways, but it wasn't as if they had a choice. Not making him available upon demand would trip all kinds of alarms for the Rebel Empire noble. They'd never get out of this system alive.

He considered the potential options as soon as he signed off the call. Each one of them involved trusting the prisoner to an uncomfortable degree. One word from him, and the gig was assuredly up.

If Lord Fielding was the man's uncle, he would undoubtedly insist on some privacy in meeting his nephew. Depending on how paranoid the man was, he might even insist it happen off the destroyer.

How could he assure they at least knew their cover was blown? Could he plant a listening device on Austin Darrah? One that couldn't be detected?

Possibly, though not in the strictest sense of the word. Princess Kelsey had Marine Raider implants, including enhanced hearing that could pick up a surprising amount of information from an amazing distance. Almost as good as a parabolic microphone.

She was also a known element to the Rebel Empire Lord. He would probably understand if the mission leader insisted one of their own keep an eye on their junior player.

That was a lot more like playing spies than Kelsey would be ready for. He dearly hoped she was as good as her counterpart at improvisation. Well, perhaps with fewer explosions.

Sean sighed and focused his attention back on the loading process. Kelsey and Fielding had loaded the drones in the fifth crate and were servicing the final ones now. Based on their previous speed, they would finish in roughly half an hour.

As a betting man, he wagered that would be when Fielding made his play. Time to try to stack the deck.

Keeping a mental eye on the loading via his implants, Sean headed for the maintenance tube where they'd concealed Elise and Darrah. Both rose to their feet as the marine guards tensed. He waved them back down.

"It's okay. I'm just dropping in to have a word with Mister Darrah."

Elise rose from her seat again. "Then sit. Looming over people doesn't make for an easy conversation."

It flew in the face of his upbringing, but he took the offered seat. This conversation was going to be difficult enough without adding elements of intimidation.

Once he'd settled in, he leaned toward Darrah. "I assume you've seen images of the man who might be your uncle. Is it him?"

Darrah nodded. "Damned if I understand what he's doing here. As I said to Miss Orison, he's not part of the mission."

Hearing the man not use Elise's title rankled a bit, but he hadn't been told. That was one of the secrets they'd decided not to share as it gave him too much background. The other was the fact she was married to Admiral Mertz.

"The facts prove otherwise," Sean said in a low tone. "He knows everything, and he's probably the head man on this end of the mission. What you should be wondering is how much he likes you."

"I don't understand," Darrah said with a frown.

"This might come as a shock to you, but I've wondered how expendable you were once the mission was complete. Unlike the others, you weren't an enthusiastic conspirator. Once they finished, they might've dropped you out the nearest airlock.

"But with your uncle being high in their plans, I wonder if that's so. Or at least if he has the intent to change the plans in your favor. He did train you, after all."

"Trained me," the prisoner repeated. "You think his assistance in learning all the systems on a ship was to enhance this mission? That was years ago."

"One doesn't hatch a conspiracy of this scale the day before one executes it," Elise said reasonably. "The leaders and other conspirators didn't have the luxury of vanishing from the public sphere with no warning. People would talk.

"In fact, now that everyone has left, people are undoubtedly trying to figure out where they vanished to so abruptly and why."

"The Lords planned for that," Darrah said. "Everyone is part of a supposed trade mission. We'll be gone for six months and then return. My assumption was that the deal was already done or that we would proceed there as soon as we finished at Terra."

Sean agreed with that assessment, only he suspected the entire ship would vanish with all hands. Done in by the fanatical leader or even the AI at Terra. In no case would the ship be allowed to leave that system.

The System Lords couldn't risk allowing the contagion to escape stellar containment. That probably meant the System Lord there had some kind of escape plan.

"In any case," Sean continued, "your uncle will be done loading the bioweapon in perhaps ten minutes. As soon as he finishes, nothing will be holding this ship here. I expect him to call for you.

"We either have to produce you or start shooting. One way or their other, you can stop us. We want to save the lives of everyone on Terra. Are you truly willing to murder millions or billions of people?"

Darrah deflated a bit. "No. Since the Lord press-ganged me, I've been powerless to change the outcome of this mission. Honestly, does helping you do more than put it off for a few more months? How long before the Lords send a second mission?"

"That depends on how long we can make them believe the mission was a success. If we can, of course. But that's dodging the question.

"If you help them, you're a murderer. If you put them off, the people might still die, but you did everything in your power to save them. Which kind of person are you?"

The man smiled a little. "I'll keep my mouth shut and help you, but I have my own price for that cooperation. When we leave this system and head for Terra, you have to tell me everything.

"I know there's a big secret you all keep talking around. You're on an important mission of your own. You didn't come to stop the attack on Terra. I want to know what it is and see if it's something worth helping you with."

Sean considered the man's counter proposal and then nodded. "I don't control when you'll be told, but it will be sometime after we leave here and no later than when we reach Terra. You have my word."

"As a Fleet officer?"

That made Sean blink. They'd been so careful to keep that under wraps.

"What makes you think that I'm a Fleet officer?"

"My eyes and my experience interfacing with men like you. Just like I know these two fellows guarding me are marine officers. Do you deny it?"

Sean shook his head. "No. I suppose you don't need my confirmation, but you have it."

He blinked as Jared called him through his implants.

Fielding just asked to speak to our prisoner.

Sean checked the vid feed and saw the crates were all closed now. Kelsey and Fielding were stripping out of their suits. It was showtime.

We'll be there in a few minutes.

Sean rose to his feet. "He's called for you. I guess we'll find out what kind of man you are now."

35

Kelsey hadn't known what to expect when the dreadful task of loading the bioweapon was done, but she'd been praying for the rapid departure of Lord Fielding and his people so that she could get the hell out of here.

The sight of Sean and the prisoner they'd captured shot that down. What in the hell was the man thinking? They were so screwed.

Lord Fielding smiled at the prisoner. "Austin, I'm sure this is quite the shock, but I'm pleased to see you."

"Shocking indeed, Uncle Oscar. I didn't know that we were coming to Raidon, much less that we'd meet you here. You obviously know far more about all this than I ever expected."

"Life is a great circle, nephew. It turns, and past becomes future."

The man turned to Sean. "I'll want some time with my nephew. No need to displace anyone. I'll take him back to my cutter."

"I'm afraid we have an obligation to keep an eye on him. Lady Jocelyn can accompany you while staying out of earshot."

The Rebel Empire noble considered him coolly for a few seconds. "I suppose we all have to make compromises. Lady Jocelyn, if you would please escort us to my cutter."

She shot Sean a sharp look. *What's happening?*

We're making lemonade. Keep an ear on them and let me know if our little mouse betrays us. If so, take them down, and we'll try to make a run for it.

Kelsey had seen the scanner readings, so she had no illusions how that would turn out. If the man betrayed them, they'd die here.

No pressure.

She nodded to Sean and fell in beside Lord Fielding. The prisoner—Austin, she corrected—might be his nephew, but she was masquerading as someone higher up the societal food chain, so she got the more prominent position in the parade.

The trip to Fielding's cutter was short, and he walked in silence. He'd already told her more than enough about the damned weapon as they'd loaded it. She'd definitely have even more nightmares now.

She was grateful that she'd managed to do what she needed to do in assisting him with the grisly task. The engineering people and Lily Stone had given her what she needed via her implants, and she hadn't screwed up.

That was a refreshing change of pace.

Lord Fielding's cutter was different from the Fleet models Kelsey was used to, not larger on the outside, but significantly more luxurious on the inside. Rather than allowing for as many people, it could hold a far smaller number in absolute comfort. Gold finishes, dark woods, and expensive-looking cloth abounded.

The sight didn't seem to surprise Austin. This must be more common in his sphere than Kelsey had thought.

Fielding turned to her. "I'm going to step into my private compartment with my nephew. I'll leave the hatch open so that you can carry out your observational duties. Feel free to sample something from my bar. You've more than earned it."

Kelsey inclined her head and watched them go through the unobtrusive door at the rear of the compartment. This was it. If the prisoner was going to betray them, it would be now.

As she might be under observation, she did pour a glass of something. The dark liquid burned smoothly as she sipped it. Not bad.

When Lord Fielding spoke, even though he kept his voice low, Kelsey could clearly hear him.

"Austin, I'm sorry. I truly am."

"Are you really, Uncle Oscar? It seems to me that my presence here is your doing. Far from being accidental, you've put me in a situation I probably won't survive. There are two major paths in front of me, and neither seem to have a good chance of me getting back home."

The older man grunted softly. "Contrary to what you think, I didn't take this step lightly. Like you, I have to balance the demands of the Lords against my family. I made the best choice I could."

"Against your family or against your own interests? It seems as though you've abandoned me to enrich yourself."

"Don't be more of a fool than you have to be, boy," the older man grumbled. "Life isn't simple. We have to navigate the shoals and whirlpools that are determined to sink us. I did what I had to."

There was a short pause before Darrah answered him. "I see. Well, let me tell you what I know. They put a bomb in my head, and I have little doubt they'll dispose of me as soon as this mission is done. You'll forgive me if I don't see how you've done what you could for *family*."

"You think you were the only one the Lords forced into their plans against their will? Do you think I wanted to concoct this devil's brew? Bah.

"The Lords ordered me to do what I've done, and I did it. Here's a little surprise for you. I have a bomb in my head, too. Don't think I'm unaware of how this might turn out."

Kelsey relaxed a little. Maybe the boy wasn't going to betray them after all. She sipped the drink again.

"I think you've missed the point," Austin said. "You betrayed me personally. I didn't have to be part of this. I'm sorry the Lords came after you for this terrible task, but why give them my name? Why train me for a task that will kill your sister's son? Do you hate us that much?"

Fielding sighed. "I don't hate you, and you know it. I love you both. In fact, I have a gift for you. The code for disarming the bomb in your head."

Kelsey perked up. They'd removed the device. Even the code controlling it was gone from the prisoner's implants. What would happen if the older man tried to disarm the bomb and it failed to respond?

"Even that won't save me," Austin said. "They can shoot me down at any time or shove me out a handy airlock. Don't think they won't. That said, I'll take the code and hold it in reserve. They might know if I turn it off."

"Here you go. I doubt they'll know if the device is deactivated, but keep it to yourself."

"How did you get it, and do you have your own code?"

"Let's just say that I have ears in many places, and I'm not worried about my head exploding. I have a plan to keep you safe once the mission is completed, too. I'll need to speak to Lady Keaton, but it should more than serve to protect you."

"You sound very confident," Austin said cautiously. "What will you do?"

"Something that will more than prove I love you, boy. Come on. Your watcher is probably growing concerned. You can watch me work my magic in person."

* * *

JARED SAT in *Athena*'s small conference room with Olivia and nervously waited for Lord Fielding to arrive.

Sean walked in a few seconds later. "We're ready to break orbit as soon as you give the green light. All of the workers have departed in the cargo shuttle that brought the bio agent. Only Fielding and his guards are still on board. Once they leave, we can get the hell out of here."

"Kelsey said Fielding has some kind of plan to protect his nephew. I hope it doesn't screw us up. They're in the lift now. Park it, and we'll find out what curve ball he's going to toss at us."

The hatch slid open a few minutes later and let Lord Fielding, Kelsey, and Austin Darrah into the briefing room. Olivia stood, so he and Sean joined her.

"Please sit," Fielding said. "We have just a few more items to discuss before you embark on the final stage of your mission. Allow me to compliment you on how well you've done so far. Excellent work, particularly from Lady Oldfield."

Kelsey silently inclined her head as she took a seat next to Austin. The young prisoner eyed everyone at the table with what Jared suspected was secret amusement glinting in his eyes.

Once everyone was comfortable, Fielding continued. "First, I need to warn you just how dangerous the agent is. While it's locked away in the drones, it should be safe enough, but due care *must* be taken.

"The Lords tasked me to use my labs to bring this ancient weapon back to life. Gods only know why the dictator felt the need to kill every human being on a world and render it uninhabitable forever. Let me tell you, creating this organism from scratch was no easy task and had more than its share of setbacks. Lethal ones."

Olivia studied the noble for a long while before she added her thoughts. "While I've seen a summary of what to expect, why don't you fill me in on the details. We have to get this right the first time. What kind of setbacks are you speaking of?"

The man grimaced. "We used all due caution. This mining orbital oversees extraction of rare gases on the giant below us, so it's isolated. Perfect to maintain the secrecy the Lords demanded.

"In addition, there are smaller stations used for specialized refining. One of them became the primary laboratory. After several months of work, they recreated the correct genomic sequence. That was a tremendous achievement for them. The accidental release of the agent inside the station was equally tremendous but in a very negative manner.

"We all got to see the terrible progression of the disease up close and personal. The System Lord insisted we allow the scientists to perish so we could record the data rather than ending their lives quickly. It was just as horrible as you might imagine.

"Once the last person was dead, we deorbited the station and allowed it to burn up in the gas giant's atmosphere. That was more than sufficient to sterilize everything."

"That's awful," Jared agreed. "But as you say, we have the agent in the drones now. What risk is there?"

Fielding fixed him with a cool smile. "I suggest you keep the cargo hold hermetically sealed. The little beast is pernicious. It can cross any air gap you'd care to place around it. Only hard vacuum will keep it at bay.

"I don't think it will leak, but you dare not take chances. Given one moment's inattention, you won't be allowed to survive. And you won't want to. Diving this ship into the nearest stellar body will be the only way to be sure you've cleansed it."

That sounded pretty dire to Jared. They'd be ultra-careful.

"We could detonate the plasma charges to eliminate the threat," he suggested. Getting the codes for the antitampering devices would be a huge relief, if he could manage it.

"Sadly, the Lord has forbidden dispensing them," Fielding said with a small smile that seemed faked. "Still, what you say has some merit. The damage to the ship would be severe, but if the agent was limited to the cargo holds, the plasma would cleanse it.

"Your thoughts parallel something I've been pondering. The trip to Terra will take two weeks. Secrecy and safety are paramount. I've come up with a way to expedite your journey while increasing your odds of arriving at Terra safely."

Jared felt himself tensing.

"How would that be?" Olivia asked in the guise of their leader. "If we don't have the codes to the plasma charges, we can't very well use them to protect the Lords' secret."

This time Fielding's smile was large and genuine. "The original plan calls for you to meet another ship a week out from Terra so they can extend the timer on the charges. An encouragement for you to be speedy and remain on task.

"After discussion with the System Lord, he has allowed that there is another way to accomplish the same thing while increasing the overall odds of success on this mission."

"How is that?" Jared asked, a sensation of dread settling in his stomach like a lead ball.

"It's quite simple, really," Fielding said with a grin. "I'm coming with you."

"Well," Austin said into the deafening silence with a wry smile, "this is promising to be a much more exciting journey than I'd expected."

That was the understatement of the year.

36

Nine hours later, Elise snuck out of the maintenance tube where she'd been hiding and made her way to the cramped storage room just off the enlisted crew's mess.

By *Athena*'s clock, it was the middle of the night. Their unwanted guest was safely tucked away in the quarters he'd appropriated from Sean earlier, much to the commodore's annoyance.

The destroyer had just flipped out from Raidon, and she had no trouble admitting to the relief she felt. They were no longer under the guns of all the ships and fortresses.

Now, if push came to shove, they could deal with the intruding Rebel Empire noble should he discover their deception.

That wouldn't save *Athena*, though. The man was the only person aboard who had the codes to reset the timer on the plasma charges that would gut her. All he needed to do to destroy the ship was sit idly by. In five days, the destroyer would be wrecked, and they'd be screwed.

Elise was the last to arrive in the storage room. Jared, Sean, Olivia, Lily, Princess Kelsey, and Commander Roche were already seated on portable chairs around a makeshift table.

Her husband gestured for her to sit beside him. "I'll bet you're happy to get out of that tube."

"I'd be much happier if I could sneak into my husband's quarters for the night," she said grumpily. "And before you tell me that's much too risky, that doesn't change how I feel. Has there been any change? How are we going to deal with Fielding and his six guards?"

Jared shrugged. "Anytime he is outside his quarters, we keep a close eye on where he goes and what he sees. We're doing what we can to make certain that he only interfaces with our senior officers. They've got the best chance of maintaining the charade.

"I don't see that situation changing. The odds of us being able to get the codes for the plasma charges is almost nonexistent. That's the only trump card he has to play, and he'll never just hand them over."

"I think it's much more serious than that," Olivia said, shaking her head. "He's playing some kind of game. There's very little reason for him to come along on this mission. Oh, I know he says he's doing it to save his nephew's life, but that's bull. If we were truly the Rebel Empire nobles in command of this mission, his presence would only assure his own death in the end."

"So we've got a player," Sean said slowly. "If his end goal isn't to save his nephew, then what does he hope to accomplish? He's one man against a ship full of people. Even with his guards, we wouldn't have any trouble suppressing him.

"Just look at how everyone was armed when we left El Capitan. With the exception of our techie, everyone was armed at all times, and their neural disruptors were set to kill. Whatever plan Fielding intends to set in motion, he can't reasonably expect to overpower us."

"I've discovered that when a bastard is smiling, he knows something that you don't," Kelsey said with a grunt. "Are we absolutely certain he doesn't have access to the computer systems? Is it possible that he could set off the antiboarding weapons? If he stuns all of us, then he has control of this ship."

"Not happening," Sean quickly responded. "While we were removing the lockout that our new ally put in place, we checked the entire system to make certain that we had total and absolute control. There's no way that Fielding can subvert the system, not even by digging through the manual controls."

"You'll forgive me if I'm unconvinced. It seems that things haven't quite gone as planned on this mission. At this point, I keep wondering when the next disaster is going to happen and if it'll be our last."

"I understand how you feel, Kelsey," Elise said, clasping her hand around the other woman's. "This has been a very chaotic experience. We came into this mission with a certain expectation of how it was going to work that didn't work out. We're improvising."

"The Rebel Empire has never done anything like this before," Jared said. "We had no reason to expect this side mission when we delivered the report. All we can do now is try to accommodate the unexpected and turn the situation to our advantage.

"Look at it this way, so long as we play along with the Lords' plan, they'll welcome us into the Terra system with open arms. We don't have to fight our way in. We don't have to trick the System Lord stationed there. It will be expecting us."

"Lord Fielding might not have known the people he was meeting, but the System Lord will," Kelsey said. "As soon as it sees what you look like, it will know that something has gone wrong. What do we do then?"

"The best we can," Jared said bluntly. "I've got some people working on a filter in the com system that will swap out Olivia's appearance with that of the dead Rebel Empire noble who was supposed to be running this mission.

"I don't know how effective that'll be, but at this point we don't have a choice. We're committed to making this run."

He turned to Lily. "Is there any chance of getting a sample of that virus and concocting a vaccine or an antidote that could be administered after infection?"

The doctor nodded. "Kelsey was able to capture the code that opened the crates. The drones themselves don't have specific antitampering functions. I should be able to get into one of them and extract a sample safely.

"That said, the laboratories aboard the ship are not exactly cutting edge. I can't guarantee I'll be able to discover a vaccine in the short amount of time we still have available. Or at all, for that matter. Not without the labs aboard *Caduceus*."

From what little Elise had seen of the massive hospital ship, she could well believe the capabilities on the destroyer might be a little short of what they needed.

"Is there any possibility that we'll be able to rendezvous with the fleet as it makes its way around toward Terra?" Elise asked. "If so, we might be able to use those labs to make this happen."

Jared shook his head. "The flip-point layout makes that impossible. We're going by the most direct method, and the fleet is taking the long way around. At flank speed, they're still going to arrive at Terra at least a week after we do, and they won't be at the same flip point."

He looked gravely around the table at all of them. "Whatever happens on this mission, we're only going to have the resources we have with us now. It's going to be up to us to make lemonade with the lemons we've been given.

"Once we arrive at Terra, we're going to look the situation over as we make our way to the home world. It's possible we could gain access to the System Lord and, through it, all the defensive fortifications that protect the system. If that happens, we can let the fleet in when it arrives."

"And if there is no reasonable way to access the System Lord?" Kelsey asked. "What do we do then? It's going to have access to offensive weaponry that could turn this ship into scattered molecules. Not only that, if we deviate from the mission parameters, Lord Fielding is going to know.

"Just how far do we go to maintain our cover? Just how close to an occupied planet do you intend to take this virus?"

Jared grimaced. "If we can't get access to the System Lord, our options are extremely limited. To answer your basic question, we'll most likely die, but I have no intention of allowing this virus near Terra."

"We've been in more difficult situations," Elise said firmly, keeping a resolute expression on her face. "The odds might be stacked against us, but the Rebel Empire isn't going to win this fight. The AIs will not triumph in the end."

She sat back, hoping that her bold words actually foreshadowed success. Despite what she'd just said, she knew the odds stacked against them were damned high.

Jared began laying out potential courses of action. Since they didn't know precisely what they would find at Terra, everything was suitably vague.

Elise consulted her implants and made note of the time. They had about four hours before Lord Fielding would join the rest for breakfast.

She set an internal alarm for two hours. If the meeting hadn't concluded by then, she'd bring it to a close herself. An hour alone with Jared in their quarters would be painfully short, but she was determined not to waste what might be their last days together.

* * *

KELSEY LEFT the meeting in a fairly depressed state of mind. They were probably screwed. She honestly couldn't figure out any possible way they'd come out alive and in possession of the one thing her people absolutely needed to survive: the AI override from the vaults underneath the Imperial Palace.

When she made to turn toward her quarters and catch a few hours of sleep before she had to be up, Scott turned with her. "If you've got a few minutes, I'd like to go over a couple of items with you. Nothing too big, but I'd rather not risk any of our unwelcome visitors overhearing them."

"Sure."

When she'd let them both into her quarters, he raised an eyebrow at her. "Do you suppose our associates are monitoring you?"

"No," she said with a shake of her head. "I used the information in my raider implants to build a handheld scanner with a lot more resolution than the ones generally available even to the New Terran Empire in this universe.

"Frankly, it was just to test out my capability to use the data. Something to pass the time. I used it to scan my quarters because I was curious about how far they trusted me, too. No bugs."

"Could you show me how it works?" he asked politely.

She shrugged, retrieved the scanner from her nightstand, and ran it around the room. The process took less than sixty seconds and came back clean.

"All secure," she said. "It doesn't sound like you want to discuss mundane issues. What's going on, Scott?"

He took a second to verify the hatch was locked before sitting at the small desk built into the bulkhead. He waited until she'd sat on the edge of her bunk before he continued.

"Highness, I'm more than a little concerned that you've thrown our lot in with the Bastard and his associates. Granted, it doesn't appear that he's the same man here as he is in our universe, but his primary goal on this mission is the salvation of his own people. If anyone is going to look out for ours, it needs to be us."

Kelsey frowned, crossing her legs. "I'm not quite sure where you're taking this. If it seems as if I've thrown my lot in with them, it's because they have the only viable plan to get what we need. There's only one override. If I want to take it home, I've got to help them defeat the AIs in this universe."

"That's not true, Highness," he said deferentially. "We can follow their plan up to a point and still get what we need. Our agreement to assist them wasn't meant to be a suicide pact. In case you haven't noticed, these people take unbelievable risks. How long before they overestimate their own capability and take us down with them?

"And you can't forget that no matter how reasonable he seems now, he's still the Bastard. How far can we really trust him? Don't let him pull the wool over your eyes. Don't be his willing accomplice in this at the cost of our people's lives just because he puts on a good front."

"I don't appreciate even the implication that I would ever cooperate with someone like the Bastard we all know and hate," she said coldly. "You'd best retract that insinuation right now."

The Fleet officer bowed his head slightly. "My apologies, Highness. I didn't mean to suggest that. Let me try to phrase my thought a different way. As decent as these people appear to be, they aren't *our* people. We have an obligation to do whatever is necessary to save *our* Terran Empire, even if that harms the people in this one."

A cold chill washed through her. "You're suggesting we betray them. That we help them along until an opportune moment and then seize the override."

Scott scrunched his face up slightly. "Nothing so blatant. While I have a mustache suitable for twirling, I'm not a villain. All I'm saying is that we should keep our options open. As distasteful as it might be, saving our Empire is worth any price we might have to pay.

"Jared Mertz and his associates are raving lunatics if they think they can dupe the AI in control of Terra. One misstep, and we will be praying for death. You met the Pale Ones the hard way. Do you really want to experience something like that again?"

Kelsey couldn't repress the shudder before it took her. No, she absolutely didn't want to give anyone control of her body again. She'd kill herself first.

She considered him and then sighed. "Even if I stick a handy knife into Jared Mertz's back, we'd still be stuck in the Terra system. We have no way to escape.

"You heard them. The AI controls all the defensive stations at every flip point and all the mobile platforms. We can't control this destroyer by ourselves. Hell, we can't take it away from them either. I'm tough, but I'm not *that* tough. Like it or not, all our fates are intertwined."

"For the moment," he agreed. "Yet we don't know what the future might bring. Let's say that something happens that allows us to bypass the System Lord and gets us to Terra. What are we going to find there?

"That's all I'm asking you to keep in mind, Highness. These people have made great promises to assist us in our universe, but if it comes down to their survival or ours, I know what they'll do, and so do you."

She shook her head sharply. "They gave us four intact *battlecruisers*. Fully operational warships that are individually a match for the one the Bastard stole. They've transferred an immense amount of information to us. They're training our people to utilize implants that they are giving us. That is huge.

"And before you suggest they've tampered with the implant designs, I found other references to them in places they can't have gotten to. Not to all of them. They're being upfront with us. They're helping us when they didn't have to."

Scott shrugged. "Let's say you're right. Let's say that they're generously helping us. In fact, I'll even concede that is the truth. If push comes to shove, are you going to allow these benevolent folks to survive if it condemns us to death and slavery?"

He let his words hang in the air before he continued.

"I just want you to keep our options open. Keep considering what's best for the Empire. If you decide that's continuing to assist these people, so be it. If you see that the situation is spiraling out of control and the choice is either to join them in death or act in our own self-interest, I hope you'll be ready when the time comes."

Kelsey felt numb. She knew these people were honestly helping her and her people, but Scott was right. This wasn't her universe. She had to keep in mind that their interests might not always coincide.

She prayed it never came to that, but if these people got themselves into an irretrievable situation she had to have other plans in mind.

"As much as I want to disagree, I understand," she said slowly. "I refuse to see betraying these people as an unavoidable event, and I pray that we can come up with a plan that saves everyone. But if the crisis comes and I see no other choice, I'll do what I have to."

That broke her heart, but she had to stand for the Empire. *Her* Empire.

She prayed that Jared Mertz found a path to success, because if it came to a choice between her honor and the safety of the Empire, she'd do what had to be done.

MAILING LIST

The Empire of Bones Saga
Empire of Bones
Veil of Shadows
Command Decisions
Ghosts of Empire
Paying the Price
Reconnaissance in Force
Behind Enemy Lines
The Terra Gambit

The Empire of Bones Saga Volume 1

The Humanity Unlimited Saga
Liberty Station
Freedom Express
Tree of Liberty

The Fractured Republic Saga
Storm Divers

The Scorched Earth Saga
Scorched Earth

The Vigilante Duology with Glynn Stewart
Heart of Vengeance
Oath of Vengeance

ABOUT TERRY

#1 Bestselling Military Science Fiction author Terry Mixon served as a non-commissioned officer in the United States Army 101st Airborne Division. He later worked alongside the flight controllers in the Mission Control Center at the NASA Johnson Space Center supporting the Space Shuttle, the International Space Station, and other human spaceflight projects.

He now writes full time while living in Texas with his lovely wife and a pounce of cats.

www.TerryMixon.com
Terry@terrymixon.com

http://www.facebook.com/TerryLMixon

https://www.amazon.com/Terry-Mixon/e/B00J15TJFM

Made in the USA
Lexington, KY
20 April 2019